Maid for the Rock Star

DEMELZA CARLTON

Book 1 in the Romance Island Resort series

ISBN-13: 978-1-925799-05-7
ISBN-10: 1-925799-05-0

DEDICATION

This book is for Joe.
Without his stories about fishing and living in the
Kimberley, the Romance Island Resort wouldn't exist.

ONE

"Rock stars don't retire at twenty-five! I'm way too young. And there's no way in hell I'm taking up lawn bowls." Jason stared moodily out the helicopter window at the pearl farm below.

Beside him, Jo shrugged. "So get a job. Find a different hobby. And no, banging every girl you meet isn't a hobby. It's more like an addiction you should kick."

"It's not my fault women find me irresistible," he said smugly. "I'm a fucking rock star. C'mon, sis, name two women who wouldn't sleep with me if I asked them."

"Well, there's me, for a start." Jo spotted the pearl farm. "Ooh, I should stop there before I leave town. I could wear pearls in the office…"

Jason snorted. "You're family. You don't count."

Jo favoured him with the glare he'd seen her practising in the mirror – the one she planned to use on staff who'd blown their budgets. "My dear stepbrother, in case you've forgotten, there's no blood relationship between us. So if you truly are irresistible, your charms should work on me. And I'm just not interested."

"No, you're just crazy." Jason waved a hand up and down the body he knew was sculpted to perfection. "No sane woman can resist this."

"Approaching Romance Island now. I'll have you on the ground in five minutes," the pilot said flatly.

Jason considered her. No, too old. She had to be well over thirty. He peered back out the window, hoping to catch a glimpse of bikini-clad bodies on the beach as the white and green streak on the horizon expanded into a heart-shaped atoll.

He couldn't help feeling a thrill of excitement. This was the place, he knew it. This exclusive tropical resort was where a rock star could get a bit of rest and recuperation, with plenty of female company to keep him busy at night. And when Angel came to her senses and set out to find him…well, here he'd be. In paradise. What more could she ask for than the perfect man in the perfect setting? Maybe she'd reconsider her decision to break up the band, agree to do a comeback tour, and realise that nothing was better than living the rock star life. She just needed a bit of time, that's all. Time he'd spend in paradise, living it up.

He wondered whether he wanted blonde, brunette or a rare redhead tonight. When the helicopter bumped to the ground, he decided to leave it up to chance. After all, he could try something different tomorrow.

TWO

"Audra, you'll take care of the Pearls this week." Annette didn't lift her eyes from the staff roster in her hands.

Audra raised her eyebrows at hearing the name of the resort's crown jewels. "I thought only Jackie cleaned the Pearl Villas." Casual housekeeping staff like her didn't have a hope in hell of getting near the VIPs who stayed in the Pearls. She usually ended up dealing with the motel-style rooms in the main building. Families, honeymoon couples and well-paid professionals who didn't have secrets to keep like the Pearl guests did on the other side of the lagoon.

Annette shrugged. "Jackie's off sick. Injured her knee when she slipped cleaning one of the bathrooms. I can assign one of the other girls – Penny, maybe – but you asked for more responsibility, and if you want to stay on after the dry season's over, you'll have to know how to deal with VIPs."

And if she didn't, Penny might get the permanent position instead, was what Annette didn't say. She didn't have to. Audra needed the job and she couldn't afford to lose it to Penny. This job would see her through until next year's round of graduate job offers, if she could win the contested full-time position in the off season. Otherwise, she'd be forced to return to endless rounds of job-hunting between queuing up for unemployment benefits. Just like her brothers and her father. "No, I'll do it," Audra replied. "Thank you."

"You should thank me. Maxima's the only villa occupied at the moment. One VIP whose only request is privacy and solitude. Should be easy."

Audra nodded, but she didn't agree. Nothing in her life was ever easy.

Annette set the roster down on the table and pulled her phone out of her pocket. "I'll just send a message to Dennis and get him to authorise access for you." She tapped at her phone screen. "There. Run on over to Reception and he'll take care of it."

Thanking her boss one last time, Audra left the staff dining room and wended her way past the staff accommodation, through the palm trees and up to the main building. It wasn't until she reached the doors that she caught more than a glimpse of the heart-shaped lagoon that gave Romance Island its name. Not for the first time, she marvelled at how well the luxury resort's service areas were hidden among the dense palms and pandanus. When the guests paid a fortune for every night they stayed on the island, they didn't want to be reminded that the small army of staff who served their every need also lived there, rent-free.

Audra breathed in the faint scent of frangipani as she entered the air-conditioned foyer, wishing she could wear one behind her ear like the Reception staff did, but the flowers scarcely stayed in place through the first room she cleaned, let alone the whole day, so she'd given up on them.

Hana, the Japanese tour guide, stood alone at the Reception desk.

"No tours today?" Audra asked.

"Just heli-fishing this morning. This afternoon I have a large group snorkelling in the Rose Garden, if you want to come." Her dark eyes shone with eagerness. Audra suspected Hana preferred being in the water to staying on land, but she didn't understand it.

"Only if you tell the sharks to stay away," Audra replied.

Hana giggled. "Oh, but the reef sharks are the best part! They're so very shy."

"Not with me." Audra still bore the scars of her first meeting with a reef shark. She'd stood knee-deep in the shallows of what had turned out to be the reef shark nursery and one of the beasts had bitten her on the leg. She wouldn't venture into the water again in a hurry.

Speaking of hurrying… She caught a glimpse of Dennis entering the security office, made her excuses to Hana and headed after him.

Dennis gave her a curt nod of recognition and held out his hand. "ID?"

Audra slipped off her wristband and handed it over.

Dennis dropped it into the scanner and drummed his fingers on the keys. "So now you have access to all the Pearl Villas, too. Anything else I can get you?"

Audra shook her head and fastened her ID around her wrist. "Thank you."

"You watch out over there," Dennis said darkly, glaring at the lagoon.

Audra followed his gaze. "Believe me, I'm not interested in getting up close and personal with any more sharks."

He snorted out a laugh. "Not just the sharks in the water. The ones in the villas, too. Rich snobs, people with more money than morality. Or sense. Be careful, or you'll lose your job."

"How? I'm not going to steal from them, and I know all about our confidentiality and non-disclosure clauses. I'm not stupid enough to take any stories to the press."

"That's good, but it's the no-fraternising rule you'll need to remember." His gaze seemed to be searching for her soul.

"I haven't fraternised with anyone, guest or staff, since the day I arrived, and I don't intend to," she replied. "Do you seriously think I'd seduce some old mining tycoon for his fortune?" The money would be handy, she couldn't deny it, but the thought of sleeping with some old man… it just wouldn't be worth it. She wasn't desperate enough to do that.

"No, you're a good girl, but your dad would want me to look out for you, is all. We worked together for long enough, he's almost like family, which makes you family, too. And your mum would kill me if I let anything bad happen to you up here. I'm already in hot water over the shark." Dennis coughed. "There's a reason only Jackie services those houses."

"Because she's the most senior housekeeper under

Annette," Audra snapped. "She's damn good at what she does. She still holds the record for being the only person capable of cleaning the entire main building in a single shift, and she managed that ten years ago. No one else can do it."

Dennis nodded thoughtfully. "That's why she's senior staff, yes, but not why she gets the Pearls. We used to send younger staff out there, but I've had to escort too many of them off the island. Seduced by the guests. Money or love or…some of them said they were bullied into it by the VIPs, told they'd lose their jobs if they didn't cater to the guests' every whim. I don't want to see it happen to you."

Audra fought back her anger. Dennis and her parents worried about her, she knew that, but she'd been working part-time hospitality jobs for the last seven years, since she turned fourteen. And she knew how to deal with misogynistic male customers with entitlement issues, whether they were paying a thousand dollars a night for a beachside villa or three dollars for a cup of terrible coffee. Though hot coffee to the crotch was a better defence than trying to crush his foot with a lumbering cleaning trolley full of towels. More satisfying, too.

Unless Dennis knew something he wasn't telling her…

Suspicion drove her to say, "Do you know something about the VIPs here now that you're not telling me? Is it some irresistible porn star or something?"

Dennis laughed. "Nah, no idea who the guests are. Call it a hunch, so I'm telling you to take care."

Audra took a deep breath. "Thanks, Dennis, but we both know no rich guy's going to look at me twice, unless his eyesight's failing. A welfare family girl who grew up in overcrowded public housing? I wouldn't be good enough for him. You've got nothing to worry about."

THREE

"So what do you think?" Jason asked, glancing at Jo.

She scuffed her shoes on the path. "I love the property and the location. Infrastructure looks sound, quality and environmental standards are top-notch and everything's built to withstand cyclones. That cyclone shelter looks like it could survive the bloody apocalypse. As far as real estate goes, it's beautiful and brilliant. But as a business…I'm not sure. I mean, it's a remote, luxury resort and it's peak season, yet the place is half empty. I'd buy the property as a long-term investment and let some hotel chain manage the place, but none of them seem interested. That's one hell of a warning sign. Add that to the asking price, which is much too high, and…no. I don't want to buy the place."

"But I want to live here. I'm going to stay here for the whole month, just like we planned."

His sister stared at him as if he'd spoken Chinese and

not English. "Why? I mean, I get it's nice for a holiday but the isolation would kill you. You're miserable when you're not surrounded by fans. How long would you like living out here alone?"

Jason laughed. "I wouldn't be alone. There's a hotel full of people here. Well, half-full, maybe. Different girls every night, all looking for a good time. It's like rock star heaven."

"And that's what you want, a new girl every night? That's all you want out of life?"

Jason couldn't stand seeing the pity and disgust in her eyes, so he surveyed the lagoon instead. "Until I find the right one, yeah." She'd come. She had to. And when she did, he'd be waiting on a romantic beach with open arms.

"You'll never find her that way, Jason. Instead, you're going to be very lonely."

"I'm never lonely. I can have any girl I want, remember?"

Jo rolled her eyes. "Yeah, except me and anyone who really matters. And I'm not staying at a resort in the middle of nowhere that I don't want to buy. I'll be gone tonight, so you can have your little orgies from dusk 'til dawn without me complaining that your bed partners make too much noise." She sighed. "You're still hung up on her, aren't you?"

"No!" Even Jason heard the defensiveness in his tone.

"So why are you hiding out on this island for a month?" Jo persisted.

"Checking the place out before I buy it. Working out if I want to retire here and go from rock star to hotel owner. I always figured I'd go down in history as rock star royalty like the Stones, not bail out of the music industry before I hit thirty. It feels too soon, you know?" Jason tried to sound virtuous. "I'm going to spend a month working out what I want to do next in my life. What path I want to take."

Jo snorted. "Want me to find you a career guidance counsellor? I bet the local high school or unemployment office has one. I'll see if she's willing to fly over here for a day as a consultant to counsel you on your career choices."

Thinking of the young, female teacher who'd been his guidance counsellor at high school, Jason perked up. "Is she as hot as Miss – "

"How the hell should I know? Probably not. Might even be a man."

"Fuck no. I don't need some bloke telling me what to do. Trevor's bad enough." Jason couldn't suppress a shudder. He'd never admit it aloud, but he was terrified of the band's security consultant. The man was an ex-US Marine who'd served in Afghanistan, for fuck's sake. He could kill a man with his bare hands, Jason was sure of it. Hey, maybe that was one good thing about the band breaking up. No more wondering if today he'd finally push Trevor over the edge and the man's angry face would be the last sight he'd ever see.

"I don't remember you complaining when Trevor scared off that scary stalker chick who swore she was carrying your baby. What was her name again?" Jo retorted.

He didn't remember and he didn't want to. The baby wasn't his – condoms made sure of that. And he didn't want to talk or even think about crazy girls who didn't understand the meaning of the word *no*. He waved his wristband at the scanner below the ornate sign that read

VILLA MAXIMA and suppressed a sigh of relief when the door opened. It may as well have said HOME SWEET HOME for all he cared. This was the place. For the next month, it would be rock star heaven. He was certain of it. But first, he wanted to be that little bit more comfortable.

"I need to take a piss." He strode into his villa, fumbling with his zipper as he headed for the bathroom.

FOUR

Audra tucked her dusting cloth into the hamper for dirty linen as the door clicked closed behind her, muffling the robotic vacuum cleaner's whirring as it scooted around the floors of Villa Pinctada. She had one last villa left – Maxima, the inhabited one. Deciding to leave her trolley at the bottom of the steps beside Pinctada, Audra trotted up to the grand front entrance of the hotel's most expensive accommodation.

Her wristband triggered the door as she approached, but still she hesitated. "Hello, Housekeeping," she called, crossing her fingers in the hope of receiving no reply. She repeated the call twice, before cheering inwardly that the residents weren't home. Her first day of dealing with VIPs was a success – because she hadn't seen a single one.

The dirty glasses lined up on the sink marked this villa as occupied. Audra loaded them into the dishwasher and a few swipes of the cleaning cloth later, she crossed the kitchen off her list of rooms to clean. A peep into the bedrooms revealed untouched beds and a single suitcase in the master bedroom – only one VIP, then, or a couple who packed light. Better than spoilt, snobby children who liked to smear food into the furniture. The laundry hamper was empty, as was the dry-cleaning one. That left only the bathroom.

For the second time, she crossed her fingers as she entered the sparkling white porcelain cave that was bigger than her bedroom in the staff accommodation. Toiletries, tiles…even the toilet paper was untouched, still folded into its arrow point from the last time Jackie had cleaned the villa. The only splash of colour in the room was a tiny green frog statue on the edge of the spa. It was a perfect replica of the ones that plagued the staff toilets. Good thing it wasn't real or she'd have to –

The statue hopped onto the soap dish. Of all the villas for a frog to pick, it had to choose the inhabited one. Audra spread out her dusting cloth and threw it, covering the frog and its perch. She hastily bundled the whole thing up, hoping to carry the frog outside, but it squirmed out and dropped into the tub. Where it had three fat friends. Audra swore.

She knew the hotel rules. All the wildlife on the island reserve was protected. She'd be fined if she deliberately hurt a frog. So she could either take them outside or shoo them down the drain they'd climbed up in the first place. The grating on the spa drain sat beside the hole it was supposed to be guarding, gaping a welcome to her amphibian antagonists.

Game on. Audra climbed over the edge and slid to the

bottom of the two-person tub. She grabbed the stack of fresh towels she'd brought with her and rolled a couple into a temporary fence around the frogs. She unfolded a third and spread it over the top of the enclosure. All she had to do was nudge them into the drain. Slowly, carefully…a muffled plop sounded from under the towel. One down, three to go.

Steadily, Audra tightened the enclosure, hearing another satisfying plop. She continued pushing the towels together until there wasn't space for a frog between them. Cautiously, she lifted them up. No more frogs, to her delight. That left only the escape hatch to secure. The drain grille was easily replaced, but there was nothing holding it in place to prevent the frogs from jumping right back up again. Pulling her multi-tool out, Audra unfolded the pliers and went to work on the metal, bending the edges so it wedged tightly into the top of the drain hole. Satisfied, she sat up and tucked the multi-tool back into her pocket.

The sound of running water made her freeze. The spa tap wasn't turned on and neither was the shower. The flow was too strong for the basin tap, so Audra stared in horror at the man relieving himself into the toilet bowl. Expensive designer jeans clung to what she had to admit was a very peachy bum – so shapely that it took her a moment to register that the guy was wearing jeans in a tropical climate. Her VIP was a foreign tourist, definitely. A foreigner with a fire hose.

In a tiny house like her parents', privacy was a precious commodity and soundproofing was non-existent. So with three brothers and her dad using the toilet beside the bedroom she shared with her younger sister, Samantha, the two girls had categorised the noises they heard as they lay giggling in their bunk beds at night.

There were the tinklers — usually little boys and old men who tinkled in a tiny trickle for eternity like a leaky tap. Then there were the sprayers — who didn't aim for the bottom of the toilet bowl but liked the sound of liquid falling on porcelain, or so it seemed. And the gushers — those who'd built up a whole head of pressure and were going at it like a fire hose. As both she and her brothers had grown up, she'd added a fourth category to the list — the beaters. These took advantage of the privacy of the toilet to jack off, and their tell-tale moans and groans had always made her laugh.

Mr VIP Peach-Bum — or should that be Plum-Bum, given his dark jeans? — most certainly wasn't a beater: he was the sort of high-pressure gusher you got from a three-hour drive down unsealed roads from town, then a rough boat trip through changing tides to the island. Or a bender involving a carton or two of cheap beer, a bottle of bourbon and a football match on TV so riveting they couldn't leave it until the final whistle blew. No, foreign tourists didn't understand Aussie rules football.

She considered climbing out of the bath and sneaking out while his back was turned, but it made more sense to stay where she was. At least then she had the excuse of dealing with the frogs — she could say she hadn't seen or heard a thing. And she hadn't — until the man shook himself and turned slightly to reach for the toilet paper. Then she saw what she had to admit was quite a sizeable piece of equipment before he tucked his fire hose back into his pants and zipped everything safely inside. Maybe he was a porn star.

Well. There was some excitement for a morning. A free show. Audra felt a touch of dampness on her thigh. Oh, bloody hell. Was the frog grinning at her? Little bastard. She grabbed a towel and used it to push it off her leg and closer to the plughole. Shit. She'd sealed it. Audra threw the towel over the top of the cheeky beast and bundled it up, hoping this time she had the frog inside. Now Plum-Bum just had to get the hell out so she could make a dash for the French doors to the veranda.

Water hissed and pattered into the basin, followed by the sound of someone pressing the liquid soap dispenser. She'd never hated good hygiene this much. Why couldn't Plum-Bum forget to wash his hands? The frog was already squirming its way out in another escape attempt.

Footsteps crossed the tiles and she heard a distinctly Aussie voice say, "Shit, I need a beer. What's in the mini-bar today?"

"What do I look like, your maid? Go look for yourself, lazy-arse." The woman sounded like she was in the kitchen.

"I have it on good authority that it's a fine arse, not that you'd notice, sis. I've had a couple of magazines ask to do centrefolds devoted to this perfection." Plum-Bum's voice faded as he padded off to join the woman that Audra realised was his sister in the kitchen.

Audra breathed again and lifted her head above the lip of the tub. The coast was clear. She vaulted over and sprinted for the outside door. The lock clicked and the doors swung open as she waved her wristband frantically at the scanner. Clutching the bundled towel in her arms, she bumped her certainly-not-centrefold-worthy bottom against the door to shut it. A second click of the lock told her she was safe.

She shook the frog out under the veranda and carried the crumpled towel to her trolley at Pinctada. So much for an uneventful first day in the Pearls. Could this one have been worse?

Yes, she decided. He could have seen her. He could have been doing more than pissing. The frog could have entered her underwear. Or hopped out of the bath and alerted him. Or both. Or it could've been the sister in the bathroom…

Hmm, a brother and sister who could afford Maxima. Were they some mining or media tycoon's grown-up kids? That was almost worse than the younger sort – these would deliberately pour chocolate sauce on the rug and snigger as they watched her clean it up. The sort of people who'd never had to work a day in their lives. She wouldn't let it worry her, but she wouldn't take any shit from them, either.

Audra slung a laundry bag over her shoulder and seized a fresh stack of towels. Lifting her chin, she marched back to the villa.

FIVE

Audra scanned her wristband and waited for the door to open, but it remained firmly shut. The intercom beside her emitted a persistent beep. She swiped her ID down the scanner slowly, so the stupid thing couldn't possibly misread it. She took a calming breath and the beeping stopped…but only for a moment before it resumed.

Audra glared at the intercom screen and was stunned to see a message scrawled across it.

GUESTS AT HOME.
NOTIFY?

Her finger hovered over CANCEL, but she changed her mind and pressed the ENTER button.

A soft chime sounded, echoing in the villa. "Housekeeping at the door," a recorded but mellifluous English voice announced. "Maid service required?"

"Hell yes!" Audra heard Plum-Bum's excited shout.

His sister hushed him. The front door flew open and Audra found herself face to face with a young woman about her own age. Audra lowered her gaze to the woman's expensive shoes. "We don't need anything. We just arrived today and haven't made enough mess to need a clean-up yet."

But I did, Audra thought but didn't say. The bath tub was still full of frog-tainted towels. "Towels," she said, pointing.

"Ask her!" Plum-Bum insisted, his bare feet appearing on the tiles behind the woman. "You'd fuck me, right?"

Wow. He might have decent equipment, but that's all that defined this dickhead. Probably a porn star for sure. "No, thank you," Audra said faintly.

"What'd she say?" Plum-Bum demanded.

The woman shook her head and guided Audra to the bathroom, then blocked the doorway to keep her brother out. "She doesn't understand English. Most hotel maids are foreign migrants, waiting for their qualifications to come through as they improve their English so they can get higher-paying jobs. Besides, she could lose her job for sleeping with a guest. Don't you remember what the hotel manager said about fraternisation policies during our tour? Leave her alone, Jason."

Audra snorted. In Perth, maybe, hotel staff were recent migrants, but not here in Broome. Even the casual staff were Aussie. But if the woman's words kept her oversexed brother's hands off her, all the better. She set the stack of fresh towels on the edge of the spa and stuffed the froggy ones into the laundry bag.

Glass clinked on metal. An empty beer bottle going into

the bin, most likely. The crunch and crackle of plastic followed it. Definitely the bin. She'd empty that on the way through and then she could escape the Pearls for the day.

Fixing her eyes firmly on the tiled floor, Audra marched to the kitchen to the approaching beat of helicopter rotors. Third flight today.

"Right, there's my ride returning. Don't get into too much trouble, don't make too much trouble for the staff, and enjoy your holiday. If you're not fit and ready for the band's farewell tour, you know it'll be your balls on the chopping block."

Band? Did she say he was in a band? Audra raised her gaze to scrutinise Plum-Bum's face. Even with the sexy stubble along his usually clean-shaven jaw, she recognised the face from the poster that had adorned her bedroom wall for the better part of the last five years. The one Sam kissed every morning. One she'd fantasised about since high school. Maybe she'd even kissed that poster once or twice herself. She glanced away before he could catch her staring. Oh shit. She'd already seen his –

"Promise me that if you get lonely, you'll call me. Don't do anything stupid." The sister sniffed. "I do love and care about you, you know."

"HA!" he shouted. "I knew it. Told you that you wanted me. It's not incest if I'm your stepbrother. Everyone wants me."

Audra snorted. Arrogant prick. Even she could tell the girl didn't.

"You're delusional, Jason. I love you because you're my brother, blood or no blood. I wouldn't sleep with you if you were the last man on Earth." She pulled out her phone and tapped it meaningfully. "Promise me you'll call me."

He nodded sulkily.

Her eyes met Audra's. "Don't take any shit from him. There's a place in town that neuters tomcats for half-price. You can put it on his hotel bill." She winked.

Audra stifled a snort of laughter. Mess with this man's glorious equipment? The world would weep. Especially if castration robbed him of his signature, underwear-igniting singing voice. Even she'd shed a tear for the loss.

She waited for the sister to leave before she pulled out the rubbish bin to change the bag inside.

Bare feet appeared beside the bin. "You understood every word, I bet," he said. "And I know you recognised me. If you know who I am, we both already know the answer to my question. So answer me. Would you fuck me?"

SIX

Audra didn't hesitate. "No." She turned to leave before she could take it back and change her answer.

A hand landed heavily on her shoulder. "Fuck, don't go. Do you know who I am?"

Here goes. She sighed as she shrugged out of his grasp and turned to face him. "You're Jay Felix, the lead singer of Chaya, and you have an army of fangirls the world over. Your shows are always sold out because you make yourself…accessible to your fans." And the man who'd played centre stage in all her teenage fantasies.

He laughed. "More like they make themselves accessible to me." He dropped his voice, into the seductive purr that had made her love his songs back in high school. "Go on, Audrey, tell me you wouldn't."

"I already have," she snapped. "And it's Audra, not Audrey." She peeled her badge off her breast and held it up to his eyes. "Less distraction so you can see it better." And because she wanted to hear his voice caress her name, just once...

"I like the view." He deliberately dropped his gaze to her breasts.

She itched to slap him. She'd never liked her conservative work uniform as much as she did today.

"What more could a woman want than a fucking rock star, Audrey?" he whispered.

Rock star? Man whore, more like. And one who couldn't even get her name right. Audra looked him in the eye. "Less swearing, for a start. A bit of honesty. Humility. Someone who listens and remembers her name. Being someone's one and only, and knowing your partner isn't the darling of millions, but yours."

"Mine?" He stepped closer to her so she could feel his breath warm on her face. "You want to be mine?"

YES, every cell in her body screamed, or at least those below the neck. The ones in her brain were blaring warning sirens against dickheads who didn't know her name and would cause her to lose her job without caring. Yet here was her high school heart-throb, standing so close to her she could reach out and touch him. Close enough to smell him. Audra backed away, wrinkling her nose in defence against the man's scent. He smelled like the ever-present pindan dust on the mainland, overlaid with sweat from walking outside in the humidity, with a tantalising top note from the frangipani soap in the bathroom, reminding her of what she'd seen there. Her eyes strayed to the front of his pants.

His hand slid into view, covering his crotch. "I'll give it

to you if you admit you want it."

For an insane instant, she considered it. Considered giving in to her own teenage desires to get up close and personal with a rock star. But she wasn't at high school any more. "Mr Felix, that's a lovely offer and I truly appreciate it, but I'm in the middle of my work shift. I have a lot to do today." Like round up all the robotic vacuum cleaners in the other villas. She prayed she wouldn't have to chase any under the bed.

"Working. Of course." His smile said he thought it was a joke. "When do you get off? I want to be there when you do."

Him and his bloody double-entendres. Sleazy, persistent, arrogant rock star. "Sorry, Mr Felix, but staff don't fraternise with guests. It's against the rules." She flashed a professional smile. "I have other guests to see to. If you need anything, don't hesitate to call Reception. They'll be happy to help." She forced her steps to remain confident as she walked out the front door, down the stairs and into Pinctada. When the door closed behind her, she pressed her back against it and slid to the floor.

Why did it have to be him? The image of male perfection she'd admired in his posters and music videos, dreaming that one day she'd get to meet him and maybe, just maybe, she'd know one night of bliss in his arms. That's what the press said about Jay Felix – there were dozens of stories about girls he'd loved intensely for one night. Never more than one night. Like the king in the *Arabian Nights* – one night with his queen and the next morning she'd perish. Not that Jay was known for killing women. No, he left them very much alive and singing his praises. Every high school girl the world over wanted to be the one to cure him of his tomcatting ways, to be the Scheherazade to tame him. She wondered if she'd have been as enamoured of him if she'd known his idea of seduction included staring at a girl's breasts as he casually asked to be fucked. Or that his equipment rivalled that of the Brahman bulls over on the mainland. He probably rutted like one, too. Mm, how romantic.

She laughed until tears rolled down her face. As a teenager, she'd have given anything for what had just happened, swearing and all. But now? She wondered if the veterinarian in town who offered half-price neutering would take a human tomcat. His sister had the right idea. She wouldn't sleep with him if he was the last man on Earth.

SEVEN

"Audra!" someone shouted.

She switched off the vacuum cleaner, dragging her eyes away from the sweaty, well-muscled man bench-pressing by the window. "Yes?"

The personal trainer lowered his voice. "Message for you from Reception. One of your guests needs help with the TV."

Her guests? Since when did she have her own guests? And didn't Engineering or IT normally handle technology issues? "What room?"

Serge pointed to his ID. "Villa Maxima."

Audra checked her wrist and, sure enough, Maxima scrolled across the ID display. Of course. Mr Rock Star needed a maid to turn on his television, most likely. Couldn't press the buttons himself because he didn't know how. Probably couldn't even find them.

"Get him to call Engineering," she said, reaching for the vacuum's power button without even glancing at it.

"The Pearls get maid service. Jackie used to complain about it, too. VIPs can't call tech support on their own. That's what you're for." Serge shrugged. The movement flexed his arm muscles and put the bench-presser to shame. "Can you see if any of them need a personal trainer this week? Or a fitness class? I'm low on bookings and if they don't pick up, Adam won't need an assistant any more. I'll have to go back to the farm, working sixteen-hour days again. Not to mention I won't get enough hours to be certified so I can leave the farm forever. If one of the VIPs requests daily yoga or pilates or personal training..." He looked hopeful.

Someone else who desperately wanted out of the life family and fate had forced upon him. How could she refuse? "I'll see what I can do," Audra replied. "You could always suggest wellness classes for staff, or let them attend the guest programmes. I know Pamela would love a yoga class and Penny complains daily that she can't do some sort of dance fitness programme here." She found Serge staring at her. "What?"

"If I get approval for staff classes, would you be there?"

She knew that look, but she blushed anyway. "Maybe, if my roster allows. And this VIP doesn't want to tie me up in his room for the duration of his stay. If I'm not in the staff dining room at six, can you come rescue me?"

Serge grinned. "Gladly."

Audra tucked the vacuum cleaner into the gym's cleaning cupboard and set out through the jungle to Villa Maxima. Flying fish skimmed across the lagoon and she wished she owned a camera good enough to catch them at play. One day, she promised herself. One day she'd earn enough money to come here as a guest on holiday with an SLR camera. But that day would be a long time coming.

She reached the door and paused to take a deep breath. Patience, calm and don't kill the VIP, she told herself. Then she rapped on the frosted glass door. "Maid service, Mr Felix."

"It's open."

It wasn't, so she swiped her wristband, waiting for the intercom to beep as it had earlier.

The door hissed open. Audra swallowed her surprise and strode inside. She should be used to automatic doors by now.

"In here."

Audra followed the sound of his voice to the theatre room, where he lay sprawled across the modular sofa in his black boxer briefs and nothing else. He reached down to scratch his sizeable, cotton-clad bulge.

Clearing her throat, Audra began, "Reception said you were having trouble with the TV?" She crossed the floor so she could focus on the screen and not the chiselled man tempting her like a bar of the best chocolate. The dickhead had a body that rivalled Serge's. Speaking of Serge… "If you like, I'll arrange to get a repair crew from Engineering out here. I could arrange some other activity for you in the meantime. Perhaps book you a session with the personal trainer in the gym…" She squinted at the screen. The picture seemed to be just fine, if a bit blurred. It took her a moment to realise what she was seeing projected across the wall. Then she didn't know where to look. "I take it you don't want to watch the adult movie channel?" Audra enquired, trying to keep a straight face. She'd heard every excuse in the book for why hotel guests had accidentally accessed the channel. She wondered if he'd have a new one.

Jay laughed. "Babe, I'm a rock star. Porn goes with the territory. I don't usually watch it alone, is all."

"Ah." She really didn't know what to say. Had he called her to come and watch adult movies with him? She heartily hoped that wasn't included in her job description.

"Nah, it's this awesome blowjob the chick did. Here, check it out." To Audra's horror, he flipped the movie back to a different scene and made it play. Her mouth dropped open as she watched the male porn star's genitals disappear down his co-star's throat, while he grinned beneath his moustache and made a lot of noise to express his evident pleasure. An excruciatingly long moment later, Jay paused the film on an extreme close-up of the action. "There. Can you do that?"

"No." In fact, Audra didn't think any normal woman could.

"Aw, c'mon, babe. For me. Give it a shot." His boxer briefs landed on the floor beside her foot.

Audra took a deep breath, forcing her eyes to face forward and under no circumstances glance at the hot, naked rock star on the couch behind her. If she did, she knew she wouldn't be able to resist him.

"Mr Felix."

"Babe, once you've sucked my cock, you can call me Jay."

Thank you, coarse-tongued creep for breaking the spell. Two more deep breaths and she managed to find the strength to refuse. "Mr Felix, I think you've confused maid service with the services of a prostitute. My job description doesn't include sexual favours. I can contact Reception and ask them to arrange transport for you to the brothel in town, where you can – "

"Babe, I'm a fucking rock star. I don't need to pay for sex. I have chicks lining up to suck my dick. Fuck, they'd pay me for it."

Reluctantly, Audra turned to face the arrogant prick. She held his gaze, not trusting herself to look anywhere else. "Please don't swear at me, Mr Felix. And I hate to tell you this, but there isn't anyone waiting outside. Perhaps your adoring fans aren't aware that you're here. If there were such a queue, I'd be able to escort the first lady in line inside to see to your…needs." She heard the distaste in her voice and changed the subject. "So can I report to Reception that your TV is now working fine and get back to my other duties?"

His eyebrows scrunched up so they almost met across his red nose. In fact, his whole face had turned red. "I just want you to suck my dick while I watch porn. What do I have to do to get a blowjob?"

"I don't know, Mr Felix. All I do know is that it's not my job. Perhaps I can ask Reception to call the brothel to send an expert over?"

"I don't need to pay for sex!" he bellowed. "Is that what you're after? Money? Fine. How much does it take for a man to get a blowjob from you?" He reached for his wallet and pulled out a wad of bills.

"I'm sorry, Mr Felix." She wasn't, but it sounded civil to say so. "It would take flying pigs, a cold day in hell and the sun to rise in the west, and I still wouldn't do it. Because I'd lose my job." She forced herself to smile. "I hope you have a pleasant evening." Audra turned her back and strode toward the front door. How fate could grant an arsehole like him a body so perfect…nothing in life was fair.

"You expect me to deal with this hard-on by myself?" His voice shifted up an octave.

Audra thought she heard a note of desperation. Good. Maybe it was time life evened up the score a bit. For all the nights she'd lusted after him and never been properly satisfied.

"You have two hands, Mr Felix. I understand that's all a lonely single man needs." She clamped her lips together and forced herself to remain calm until the door closed behind her. She blinked in the late afternoon sunlight, feeling like she'd been inside a surreal film and the real world was definitely a relief. Sunset tinted the path as she followed the yellow brick road away from the rock star the newspapers called the Wizard of Aus.

Once she'd rounded the corner and Villa Maxima vanished from sight, she broke into a sprint for the main building. She had to get to Dennis before the dickhead called security to get her fired. Or before she turned around and did something she'd really regret.

EIGHT

Audra hurried to Dennis' office and was relieved to find him in.

"Where's the trouble?" Dennis asked, already on his feet. The ex-minesite emergency response supervisor in him would never die.

"In some prick of a VIP's pants. Or lack of." Rapidly, she summarised her exchange with Jay.

"Let's hear it in all the gory detail." He nodded at his scanner. "ID."

Uncertainly, Audra detached her wristband and dropped it on the scanner pad.

Dennis peered at his computer screen and tapped his keyboard.

"In here," Jay's seductive purr came from Dennis' speaker.

Audra gritted her teeth as she listened to the recorded

replay of her conversation in Maxima.

Dennis eyebrows would have reached his hairline if it hadn't receded. "The sun will rise in the west, hmm?"

The tension broke as they both laughed. "I might've borrowed that one from *Game of Thrones*," she admitted. "Do you record all the conversations in the hotel?"

He shook his head. "Only the ones where staff are in the room with guests. It's to protect both parties, and we usually don't listen to any of it unless a complaint is made. It's not common knowledge among staff or guests. Based on what happened today, you don't have anything to worry about, even if he does file a complaint." He sucked in a breath. "Did he touch you at all?"

Audra shook her head.

"Damn. If he does, it's assault, and I'll have grounds to make him leave the island. But if not…he's still allowed to stay here. Let me know if anything worse happens and I'll contact the police. Just don't touch him, or he'll have grounds for an assault charge."

Slowly, Audra nodded. For the first time, she was glad she hadn't slapped him, however much she'd wanted to. Maybe he liked that sort of thing.

"Just remember to swipe your ID every time you enter or exit one of the villas and you'll be fine. Your ID will record every conversation within earshot while you're inside. I'll handle this one from here. If you like, I'll give you the highlights of his complaint at dinner. It should make for a funny story."

Dismissed, Audra relaxed as she left Dennis' office. Whatever else happened, at least her job was safe.

Idly, she wondered if there was a way to circumvent the

security system. If she did snap and tell the prick what she thought of him, she definitely didn't want it recorded for posterity. Dennis would laugh himself sick.

Or if she surrendered to her own weakness and gave Jay what he asked for…no. One night with Jay wasn't worth losing her job, no matter how good he was in bed.

Or on the sofa…

Audra ruthlessly shut that thought down before it went any further. Just because her body lusted after him, didn't mean she had to give in. She didn't even like him.

NINE

Audra raised her arms above her head in a stretch that resonated through her shoulders to her spine. "Right. Good to be in my own clothes again. Do you think they could make the uniforms any more uncomfortable?"

Pamela smiled shyly. "It could be worse."

Audra thought of the ties, tight-fitting tops and short skirts she'd had to wear in her various other jobs. "You're right. Let's get these down to the dock in time for the last boat and we can go for dinner." She counted the trolleys. "Isn't Penny supposed to be helping us? Where is she this time?"

"She said something about a sexy new sous-chef."

That meant Penny would be too busy flirting to do laundry duty like she was supposed to.

Audra sighed. "Fine. You grab that one and I'll take these two." She yanked four laundry bags off the full trolley and dumped them on the half-empty one, then added one more. "Now they're balanced."

They trundled down the path in a rattling procession to the jetty where the carrier boat waited. Baz, the captain, offered them a lazy salute. "Ladies."

Both girls laughed.

Audra waved at the bags. "Guest laundry and a week's worth of island uniforms. Please don't let the laundry service get us mixed up with the hospital linen again. The only thing worse than the maids' uniforms out here are surgeons' scrubs."

"Oh, so you liked the nurses' uniforms, did you?" Baz teased.

Pamela blushed bright red. "One day, when I can afford to go to nursing school, I'll wear one all the time."

"You'll get there," Audra said.

"And I bet the guests think all you housekeeping girls are deaf, dumb and stupid. What would they say if they knew you'll one day be saving their lives, predicting the weather or…what's the other girl want to do again?"

"Penny wants to be famous. She wants to be a reality TV star." This week. Next week, she might want to be a lounge singer. Or marry someone rich. Audra lost track sometimes.

Baz rolled his eyes. "Right. Well, see you in the morning. Don't break too many hearts tonight."

They waved as Baz and his mate cast off, before trudging up to the staff block.

"There you are! I've been waiting for you," Penny said.

Audra didn't believe a word of it. Penny's shirt wasn't buttoned right and she had a suspicious mango-coloured stain on her breast pocket. "If you'd remembered we're on laundry duty tonight, you'd have known where to look."

"Oh. That. Sorry." She didn't look it.

As Penny launched into a rambling story about her time training to be a chef at the community college in Port Hedland, Audra stepped into the staff dining room, scanning the tables for Dennis. He met her gaze and slowly shook his head, then shrugged. No, the dickhead hadn't complained and Dennis had no idea why. At least, that's what she thought it meant.

She nodded and resumed listening to Penny's story about the night her crazed housemate in Hedland kicked in a door, convinced that Penny had poisoned her. From what she'd heard about Penny's cooking and her penchant for revenge, anything was possible.

Audra accepted a plate from Pamela and proceeded to load it up with salad. An experimental sniff at the hot food told her the new sous-chef had burned the mango chicken again and the results were deemed not good enough for guests. Mango chicken salad was her favourite, so she hoped the forgetful sous-chef would be around for a while.

More fresh mango for dessert. If it wasn't her favourite…Audra laughed quietly to herself and filled a bowl with fruit.

The personal trainer jostled her aside. "Wow, you must really like mango." Serge grinned. "Pity I didn't need to rescue you today. I did an extra hour on the rowing machine, too, just in case you needed a fast escape off the island." He imitated the sculling movement, flexing even more muscles that Audra didn't know the names of.

She laughed. "Yes, I love mangoes. One of the best

things about working up here is that I get to eat my fill." She couldn't afford them at home and on the rare occasions she'd attempted to treat herself, the fruit had disappeared from the fridge before she'd had a chance to taste it. Her brothers' fault, she was sure of it.

"Have you tried that mango beer in town? I'm due two days off next week and I know your roster matches mine. Do you want to come to dinner with me at the brewery restaurant?"

She couldn't justify the expense of dinner or beer, but she couldn't tell him that. "I have a date with my laptop next week. Both days. Maybe another time." If she didn't submit her job application by the due date this year, she'd be vacuuming floors and cleaning bathrooms for another year instead of using her degree. No. Her future was more important than that.

"I'll hold you to that," Serge promised.

Audra managed a smile. Her ID began beeping, drawing the attention of everyone in earshot.

"Damn VIPs. Taking advantage of the twenty-four-hour maid service. Sucks to be on call." Serge patted her arm and headed off.

Audra uttered a few swear words under her breath as she read the digital display:

MAXIMA

Did he need someone to wipe his bum now? She slammed her bowl of mango cheeks and ice cream down on the table and decided he could wait until after dessert.

The persistent beeping continued.

"You're doing Jackie's job at the Pearls?" Penny squealed, seizing Audra's wrist so she could read the display. "Ooh, who needs you urgently in Villa Maxima? Is he rich? Hot? Single?"

Audra swallowed. "Confidential. You know I can't say. Guest privacy and all."

"Can you tell me how big his dick is?" Penny persisted.

Huge. Audra felt her face grow red. "Penny, you know it's against the rules to get with the guests."

Penny shrugged. "Wouldn't stop me. What's a low-paid job like this compared to being swept off your feet by a rich man who's hung like a horse? I'd ride him before he could ask for room service." She winked.

Maybe Penny would've been a better choice to service the villas, Audra fumed. At least she would have enjoyed dealing with the almighty prick who thought he was God. But then Penny might also get the full-time job that Audra wanted, which she couldn't allow. She'd better find out what he wanted. The sooner she dealt with him, the sooner she could knock off for the night.

Audra made her excuses and left the table.

"Have fun counting the inches!" Penny called after her.

TEN

Audra slowed her steps as she reached the front door of the villa. Reminding herself that every word would be recorded, she forced herself to put on her professional smile. Even if she was out of uniform, she'd be the consummate professional she needed to be. She swiped her ID and allowed the intercom to notify Jay that she was waiting outside.

The door opened and he stood in the doorway. "Fuck me!" He looked her up and down, wide-eyed.

Here we go again. "Mr Felix, I've already said no, thank you." She turned to go.

"No, wait!" He grabbed her hand.

Assault. She had an excuse to get him arrested. If she wanted to.

"Please." His brown eyes begged. "I'm sorry. I expected you to be in your shapeless uniform again, not —" He waved at her singlet top and shorts. "– this. You surprised me."

Audra wished she'd worn one of the laundry bags over her clothes. Then maybe he wouldn't be staring at her breasts. "Is there something you need, Mr Felix? Something that is within my job description to provide?"

He reddened. "It's my phone. It's not working."

She nodded and waited for him to step aside to let her in. She led the way to the kitchen, where the intercom phone was. "This one?"

"No. Mine." He waved his smartphone. "I can't get reception."

"That's because there isn't any. The year the resort was built, the phone tower came down in a cyclone. They replaced it, only for the next storm to knock it down again. It cost too much to replace, so no one ever did." Audra lifted the intercom receiver. "You can make outside calls with this. Just press zero for an outside line, then the number. It'll be added to your hotel bill when you leave."

"Okay." Jay took the receiver from her and frowned at his phone. He stabbed the buttons on the intercom and clamped the receiver between his shoulder and his ear. "It's not ringing." He handed it back to Audra, who held it to her ear. A recorded message told her to leave her name and number after the tone and someone named Jo would get back to her.

"Your friend's phone isn't switched on," Audra told him, wondering how much she'd have to explain.

"My sister. She made me promise to call her. I need to talk to her!" Audra recognised the panic in his eyes. It was the same look her brother got when the world overwhelmed him and he forgot to take his pills. Her heart twinged with something that might be sympathy. For Jay Felix? Never.

"Your sister. The one who was here today?"

He twisted his shirt between his hands. "Yes."

"The one who flew out today. And when you fly, they don't allow you to switch your mobile phone on?"

"Yes." It took a moment before her words sank in. "You mean I can't call her because she's flying?"

Audra kept her voice steady. "Yes."

Wrong answer. "So what am I supposed to do? I need to talk to her! She said…she said…" His panicked eyes darted around the room, not fixing on anything.

She said to call her before he did anything stupid. Too late. And she'd made it worse. Audra sighed. "She said to call if you got lonely, didn't she?"

He nodded, then sighed. "I fucked up. You don't even like me and she's going to kill me when she finds out what I said to you today. I'll keep calling her until she lands and switches her phone back on." He paled. "What if she's driving? Or she stays in a hotel where there isn't any mobile access? What if I can't get hold of her until tomorrow or later in the week? I need someone to talk to." He seized her hand again. "Don't go. Please."

For a long moment, Audra stared into brown eyes that could have been her brother's. Tad was the reason she could never leave her shaver in the bathroom, after the first time she'd had to clean up the blood he'd dripped everywhere from the shallow cuts on his arms. If this prick got seriously into self-harm, she'd have to clean up his mess, too.

Audra told herself that her motivations were entirely

selfish, as she said, "All right. I'll stay for a bit. As long as you don't demand sex of any kind, don't try to treat me like a prostitute, and don't stare at my boobs the whole time."

He managed a watery smile. "I'll try. But your boobs…the…you have to promise you won't go to the press. Whatever I tell you, no one else will ever know, right?"

Unless they hear this recording. Audra pressed her lips together. "That's right, Mr Felix," she lied. "All hotel staff are covered by a non-disclosure agreement. I can't sell guests' secrets to the press or I'll lose my job." That part, at least, was true.

"Jay. You can call me Jay." He met her eyes and then glanced away. "Let me get you a drink. We only have these weird fruit beers left. None of the normal ones. What'll you have?"

Thanking the hotel's policymakers for forgetting to ban drinking on the job, she accepted a mango beer and settled in an armchair. Savouring the taste with her eyes closed, Audra asked, "So what would you like to talk about, Jay?"

ELEVEN

He hunched over in the armchair across from her, gripping his beer with both hands for what seemed like an eternity. "This is stupid. I don't know you. You don't like me, so there's no way you could want to help me. You're nothing like my sister. And as long as you're wearing a shirt that shows your tits, I'm going to stare at them."

Yes, this was stupid, but if it saved her from cleaning blood off the floor and worrying about her brother... "Fine," she relented. "If you feel more comfortable talking to my chest than my face, do it. Not knowing me didn't stop you from wanting to get naked with me this afternoon, and talking is nowhere near as personal as that. But if it helps..." She took a deep breath. "Hi. My name is Audra. I've been working here at the Romance Island Resort in housekeeping for a few months now. Since graduation. I'll probably work here until I get a job in something more related to my degree. I have two older brothers and one younger one who've been bringing their problems to me since they could talk, and I usually find some way to solve them, so they keep coming back to me. Sometimes I don't like them much, either, but I still help. And I may not be like your sister, the lady I met earlier today, but you remind me of my brother."

"Do I look like him?"

Audra laughed softly. Jay might be a prick, but he was a perfect physical specimen. "No. Tad's…well, he has more of a keg than a six-pack. And a beard. One of those bushy, hipster ones." Because he doesn't trust himself with a razor anymore, she thought sadly. "No, you're better looking than my brother. But Tad video calls me at least once a week. Whenever he gets lonely. Just like you're calling your sister."

He chewed his lip. "I don't get lonely that often. I don't call her every week. I'm a rock star. I'm usually surrounded by people." He stuck his chin out. "What're you? A shrink?"

"Hell, no. My degree's in atmospheric science. Meteorology and weather, mostly."

It was Jay's turn to laugh. "A weather girl. I'm going to tell a weather girl my problems and then you'll forecast fine weather and sunny skies for me? Why are you here, Audrey the weather girl?"

She gritted her teeth, but turned it into a smile. "Audra. My name's Audra. Not Audrey."

"You look like that classic movie chick called Audrey. The one with the dark hair and big eyes who smoked a long cigarette with her breakfast." Jay took a deep pull of his beer.

"You mean Audrey Hepburn?" Well, there were worse

people to be compared to. Coming from him, it was quite a compliment. Especially alongside the weather girl joke. If she had a dollar for every time someone had said it, she wouldn't be doing this job, that's for sure. "Um, thank you. But my name really is Audra. And aren't you the one who's supposed to be talking? It's my job to listen."

Jay nodded, drained his drink and headed to the kitchen for more. When he offered Audra another, she shook her head and held up her barely touched beer. She didn't dare have more than one – not being able to afford much alcohol messed with her already low tolerance for the stuff.

He returned to the lounge but rejected his armchair for a sofa he could recline on instead – fortunately, wearing more than just his undies. "Do you know how Chaya started?"

Audra shook her head and sipped her drink. Damn, it was sweet, but good.

"I started getting a couple of live gigs in small bars on weeknights, just me and my guitar. It was all right, but not much money. In school, I was in a band with my sister and her best friend. That girl had…music in her head like magic, you know? She'd come in to practice and tell us to stop whatever we were doing to try something new she'd come up with last night. We'd whinge and complain, but we'd always give in because whatever it was would just be fucking awesome, better than anything we'd ever done before. And when the bars started looking for bigger bands than just some bloke with a guitar, I gave them one of our high school demo tracks by mistake. They fucking loved it – wanted to know if the rest of my band could come in and play. Except I didn't have a band. The girls were still at school and she was a year younger than my sister. So I waited, still playing small gigs and making a name for myself, until my band were all over eighteen and could play in pubs on a Friday and Saturday night. Sunday sessions. The bigger stuff.

"Then right before she turned eighteen, she disappeared. I was the last person to talk to her. She said she was buying my birthday present, but she wouldn't tell me what or where. We had a rehearsal that night and she never came. The police interrogated me, heaps of times, and everyone looked fucking everywhere for her. But they found nothing. It's like she'd been abducted by aliens or something. But in broad daylight while she was shopping."

Shaking his head violently, he fell silent. Audra waited.

Finally, he continued, "After about a month, they found her body. Well, not really her body, because she was alive. But only just. And fucked up...the things her kidnappers did to that girl. Fucking monsters, the lot of them. They broke every one of her fingers. She was a guitarist, amazing on the piano, too, and her voice just soared along with it, but without her hands...fuck. I thought she'd never play again."

"I don't remember hearing about this in any of the news about Chaya," Audra ventured.

Jay laughed mirthlessly. "And you won't. If some journalist tried to print it, they'd mysteriously disappear. Don't get me started on the things wrong with how that investigation was handled. A fucking government conspiracy worse than aliens. And the girl...it's like everything that happened to her unleashed a fucking avalanche of music. She got out of hospital and laid down something like the next five years' worth of songs. Dark stuff, light stuff, all of it more epic than anything we'd ever done before. And then she sold the story of all the shit that happened to her to some media group, who interviewed her on TV.

"From that, she got us a record deal. Nothing huge, mostly just royalties…and when we hit it big, the record company realised they'd fucked up, big time. We were raking it in and they were getting next to nothing. In less than a year, we renegotiated our contract and we were playing up and down the east coast, videos and tracks just going crazy on the internet. She had her new rock star name and wouldn't do press interviews because she said she was in the witness protection programme. Fuck, with an audience of millions, what sort of secrets did she expect to be able to keep? But I knew we were screwed without her, because she built the band. The songs, the image, the contract…it was all her. So I stepped up and took the media spotlight. Spent more time in the gym than practising the songs. Became a fucking rock star who everyone wanted." He sighed and drained his second beer in one long pull. "Except her."

"Your stepsister?"

He snorted and choked, spraying beer everywhere. "Jo? Fuck, no. I mean, no, she doesn't want me and I don't want to fuck her either. We grew up together. Since we were little kids. Our parents met when we were at playgroup together and I can't even remember my real mum. Jo's the only sister I have. What kind of crazy, incestuous bastard screws his own sister?"

"There's a whole genre of romance books about stepsiblings who do. Seriously. Check out the resort library some time," Audra said. Yeah, right next to the rock star romance section. Which she seriously needed to revisit in the near future. Maybe some fictional rock stars could help get thoughts of Jay Felix out of her head.

Jay padded to the kitchen and pulled his beer-soaked shirt off before washing his face and chest in the sink. Water cascaded down muscles in a performance that held Audra's attention far more than she expected. She tore her eyes away and turned her attention to her own beer. Pretty packaging did little to hide the mess he was inside, she scolded herself.

Jay returned to his seat, sans shirt. "Nice to know there are people more fucked up than me." The bottle cap clinked to the table as he opened a new beer and raised it in a toast before drinking.

"So if it's not your sister…you must mean the girl. The one who was attacked."

"The weather girl gets it right!"

His taunt nettled her. "And so you're at a luxury resort, sulking, because a traumatised girl doesn't fall at your feet and worship you?"

"I don't want her to fall at my feet. I just always figured if I became a rock star, then she'd want me. She didn't even want to study music at uni. She didn't. Her dream was…different. But I always figured she'd want me. I mean, what's better than a fucking rock star?" He puffed his chest out and struck a pose. An impressive one, Audra had to admit. But one that was shallower than the shark-infested lagoon outside.

"Jay, have you ever read any romance books?" Audra asked carefully.

He snorted. "What, shirtless dudes on the cover and women falling over themselves to let the bloke tie them up? Why the fuck would I want to read something like that?"

"Because it's what women want. A fantasy." She'd had this argument with her brothers before. "You know, there's a whole section of rock star romances in the resort library. Right next to the stepbrother ones you don't like. Maybe if you read those, you'd work out what women want from a rock star."

And it'd be bloody funny to see a rock star reading a romance book about his fictional colleagues, she had to admit.

"I'm not walking into a library and asking for romance books!" Jay protested. "I am a rock star. I know what women want from a man like me. Sex and plenty of it. They beg me for it all the time."

Not all of them, and not tonight. At least as long as she managed to control herself. Audra let the silence build until the pause was so pregnant it was ready to give birth to a crazy idea. "I could go into the library on your behalf and smuggle them in here, wrapped in tomorrow's fresh towels."

Jay regarded her for a long moment, as if his beer-blurred brain was trying to figure something out. "Do you read them?" he asked finally.

"Yes," she replied. "I'll try to bring you ones I've read." Just as long as he didn't ask her if she'd ever imagined herself with the books' heroes.

"Then I can ask you questions about them. You'll come back tomorrow night, right?"

She couldn't argue her way out of this one. Book club

with the rock star. What had she gotten herself into?

"Sure," Audra said wearily. "Just get Reception to page me."

TWELVE

The following morning, Audra slipped into the library on her way back from breakfast. Blushing a little, she realised Jay was right – most of the book covers featured hot men with more ink on their skin than clothing. She wondered why Jay only had the one tattoo inked down his well-muscled arm. She'd have to ask him about it some time. In the meantime, she avoided tattoos and shirtless men as she selected two books with couples on the front and then picked out one with a pink cover.

"Are you out of books?" Annette called. "The hen's party in Albina last week left a whole stack I'd never seen before. A real mix, too. Email-order brides, rock stars, virginity auctions…even a hot student-teacher romance. I've been reading them, but I'm almost done. I can pass them to you next, if you'll put them in the library when you're finished with them."

Audra held up her three new titles and thanked Annette. Maybe the rock star romances might be appropriate for Jay, too, not that she'd tell Annette that. Jay's romantic education was one joke she'd have to keep to herself.

Remembering her promise, Audra placed the books carefully between the folds of a towel before carrying the stack to Maxima. An awkward wrist swipe gained her access to the empty villa, where she left the towels on the side of the fortunately frog-free bath.

Wondering whether to leave a note or simply continue cleaning, Audra headed for the kitchen. The previous night's beer bottles were lined up on the bench, so she took care of those and dragged the rubbish bag outside to her cleaning trolley.

Jay ambled up the path, his steps quickening when he spotted her. "Did you get the…"

"I brought you fresh towels. You'll find everything in the bathroom," she replied, hoping he meant the books. She headed back into the villa, but hesitated at the front door. "Do you want me to finish cleaning now, or come back later?"

He shrugged. "I was going to head off to the beach. Now's fine." He entered the villa in front of her and made a beeline for the bathroom. He emerged with a beach towel wrapped around the pink book and a look of distaste on his face.

"Good choice," she said, nodding at the visible strip of pink.

He stared at it in horror and adjusted the towel to cover it. He left without another word.

Audra hid her smile and returned to the kitchen to wipe

down the counter. She'd have to refill the refrigerator, too, given Jay was out of beer. Probably a good thing. She wasn't sure she could discuss rock star romance with a rock star while she was sober. Or without picturing the hero as him...

THIRTEEN

She needn't have worried. After dinner, she spent an hour talking to her family on an online video call while her wristband was mercifully silent. She even managed to squeeze in a little light reading of her own, after she'd found Annette's stack of books sitting outside her room.

Jay avoided her for three days, though she caught sight of him lying on his private beach, reading, more than once. If she lingered for a moment or two to admire the lines of his sweat-sheened body, spread on a towel for all the world to see, surely no one would blame her. She was human, after all. Looking wasn't licking…and she couldn't deny that it had been a long time since she'd licked any part of a man's anatomy.

Not that Jay was on the staff menu, she reminded herself. She'd be lucky to get anything as tasty as mango chicken again this week, let alone raw rock star. A raw, hot mess of a rock star. Or maybe he'd gotten over his momentary insecurity, managed to contact his sister, and decided that he was the deity of music once more. His ego certainly seemed big enough for it.

On the third night after her book delivery to Villa Maxima, Audra eyed the evening's burned dinner offering. Penny had evidently distracted the sous-chef so much that he'd singed the garlic prawns. It wasn't that she didn't like king prawns; it was just time consuming to peel them out of their shells, and if they were overcooked, they might be inedible. She tentatively touched the tiniest crustacean with the tongs.

Someone bumped her elbow, sending the tongs flying. "Don't do it!" Serge cried.

Audra stared at the grinning personal trainer. "Why? Am I so fat I need to cut down on my protein intake?"

"You're gorgeous just as you are. But if you eat one of those, you might break a tooth. Adam did." Serge jerked his head at the gym manager, whose thunderous expression was partially concealed by the bloodstained wad of paper napkins he held to his mouth.

Overcooked prawns. Ugh. Audra reached for the beef curry instead, ladled a generous dollop onto her plate and carried it to an empty table.

"Do you have plans tonight?" Serge's plastic bowl of fruit salad clacked to the table and he took a seat beside her.

"Hmm." She deliberately delayed by taking a bite of beef. "I plan on staying on the island, relaxing for a couple of hours after dinner, before I drag myself into bed to fall asleep for a few hours until I have to wake up tomorrow and vacuum the sweaty gym carpet."

"Hey, it's not just sweat. That's my gym. There's blood, sweat, tears, toil and determination soaked into that carpet!"

Audra laughed. "Glad I only vacuum it and don't have to shampoo it. I've cleaned some crazy things off hotel room floors, but I wouldn't have the faintest idea how to get determination out of carpet."

"Me neither. Hey, do you remember that hen's party last week?"

How could she forget? The bride-to-be and her friends had cackled their way through their stay, drinking the bar almost dry each happy hour as they demanded every cocktail on the menu and a few they'd probably dreamed up just to confuse the bar staff. Not to mention the steamy reading material they'd left behind. Pressing her lips together, Audra nodded.

"They bought me a carton of beer as a thank you for running their boot camp sessions. Gazza from the bottle shop in town rang to tell me, asking me what I wanted. I could've gotten a carton of VB." Audra wrinkled her nose at the name of her brothers' favourite cheap beer. "See? I figured you wouldn't like that, and if I can't tempt you to into town to try the beers at the brewery, maybe I could bring them to you. So I asked him to send a taster pack and I've got Patel keeping it in the back of one of the Catering fridges."

Audra didn't know what to say. Finally, she answered, "But you earned it. You should enjoy them."

Serge laughed. "I intend to. Look, you said you want to relax for a couple of hours. How about you come relax with me on a beach with some of Broome's best beers and we'll watch the stars until they get too fuzzy to see?"

Audra glanced at her wristband, but the display was still dark. Just because she was on call didn't mean she'd be called, and Serge was certainly good company. "Sure. I'll swipe some beach towels from the laundry to sit on and we'll make a picnic of it."

After dinner, they met outside the staff accommodation. Audra slung a couple of towels around her neck, while Serge carried a cooler box full of ice that rattled against the bottles inside with every step.

They reached the beach, only to discover that the tide was in and there wasn't enough dry sand to lay a towel.

"Is there anyone in Villa Penguin?" Serge asked, staring at the waves trying to lick their feet.

Audra snorted. "That's a weird name for a pearl. You can't be serious. I don't believe there's a Villa Penguin."

"Sure there is. It's the little one with a private jetty. If you haven't found it yet, I guess no one's booked it." Serge led the way along the path to the Pearl Villas.

The houses were all dark as Audra and Serge crossed the compound, the flip-flopping thongs on their feet lit up by the glowing path-side lamps. Jungle abruptly ended and the cobbled path gave way to wooden boardwalk, extending out into the water.

"Villa Penguin's private jetty," Serge said, pointing to the sign that proclaimed just that.

Audra laughed softly and shook her head as she led the way along the boards. The scrape and thump of Serge's footfalls behind her was the only sound above the sibilant splash of waves on the jetty. Spreading the towels out at the very end, she settled on one and stretched her toes out over the edge.

Serge sat down beside her and flipped open the cooler box. "Smokey or Pearlers?"

Audra shrugged and reached for the nearest bottle. It was too dark to see the label. With the aid of Serge's bottle opener, the caps tinkled to the deck and they both drank. She tasted the bitter notes as she swallowed – then almost choked as it burned down her throat, as if she'd drunk whisky and not beer. "What the hell was that?" she gasped, squinting at the bottle. By the dim glow of Serge's phone, they read the label. "Chilli beer? What kind of sadistic bastard makes beer out of chilli?"

Serge switched his beer for hers. "Only in Broome. Have mine. It tasted like some sort of tropical fruit."

Not wanting to be caught out again, Audra checked the label first. "Lychee. Yeah, that's fruit. Fruit beer. Only in Broome, all right." When she felt the alcohol warming her from the inside, she lay back and stared up at the Milky Way, spanning the sky in the sort of glorious display she'd never see in the city at home. "I'll be dreaming of stars tonight."

"Me, too." Serge lay down beside her. "What else do you dream of?"

For a moment, she wondered if he was asking about her night-time dreams. No way in hell was she telling him about her fantasy involving Chris Hemsworth, a packet of Tim Tams and a jar of Nutella. Admittedly, lately Jay had taken his place in her dreams, along with an extra jar of hazelnut spread, but she wasn't going to tell Serge about that, either.

As if he'd sensed her confusion, he added, "You'll think it's silly, but what I dream of most is having a secure job. One where I don't need to worry about the weather or the economy or anything. A job where I can earn enough money to live off, and never have to worry about being laid off as long as I do my job right. And then I spend a day working for a bloke with a toothache and realise I want more. I want a steady income, yeah, but I also want my own gym. In the city, not near my family's farm. One where everyone gets one-on-one time with a personal trainer and a wrist tracker, to help them monitor their goals. And small classes, where the instructor's not just up the front, but making sure people do the moves right and get the most benefit they can out of it. With a meal service to help people who want to lose weight or improve their nutrition, too. A one-stop shop." He laughed softly. "That'll only ever be a dream, though. The amount of money I'd need to start my own gym and always have enough to live off…I'll need to win the lottery, I guess."

"Good luck. There are worse dreams than wanting a stable job." Like dreaming of a rock star you couldn't have. Especially when you had to reject his daily offers to make your other dreams come true. "It's one of those things you take for granted until it's taken away without warning." Audra hesitated, then ploughed on, "I'd like to work at a remote weather station in a place like this one. Seeing things few people get to, taking observations for posterity, but most of all…alone, I guess."

"You don't like people?" Serge sat up in surprise. "I wouldn't have thought that about you."

Audra bit her lip. "It's not that. I do like people. I've lived most of my life in the city, in a household with five kids where you barely get five minutes to yourself. I…you'll laugh at me when you hear this. Annette warned me about the accommodation here, saying it was just like a minesite with single rooms and all, but I almost squealed in delight when I saw it. It's the first time in my life that I haven't had to share a room with someone else. I love my family, but they always seem to need help with something. For as long as I can remember, I've done the laundry for all seven of us, just to make sure I had clean shirts for school and then for work. Cooked most nights that I was home, because Mum just never had the time or the energy by the end of the day. Is it a dream to want to only have to worry about myself?"

"Nah, I know what you mean. When I'm on the farm, Dad always worries about the price of wine and grape yields and who's been bought out by the big wineries. Whether he'll get enough workers for the harvest or the pruning, and whether drought or fire or hail will ruin this year's crop. Whether he's better off selling the whole crop to another winemaker, or going to the trouble of pressing the vintage himself. My brothers all went to uni, did agriculture or viticulture or courses in how to make sheep cheese, and now they're all planning on getting married and having kids, to Mum's delight. I'm the youngest and Dad damn near disowned me when I said I didn't want to go to university. As for getting married…I was more interested in health and fitness, not wine. Family…shit, I love them, but they're not the ones living my life. That's me. I have to make my own choices." Glass clinked. "Want another beer? I think these are both normal ones. No fruit or vegetables this time."

Audra accepted the drink and hugged her knees to her chest as she stared out over the dark ocean. "Thanks. Yes, I love my family. But it feels like I do less work out here, even when I'm still on laundry duty. I have time to myself.

Almost makes working here feel like a holiday." She laughed. "Don't tell Annette I said that. When we're fully booked and I've had to clean a record number of rooms in less time than it takes to drive here from town, sometimes I vacuum so many rooms and scrub so many showers that I can still hear the hum of the vacuum cleaner at dinner, or I wake up with my fingers cramping around an imaginary spray bottle in the middle of the night."

"Why don't you have a job at a weather station? I haven't finished my qualification yet, but I thought you said you'd graduated."

Audra sighed. "Yeah, I graduated earlier this year. Most of the meteorology jobs in Australia are through the Commonwealth Bureau of Meteorology. They have one graduate intake a year." It still hurt to think about it.

"Did you miss out last year?"

She thanked her lucky stars that it was too dark for her to see the sympathy on his face. Or for him to see the tears escaping from her eyes at the memory of Leon's mangled car and him lying in hospital in a drug-induced coma, like an ad for why seventeen-year-olds shouldn't own V8s, drive fast and drink alcohol. "Sort of. I didn't get my application finished before the deadline. So they didn't accept it and I had to wait another year."

"When's the deadline?"

"In two weeks. My application's mostly written, but I want it to be the best it can be so that this time next year, I'm cleaning a cup anemometer, not some VIP's carpet. So every day off between now and then, I'll be picking through the words, trying to put them together better, practicing responses to interview questions…the best applicants get the best locations, or that's what I've heard. And I've never been outside Western Australia before."

Serge clinked his beer against hers. "Then good luck. To you achieving your dreams, because they sound like they're a damn sight closer than mine. Mine are up there with those stars somewhere." He waved at the Milky Way.

"Thanks." Audra drained her beer.

"Want another one? The last two are mango and ginger, I think. Guess I saved the best for last. Here's the mango one."

Just like she'd had that night with Jay. Audra reached for it and her wristband beeped. The LED illuminated the name of Jay's villa. Had he read her thoughts? "Shit."

Serge dropped the bottle back into the ice. "I'll keep them for you until you come back."

Book club with the rock star. Good thing she wasn't sober. "No, don't wait up. Who knows what the VIP wants this time. You enjoy them, or save them for another night." She rose and dusted off her shorts. "Can you drop the towels in the laundry on your way back?"

Serge nodded. "I'll save the last beers for the night you find out you've got the job, managing your own weather station in paradise."

"You mean when I get sent to the arse-end of nowhere." Audra laughed. "Wherever. You're on."

FOURTEEN

The swish of waves on the shore still permeated the jungle as Audra headed for the only illuminated villa on this side of the lagoon. Once again, work won over any chance of enjoying herself. Was Serge right – would her life one day hold something different? Or would she just work herself to death, without getting to enjoy any of life's pleasures the way normal people did?

Jay hadn't drawn the blinds, so skirting his villa was oddly voyeuristic as she watched him check his watch and glance at the door every few seconds, clenching a book in his hands. He looked like the poster boy for money's inability to buy happiness. She and Jay could be miserable together, then.

Audra swiped her wristband and waited for the door to slide open as the intercom announced her arrival. The sound of tumbling glass greeted her as she entered the lounge room — what hadn't been visible from the window were the empty bottles lined up on the tiles at Jay's feet. She leaped into action, grabbing as many as she could before she had to clean up broken glass instead of just beer-basted bottles.

Two armloads later, she'd filled the recycling bin in the kitchen. Audra eyed the tiles critically. "Do you want me to mop that now or wait 'til morning? It's only a few drops and I'd hate you to slip…" Her beer-befuddled brain caught up with her mouth. "But a fresh-mopped floor would be slippery, too. Morning's probably best."

Jay nodded, his unfocussed eyes making her wonder if he'd even understood her question, let alone her dilemma.

"You paged me. Was there something else you wanted me to help you with?" Audra wet her lips. "Or did you just want me to clean up the bottles?"

"Your rock star romance books don't help," he slurred, throwing them down on the sofa.

Audra eyed the pink book and one with a couple on the front. "How so?" she asked lightly.

Jay waved at them. "These are about girls still hung up on their high school crush, who never noticed them, until they're rock stars and suddenly they do. If I was a chick who wanted to seduce a rock star, fine, but I'm the fucking rock star."

Audra rubbed her fuzzy eyes, wishing she could do the same to the inside of her head. He wasn't making any sense. "I thought you said the girl you've been pining over since high school is a rock star, too. Your guitarist…isn't that what you said? You're out here sulking, all sad and lonely, because she's thrown you out and you're trying to find a way you can crawl into her good graces again so she'll take you back?"

"Fuck no!" Jay roared. "Rock stars don't sulk and they don't crawl for uppity chicks, either."

Audra tried to hide her scepticism. "So why are you hiding out here?"

"I'm not hiding!" With what appeared to be considerable effort, he lowered his voice to a more normal volume. "I'm planning. Regrouping. Taking some much-needed time to consider my future. The next stage in my career."

Rock stars had to make career choices? She'd never really thought about it. They wrote and recorded albums, performed the songs at concerts, while millions of fans screamed their names, bought their music and obsessed over them. But the wrong choices could end his career just as surely as they could hers. And while she could always find another job somewhere else, cleaning hotel rooms or serving food, that wasn't an option for a rock star whose meteoric rise had turned into a freefall that could only end in a crash to Earth. Did he mean he had to decide on which country to tour next or what style of music to write for his next album? Sobriety descended on Audra like a cold shower. It wasn't his career future he was considering — it had to be the girl he denied having feelings for. Career angst didn't create chaos with your emotions the way love could. Jay wasn't just a rock star — he was a man, too.

"What are you going to do next?" she asked softly.

It seemed like his macho mask slipped away and she saw genuine fear in his eyes. "I don't fucking know."

Silence hung between them for a moment. In two strides, Audra crossed the room and hugged him. One minute she was safely, dispassionately ensconced on her own seat, the next she had her arms around a slab of miserable man-muscle and she didn't want to let go. She had no idea how to disentangle herself from the crazy situation, but she knew her wristband would record every word she said.

His arms encircled her far less awkwardly, though no less firmly. He emitted a muffled "thank you".

Then he lifted his head and his eyes met hers. His mouth was so close and still slightly open, as if preparing to kiss her. Audra's lips parted to take a shaky breath before she surrendered to her desire for Jay.

"You know what'd make me feel even better?" Jay began, looking hopeful. "If you got your tits out. Then we could – "

Thank God his rock star ego had broken the moment.

"No. I'm sorry, Mr Felix, but we can't." Audra took that as her cue to retreat a few steps before collapsing into her chair again, relieved to be on the other side of the coffee table from the mess of contradictions that was Jay Felix.

"Bugger." His pause was barely perceptible. "Want a beer, then?"

She nodded silently. Better to wrap her lips around a bottle than do anything dangerous with them.

FIFTEEN

Morning light stung Audra's eyes and she cursed. She must have fallen asleep with the blinds open. She forced her eyelids up and blinked away the bleariness. This wasn't her room. It looked like...Maxima.

Uncurling her stiffened limbs, she rose from the armchair that had cradled her all night, it seemed, as Jay's recounting of the all-too-familiar plots of those two romance novels had made her nod, then close her eyes, until finally...she guessed she'd drifted right off into la-la-land. Well, she could cross one thing off her bucket list that she'd never expected to achieve: she'd spent a night with a rock star. Jay Felix, no less. And hadn't she hugged him for a moment, too?

She ran her fingers through her hair, hoping to smooth it out enough so that no one would know where she'd spent the night. Though sneaking out of Maxima at this time in the morning would probably give her away, anyway.

Audra almost made it to the door before she met Jay carrying a covered tray.

"I ordered you breakfast!" He seemed really proud of himself and not put out at all that she'd passed out on his couch.

"I'm sorry – " she began.

He waved her into silence. "Nah, you looked wrecked last night. I asked if you wanted me to read you to sleep and you sort of nodded, so I cracked open that last – " he coughed " – *romance* book you got me and started reading aloud. Haven't done shit like that since I was at school. Got to admit, it was a bit of a relief when you started snoring. Doesn't do much for my rock star reputation, reading romance books." His eyes strayed to the sofa where he'd been sitting last night and Audra felt a little smug to see that the book lay face-down, open at a page well past the middle. So much for his reputation, if this ever got out.

Audra sighed inwardly. It wouldn't get out – it was her job to protect the VIPs' privacy, no matter how many ridiculous things they did. Romance novels were barely a blip on the radar, from some of the whispered stories she'd heard in the staff dining room.

Speaking of which…"I'd best grab some breakfast. Busy day of work ahead." She moved purposefully toward the door again.

"But I got you breakfast! Look, look!" He uncovered the tray and held out a sandwich on a plate. "It's for you!"

Audra smiled politely and continued backing away.

"You can't say no to a bacon sandwich! Breakfast of rock stars!" Jay started to look desperate.

"Sorry, I don't like bacon. And I'm expected in the staff dining room." Audra escaped, jogging down the path until she knew she was out of sight of the villas. Only then did she take a deep breath.

Bacon. Her kryptonite. Actually, any sort of pork. Ever since that field trip for uni, checking out the ventilation and odour management systems for the abattoir, and watching the live pigs get slaughtered and sliced and…

She dropped to the ground, hoisting her knees up until she could wedge her head firmly between them. Breathe. Smell the brine and the ocean and the sand and the jungle and the…had someone burned breakfast again? If Penny didn't leave that poor sous-chef alone, he'd lose his job for sure. Better burned cinnamon than bacon, though.

Rising to her shaky feet, Audra continued on to the dining room. If she finished first, she might get a few extra minutes in the communal showers before one of the other girls tried to beat down the door. Hey, she could hope. Warm water caressing her skin for a few more minutes was the best she could hope for, after all.

SIXTEEN

Jason climbed into the helicopter, irritated and intrigued and itching to get off the island. Hence the helicopter. Not that he was flying it; he left the difficult stuff to other people like the pilot. He knew the press release would go out today, telling the world about Chaya's farewell tour. His days as a hot rock god were numbered and it fucking pissed him off.

And that girl…refusing him like he was a nobody already. Who did she think she was? She was a hotel maid, for fuck's sake. Not a rock star or a doctor or even the hotel manager, but the girl who cleaned the floors and took out the rubbish. He wanted some solace from normal girls. The sort that swooned at his feet. Not made him read fucking romance books full of shit no rock star would ever do. Cook a girl breakfast? Put her pleasure before his own? Tell her stuff no self-respecting rock star would ever admit to feeling when there was enough alcohol in the house to deaden it? Shit, he needed a drink just thinking about all that emotional crap. The stuff crazy people told their shrink.

He scratched his chin, or at least the hair sprouting from it. Could a rock star get away with a hipster beard? He was almost there. It'd be a shame to shave it off now.

As they lifted off the helipad, he watched the hotel staff spilling out of a building hidden among the palm trees. His eyes zeroed in on the one person he'd recognise anywhere — the maid who'd fallen asleep on his couch. When she lifted her gaze to the rising plexiglass bubble, he deliberately turned away.

Why hadn't he reported her? Called Security or Reception and had them remove her from his house? He'd even felt sorry for her and bought her breakfast, but she'd refused. What kind of girl refused to join a rock star for breakfast after sleeping with him? Well, sleeping in his house, anyway.

He'd pick up some girls in town and bring them back to the island for a few nights. That'd make him feel better. Let the maid know what she was missing out on. What was her name? Audrey, like the fool's shepherdess…Jason fingered the tattooed words on his arm, a constant reminder of who he was. At least until Chaya fractured and they all went their own ways. Then what?

Fuck, it was too early to be thinking about a future beyond the rest of the day. He wanted a drink. Then he wanted some damn accommodating chicks who'd do whatever he asked, because he was a rock star. He stared moodily out the window, where the clashing colours of red rock, aqua ocean, the muddy brown of rivers and the green swirls of vegetation marking the riverbanks looked more like an abstract painting than real land. Everything about this place was surreal, including the way all the rivers and inlets looked like tortured trees full of snakes. Next to them, the heart-shaped island that housed his hotel seemed nearly normal.

Not that he could get away with rubbishing the town in the residents' hearing, though. He knew that already. One chance comment that ended up in the news could linger for weeks. Talk about hypocrisy. He could do whatever he liked to his appearance, get drunk and sleep with half the town's female population, and all anyone would say is that he was living it up in Broome because it was paradise. Say the town had a trippy river and he'd get hate mail.

Beside the town helipad, he could already see the car he'd ordered. A brand-new, black four-wheel-drive with air conditioning that could bring an Antarctic blizzard to the Kimberley. He itched to drive it. Maybe even take it off road a bit.

The helicopter bumped gently to the ground. Driving time.

"I'll drive up to the pearl farm myself and meet you there with the chopper later," he told the pilot as he slid to the ground, doubling over to stay out of reach of the still-spinning rotors. "Oh, and make sure they know I'll be bringing guests!"

He climbed behind the wheel of his new car and pulled the door closed, sealing himself inside with the new-car smell. The cloying humidity could stay outside the glass as he drove with dream-like precision to the morning haunt of all rock stars: the nearest pub.

SEVENTEEN

"So how'd your hot date with Serge go last night?" Milk splashed out of Penny's bowl of cereal as she shoved it across the table.

Audra stared at Penny. "It wasn't a hot date. We just had a few beers, sat on the beach and talked."

Penny snorted. "Talked. Yeah, right. You're still wearing the same clothes you had on yesterday, Adam's threatening to strangle Serge because he won't stop whistling, and I know you didn't come home last night because I didn't hear your door."

"You must have been asleep, then," Audra said lightly, rising to leave.

Penny grabbed her wrist. "I wanted to borrow your argan oil. I'm out and Patel loves to stroke my hair, but I went for a swim yesterday and the salt's stripped it all dry. C'mon, I know you had heaps the last time you let me borrow it." She smirked. "Or are you saving it to grease up your lover boy?"

"Yeah, maybe I am," Audra snapped, yanking her arm free. Last time Penny had borrowed the bottle, she'd used a third of the expensive stuff and she certainly hadn't paid for it. Audra had no intention of being so gullible a second time — she wasn't sure when she'd be able to afford more for herself. "So no, you can't use it."

"You'll need all the lube you can get so that hunk of meat can slide into your puckered-up hole, Grumpy Guts," Penny retorted. "How long's it been since you spread your legs for a man? Months, definitely, seeing as you haven't had anyone over since we got here. Or longer than that? Was your boyfriend back home saving himself for marriage? Or is that you?"

Audra wanted to punch Penny for voicing what she was already thinking, but even she had to admit it wouldn't be fair. "It's been a while," she confessed quietly.

Penny hooted with laughter. "So kiss that personal trainer of yours, get him to back you up against the wall and do you in the shower block. With arms like his, I bet he could support your weight for hours." She smiled mistily. "I'd do him." She eyed Audra's top. "Looks like you already did last night. I knew you were lying. What's that, then?" She pointed at a blotch.

Peering at her shirt, Audra sighed. "Ice cream from dessert, most likely."

"Ha! You blew him! I'd never have thought it of you. That hot man practically owes you a decent screw now. If you were out with him all last night, why didn't you collect?"

"I wasn't…" Audra trailed off, knowing Penny would only get louder and more insistent the longer she protested. The fewer people who knew about last night, the better. "We were just talking and then I got paged over to the Pearls. I…it was a mess, and I was there most of the night, dealing with it." She avoided Penny's searching eyes.

"You blew a VIP? What'd he taste like? Did he tip you? How big was he? Was he hot?"

Audra winced. "Penny."

Penny finally noticed that they were drawing attention and lowered her voice. "Was he hot?" she repeated.

"I didn't do anything with anyone last night. You know we can't."

"If no one knows, it never happened," Penny intoned, waving her hands around as if she was casting some sort of spell.

Audra snorted. "Well, it didn't. It's all in your imagination." She glanced at her watch. "And now breakfast's over, so I should grab a shower before I have to finish cleaning the villas. Reception said we have a booking for Albina on the weekend." She hurried out, hoping Penny wouldn't follow.

"Tell me his name!"

Audra shook her head and kept going. Thumping helicopter blades make her glance up – surely the guests for Albina weren't arriving already? They weren't due until tomorrow. It was taking off, not landing, though, and she thought she recognised the passenger before he turned his head. Jay was headed off for an outing – a private heli-fishing expedition, a tour of the gorges or what she'd been told was a magical flight over Horizontal Falls, maybe. Stuff she'd never be able to afford. Especially not if she didn't get a shower before work.

Fifteen minutes later, when the hot water had run out and she'd buttoned herself into her work uniform, Audra stared critically at her reflection. Yes, the shadows under her eyes were almost darker than her irises. She needed a decent night's sleep in her own bed without worrying about rock stars, sleeping on their couches, drinking too much beer or...sweet dreams about sex with Jay Felix. She hoped Jay enjoyed his excursion today so much that he was too tired to call for maid service tonight.

As if it had heard her, Audra's wristband beeped, summoning her to Reception. She reached for her shoes.

Heloise stood at the reception desk, wearing a pink frangipani because the white ones blended into her fair hair.

"You paged me?" Audra waved her wrist in the air.

Heloise found the message. "The guest in Maxima will be bringing more people to the villa tonight. Can you make sure it's ready?"

"Sure thing. Did he mention what time?"

Heloise shrugged. "When the helicopter comes back. The pilot's the one who relayed the message from the mainland."

So the only warning she'd have would be the sound of the pearl farm's helicopter returning. Fine. She'd deal with Maxima first, then. Audra thanked Heloise and headed for the Pearls.

EIGHTEEN

"You want pancakes and a pint of beer?" the waitress repeated, puckering her lips like a puzzled duck.

Jason folded his arms behind his head, reclining in his seat. "That's right, babe. And extra syrup. I'm looking for a little more sweetness today." He winked, then realised his sunglasses hid his eyes. He thought about taking them off, but it was a bloody bright morning. Besides, if the girl couldn't even take his order properly, she didn't deserve a wink from a rock god.

Shaking her head, the waitress wandered back to the kitchen.

Jason shrugged. Her loss.

He resumed reading his newspaper, scanning for the story about Chaya's farewell concert, growing more and more annoyed as he kept turning pages and found no word of it. It should have been front-page news, but some plane crash had claimed that headline, and the paper was full of pictures of the wreckage and the people who'd been on board. He had enough bad news in his own life today – he didn't need to be depressed even more with stories of lives tragically cut short. In frustration, he tossed the paper onto another table. Maybe he'd have been better off staying at the resort.

The sweet smell of chocolate changed his mind as his pancakes arrived. Chocolate chip pancakes drowned in maple syrup with ice cream and a cherry on top, no less. Fuck, if they tasted half as good as they smelled, he'd have to stick them on his list of requirements for Chaya's next tour. Their final tour.

He stabbed the cherry with his fork, but somehow it slipped off before it made it to his mouth, splashing maple syrup everywhere. Swearing, he yanked off his syrup-smeared sunglasses and threw them down on the table. Fuck daylight. Fuck breakfast. Fuck hiding. No one knew who he was and soon Chaya would be nothing but a forgotten memory. He was nobody again.

"Oh my God, it's Jay Felix!" someone squealed.

Maybe not yet.

Jason found himself signing autographs and posing for photos with the group of backpackers who'd stopped in to grab breakfast on their way to the beach. One glance at the string bikinis barely covered by transparent shirts and skimpy shorts was enough to lift his spirits. And harden his resolve. A pack of fangirls to play with was exactly what he needed right now.

He invited them to join him for breakfast and grinned as two of them started fanning themselves. There had to be something wrong with that hotel maid. No one refused breakfast with a rock star.

He called the waitress over and insisted she arrange for a bigger table, more chairs and pancakes for everyone. And where was his beer?

Giggling washed over him like a bottle of shaken-up champagne. Balm to his rock star ego and enough to send his hangover away.

He lifted up the badly behaved cherry by its stalk. "Who wants me to a pop a cherry?"

Jason grinned as several of them blushed. He didn't care if girls were virgins or experts – he was their first rock star, enough to make any girl forget every other man she'd slept with. He selected a girl whose blush was so red it rivalled the fruit in his fingers. "Open your mouth," he purred, widening his grin as she obeyed, before popping the cherry inside. He paused while she ate it. "I like a girl who swallows."

More giggles erupted and he basked in their adoration. Almost as good as sex, though he was pretty sure he'd be getting that, too.

NINETEEN

Fresh towels, fresh linen, fresh milk, replacing the plundered contents of the refrigerator…Audra hummed to herself as she worked, wanting to make sure Maxima glowed like the pearl it was for Jay's VIP guests. Foreign VIPs gave tips, which were an always welcome addition to her income, and if she could get one or more of them to put in a good word for her with Annette, she'd be one step closer to the off-season position.

And perhaps Jay would conveniently forget that she'd fallen asleep in his house.

She set off the robotic vacuum cleaner in Maxima and headed to Albina to prepare it for tomorrow's guests. Albina had been booked for an executive retreat, she found, so she had to contact Engineering and IT to make sure they provided a long list of computer and communications requirements for the visiting executives.

Once the men started plugging in cables, talking about bandwidth and racks and some new game that had just been released, Audra escaped back to Maxima. One robot replaced another as she set off the one that mopped, listening out for the rotor blades of Jay's returning helicopter. Who would he bring? Other celebrities? Or the rest of the band, perhaps?

What if he brought the guitarist girl he wanted to win?

He'd rejected romance books and rubbished any suggestions she'd made, so Audra doubted the relationship between the two would change unless he did.

Though if he had a little help…

She contacted Catering and asked for a honeymoon supper package, delivered cold to the villa to be prepared at the right moment. Audra stuck the champagne in the fridge, alongside the tray of chocolate fondue, complete with instructions on how to heat the chocolate. The strawberries looked so perfect, Audra felt hard-pressed not to steal one, but she wasn't the one Jay would be romancing, so she closed the door firmly on temptation.

She took the rose petal bath mixture and massage oil to the bathroom, then changed her mind and left the oil in the master bedroom instead, adding it to the innocuous-looking, heart-shaped box of condoms and flavoured lubes.

Audra finished the romantic atmosphere with the addition of mood lighting – every battery-operated tealight she could gather, lined up along the edge of the spa, the flat surfaces in the bedroom and even on the lounge room coffee table. Pleased at her handiwork, she resolved to return at sunset to turn the little lights on.

For a moment, she wished a man would romance her

half as well as she was helping Jay do for his mysterious woman. Audra hoped the girl appreciated it as much as she would.

TWENTY

As the afternoon sun turned its slanting rays into his eyes, Jason peered at the menu, trying to decide if he needed to eat something else with his next mango beer. His lunchtime steak sandwich had been a long time and several beers ago, but it wasn't really time for dinner yet. Besides, he didn't want to stay for dinner. He was hungry for something far hotter and tastier than food.

He'd narrowed his harem down to four girls, after some had deserted him to go to the beach or other tourist shit. Three blondes and one brunette, though he was pretty sure they were all natural brunettes. Not that he cared about their hair.

One of them seemed to be reading his mind, because she met his gaze and then slowly, deliberately, started sucking on her empty beer bottle. He felt his shorts grow tight as half the bottle vanished into her mouth.

Another girl's hand landed on his thigh, so close to his hard-on, he was certain she could feel the heat of it. "You're a big boy, Jay," she whispered. "Would you like some help taming that beast tonight?"

Jason flashed his best rock star smile. No girl could tame him, but he'd have a lot of fun letting her try.

"So is it true? Chaya's breaking up and it really is their last tour?"

Irritated, he glared at the girl who'd spoken, but she didn't seem to notice his displeasure.

The bottle came out of blowjob girl's mouth with an audible pop. "What? You're retiring? But we all love your music so much. You can't quit!"

"Don't you love your fans, Jay?" The hand on his thigh abruptly pulled away.

"Why do you want to retire?"

Fuck. He didn't want to retire. He wanted to be a rock star until the day he died, and enjoy good booze and good company every day of his life. Rock stars didn't talk about their fucking feelings to chicks; they just wanted to fuck to forget they had any feelings other than physical ones.

After a day of drinking himself into a state where he could forget about his impending retirement, now these bitches had brought his despair back with a vengeance. Well, fuck them. Or not. He wouldn't, anyway. They could go screw some of their backpacker buddies. Any desire he'd felt for these girls had died.

"I need a piss," he mumbled, jumping up. He swayed a bit, then righted himself and stumbled in the direction of the bar's bathrooms.

He relieved the considerable pressure in the men's

room, glad that none of the nosy girls had had the guts to follow him in there.

"Hey, I know you. You're Jay Felix. Shit. Wow. Heard about your retirement, man. It must feel pretty awesome to be retiring at your age. What're you planning on doing? Shacking up with some hot sheilas and living it up for a bit?"

Fuck. What kind of bloke thought he could talk to a guy while he was pissing? Fucking rude, that's what it was.

"Something like that," Jason mumbled, tucking his tackle away. He shoved through the door and strode to the bar.

What was wrong with people? His plans were none of their fucking business. Why couldn't they see that? All he wanted was a bit of sympathy and distraction, and to take a piss in peace. Was that too much for a man to ask?

The maid at the hotel had understood. She'd looked sad, like she felt his pain, given him a hug and not protested when he'd stared down the front of her shirt at her tits. Admittedly, she hadn't gotten them out for him, but she'd still shown more sympathy than anyone else. And those perky tits…

Why the fuck was he here after some random, nosy chicks when the one he wanted was at his hotel? He just needed to persuade her to get over her inhibitions and sleep with him. Maybe if he bought her a present and then got her drunk, she'd agree…

What was taking the bartenders so long to serve him?

He held up his hand to catch the older bartender's eye.

"Yes, sir?"

"Finalise the bill for my table. I'm closing the tab."

"Yes, sir." She paused. "A receipt, sir?"

"Nah." Shit, he needed a present. He thought of the hotel maid and her Cupid's bow lips kissing the top of a beer bottle last night. More than once, he'd caught her closing her eyes and humming as she savoured the taste of the sweet brew. "Get me a case of your mango beer to take home, though."

She beckoned to one of the glassies and he returned less than a minute later, carrying a carton. Jay nodded his thanks, hoisted the box onto his shoulder and headed out to his car. He shoved the box in the back seat and slid behind the wheel.

Jason gunned the engine, then crunched the car into gear. Now he remembered what had gotten into him last night, why he'd begged the girl to stay. It was all that pent-up passion inside her. He could see it in every sip she took of her beer, every time she glanced at his bare chest — of course he'd taken his shirt off; he knew what the sight of his six-pack did to women. She played her part in life as well as he did. Showing one thing while feeling another. Always putting on a show. But she'd seen through his act just as he'd seen through hers. He wanted to be the one to shatter that brittle shell so she could shine like a fucking beacon.

The only girl he wanted in his bed tonight was Audra. Shit, he even remembered her name. It had to be love.

Jason slammed his foot down on the accelerator and screeched out of the parking lot. He had a helicopter to catch, and a woman to romance.

TWENTY ONE

"What in hell did you do in here?" Audra surveyed the grisly scene in the gym. It looked like there'd been a bloodbath and there were suspicious, red splatters on the ceiling, too. "Where are the bodies?"

Serge coughed. "Um, he's resting in his room and his girlfriend's tending to him."

Audra waved her arms at the blood-soaked walls and floor. "One man lost this much blood and he's still alive?"

"It's not all blood."

Audra sighed. "Does Annette know about this?" He nodded. "Fine, then. I'll help you clean it up, but you're going to do half the work and while we're working, you'll tell me how you turned the gym into a slaughterhouse."

"Well, it started with this kid who wanted to impress his girlfriend, so he showed up at the gym but refused a session with the personal trainer…"

Audra wiped down the walls on one side while Serge took the other, telling her the whole story.

The kid had come to keep his girlfriend company at the gym. While she did her cardio on the bikes, he'd decided to show his awesome muscles off by bench-pressing some weights. His sweaty, straining hands had slipped, though, and he'd managed to smash the barbell onto his nose. Blood spurted, he'd sneezed and most of the weights area, along with the wall behind it, had gotten sprayed in blood. A trail of it had followed the kid and his angry girlfriend out the door to the first aid room.

Serge had called Housekeeping and Annette had sent Penny, who'd claimed she was an expert in cleaning carpets and using the shampooing machine.

Audra knew otherwise, but she just shook her head. Perhaps it hadn't been quite as bad as she suspected.

Actually, it was worse.

Penny had filled the machine with foam, switched it on and set to work. Serge had headed over to the free weights area to work with a client. The next thing he'd heard from Penny was some shrieked swearing before the carpet cleaning machine exploded. Bloodstained water coated the walls, the ceiling and the carpet. Penny had picked up the gym phone and called Annette, whining about the faulty equipment that had almost killed her. Before she could hang up, Serge grabbed the phone off her and requested a more senior member of the Housekeeping staff to help with the mess, as this girl evidently needed first aid.

He'd rid himself of Penny and Annette had suggested Audra. So there they were.

Audra sighed again. "I'll go get the shampooing

machine. I'm sure it'll be fine when I put the reservoir in properly."

Serge shook his head. "No, that thing exploded. It's too dangerous."

"Were you or your client flexing your muscles during the training session?"

He snorted. "Weights training. It builds and flexes muscle. Of course. I'll show you, if you like." He dropped his cleaning cloth and took an eager step toward the dumbbells.

Audra waved him away. "I believe you. Some other time, maybe. Penny's easily distracted. She probably put too much shampoo into the machine, wasn't watching the foam and the pressure popped the reservoir. It's not the first time it's happened, though it wasn't quite as messy then."

Together, they finished cleaning the gym with the now-operational carpet shampooer and switched the gym sign from open to closed while the carpet dried. Afterwards, they walked back to the staff accommodation together to shower and change into their civilian clothes for dinner.

When they met again outside, Audra eyed his wet hair and her thoughts strayed to what would happen if she took Penny's advice and shared a shower with Serge. She'd never done anything aside from wash in a shower before, given how both hot water and shower time had been rationed at home in a house with seven people and one bathroom.

Serge gave her an exaggerated bow. "I owe you my eternal servitude for saving me from that mess."

"Don't you mean gratitude? You know, you're grateful for what I did? Servitude is like slavery and that was abolished years ago."

He waved a hand airily. "Either. Both. If you ever need a favour, just ask me." He grinned. "Now, the least I can do is take you to dinner."

Audra laughed. "The finest the staff dining room has to offer, I'm sure. I wonder what's been burned tonight."

Mango chicken, as it turned out, and they talked and laughed through the meal, as easily as if they'd known each other for years. Scrubbing blood off a ceiling together evidently did that to people.

After they were finished, Serge wanted to check on the dampness of the gym floor, so Audra bade him goodnight and headed back to the staff accommodation on her own. She glanced at the empty helipad, wondering if the pumping music and the shriek of the shampoo machine had drowned out the sound of Jay's return to the island. She hoped he was safely ensconced in his villa, entertaining his guest. If he needed her, he'd surely page her, but her wristband had remained mercifully silent since Serge's emergency call just after lunch.

Hoping to get an early night, Audra trudged back to her room and locked the door. She figured she'd check her emails and messages on her laptop, then go to sleep. Most of the messages were advertising, so she scrolled down the list, deleting as she went, until she came across an email from her sister, Sam, asking if she'd be free for an online video call. She'd sent it twenty minutes earlier, so Audra quickly responded that she was free now, if Sam wanted.

Five minutes later, Sam's excited face filled her screen. "Guess what, guess what!"

Thinking of her conversation last night with Serge, she said, "Mum finally won the lottery?"

Sam giggled. "She won thirty bucks last week – her first win in months – but no, she didn't win the jackpot, even though Mum still buys a ticket every week. No, better than that."

Audra couldn't think of anything better that she'd want to voice to her fifteen-year-old sister. "I don't know, Sam."

"Josh kissed me today!"

"Oh…but that's not your first kiss, is it?"

Sam rolled her eyes. "No, of course not. I'm fifteen, not ten. But it's my first French kiss with the captain of the Year Ten basketball team. And he didn't drool much!"

Audra fought laughter. "So this Josh is a good kisser?"

"Well…" Sam scrunched up her nose. "He wasn't at first, but we got better with practice. He only licked my nose once. After a while, like, all of lunch, my tummy felt all fluttery. Almost like I was in love. Tad laughed and said it was all the saliva exchange making me sick, but he's just jealous. Maybe he's right, though. Does kissing make you sick? Because I can't be in love with Josh."

Aw, first love. Audra couldn't hold back a happy sigh. "Why not? Love's not something you can control. It just sort of…" Creeps up on you, wrenches at your heart and breaks it when he leaves you.

Sam groaned. "I'm so not a kid any more! I'm in love with Jay Felix. Kissing Josh doesn't make me anywhere near as hot as kissing Jay would. I mean, just kissing his poster…" She blushed.

Audra fought to find the right words. "Rock stars like Jay aren't worth your time, Sam. He wouldn't notice normal people like us over his enormous ego." Even as she spoke, she knew it was a lie. Jay had poured out his heart to her, read her a story and even ordered her breakfast. He was worth her time, and not just because she got paid for it. "Don't pin your hopes on something that'll never happen," she finished lamely.

"One day it will. Ooh, they announced concert dates for Chaya's next tour. Jay's coming to Perth for their farewell tour next year. Guess that means he won't be a rock star any more and I'll have even more of a chance. Do you think if I…" Sam continued, but Audra stopped listening.

Chaya's farewell tour.

The missing pieces fell into place. No wonder he kept insisting he was a rock star – when Chaya broke up, he'd be just an ordinary bloke again. No longer rock royalty. He was running out of time to impress this girl with his rock star charms. Poor Jay. Audra hoped the fondue she'd left would help. To lose your identity and the girl you loved all in one hit would be quite a blow to anyone. If he needed help with anything…

Audra's eyes darted to her ID, but the display was still dark. She wasn't wanted in Maxima tonight.

"So what d'you think?"

Audra blinked. "Um, sure," she replied, hoping it was the right thing to say.

Sam cheered. "Awesome. I'll pay you back, I promise. Tickets go on sale for the concert tomorrow and if you're coming, then you can drive us."

"The Chaya concert? Yeah, okay." Standing in the audience, watching Jay and his band perform for the last time. As long as he didn't spot her in the crowd, it would be fine. The tickets wouldn't come cheap, though. There goes this week's pay, she thought.

After a few more minutes of small talk, Audra ended the call and closed her ageing laptop.

She could ask Jay for tickets. Maybe even the chance to go backstage. She wouldn't ask for herself, but she'd do almost anything for Sam. The worst he could say was no, and then she'd just buy them like she'd planned. But she'd have to do it tonight, before tickets went on sale in the morning, because if it was anything like other Chaya concerts, they sold out fast.

Audra slipped on her shoes and headed for Villa Maxima.

TWENTY TWO

How were you supposed to see the road when it was the same red dirt as the bush on either side and there weren't any street lights? Every road should have fucking street lights, Jason fumed as his car bounced over another rut. So much for the best four-wheel-drive the dealership had to offer. The suspension on this was shit. He may as well have been driving the little shitbrick of a hatchback he'd owned before Chaya made it big. And where was the damn hotel, anyway? The helicopter flight hadn't taken half this long and he couldn't see a single building anywhere.

Jason floored the accelerator, trying to get the stupid car to go faster, but all it did was bump harder down the unsealed road. Maybe he should call the helicopter to come and pick him up. It couldn't be that hard for it to find him — the headlights of his car had to be the only lights for miles. He fished around in his pocket and withdrew his phone, glancing between the screen and the road as he searched for the pilot's number. Or the hotel's. He didn't care as long as he got back.

Jo's number came up. That'd do. She could fix anything. He hit the call button and held the phone to his ear.

It emitted an irritating beep, followed by silence. Why wasn't it calling?

He glared at the screen. "No mobile access – emergency calls only," he read, then punched the dashboard. "It is a fucking emergency! I need to get back to the hotel so I can…can…" Tits. Something about tits. Scooping them out of a skimpy French maid's uniform and…

No, there weren't any frills. He didn't want her in her maid's uniform, French or Aussie or fucking Chinese. He wanted her naked. Wanted to see if her arse was as sweet as her tits.

Wondered what she'd taste like – salty like the sea around the island, or sweet like the mango beer? Fuck. If it wasn't an emergency before, it was now. His pants were too tight. He needed her now.

He tried, but the phone only beeped and beeped again, until he threw the stupid thing into the back seat. Fuck the phone. Fuck the helicopter. No, wait. He wanted to fuck a woman. Sweet and sassy and sympathetic and on call…

He'd never gone without sex so long in his life. Not since high school, anyway.

What the fuck was that in the middle of the road?

Jason squinted at the tall shape. Was some fat bloke standing in the middle of the road? Nah, no one'd be that stupid. Or that huge.

Jason found himself staring at the biggest cow he'd ever

seen, lowering its horns and charging his car. Fuck.

Jason wrenched the steering wheel right, taking the car to the other side of the track. Lights blinded him and the deafening blare of a horn sliced into his head. It sounded like a car, not a cow.

There was a jarring crunch, accompanied by the sound of a million tinkling bells before he was in flight, spinning like a skydiver in freefall. Only what skydiver took their car with them and opened their parachute in the car? Parachute everywhere. In front of him. Beside him. Sticking out of the dash like a big balloon. Holding him in his seat so he couldn't move.

Upside down. Sideways. Right way up. No, sideways again. Fuck. Upside down in a car full of parachute, but the landing was gentler than he expected. Skydiving in a car was awesome. Jason unclipped the straps holding him upside down and slid to the roof of the car. Pain flared in his hand, but he ignored it. Adventure sports came with a bit of pain, didn't they? And chicks dig scars.

Ooh, there's one.

A moving blue blur outside resolved into a woman bent double so she could see into the car window. Purple. No, blue. Purple again. Why was her shirt changing colour? She looked concerned. "Can you hear me? You hit me with your car! You could've killed me!"

He'd landed on a hot chick? Cool. Jason grinned lazily, hoping she looked as hot as she sounded. He couldn't see so clearly right now. There was something in his eye. Probably his hair. He reached up to casually flick it away in the sexy way he knew melted any woman's underwear, and tried to catch the niggling thought in his head about car crashes. Car crashes and rock stars. Numbers! That's what he had to get. Give. Whatever.

"Get me out of here and I'll give you my number, babe," he said.

Lights were flashing. Why were they flashing? They made it hard to think. Lights only flashed at concerts and he couldn't see his guitar, or the rest of the band. And why did his hand hurt?

Jason held up his fingers so he could see them better. Something black was oozing over his hand. Like tar, with sparkling diamonds in it. The light flashed red and the ooze wasn't black any more. It was ruby red. Like…blood. Fuck. It couldn't be. When he saw blood, he…

"Sir! Can you hear me? Are you all right?"

All the lights at the rock concert in Jason's head went out.

TWENTY THREE

One of the path lights flickered. First it was blazing white, then off, then blue before brightening to white once more. The solar panel or the batteries must be on the blink again. Audra tapped her ID and knelt by the path beside the light until her display read LOGGED. Maintenance would receive her report in the morning and hopefully do something to fix it.

Rising, Audra shivered in a night breeze. Back home, she wouldn't dare walk outside this late after dark. Here, the only low-lifes who'd attack a lone woman were the rats rustling in the palm fronds above. No matter how much baiting the resort did, wherever there were people, there were rats.

Maybe they were seabirds getting comfortable, she told herself. That's what she usually told the tourists, but she didn't believe it. She'd only seen a handful of rats in her time here, but for every one she saw, she knew there were a dozen more watching. So much for paradise.

She took the long way round, circling Maxima to see which lights were on, but the whole villa was dark. Even with the blinds drawn in every room, some light should've leaked out the edges. Unless Jay and all his guests were asleep…or they were only using the romantic tealights she'd left in the house.

Audra stopped dead. What if the romantic lighting and all the other stuff she'd arranged had worked for him? What if Jay and his lady love were getting it on in the villa right now? She didn't dare interrupt them.

She forced herself up the steps to the door. The scanner wouldn't allow her entry if he was inside, and there were protocols in place if the guests were in bed: if all the guests' wristbands stayed in bedrooms for more than ten minutes, they triggered the electronic version of a DO NOT DISTURB sign on the door. The guests could set that manually, too, though none of hers ever had. She'd expected the hotel to be full of couples having kinky sex, but she'd never encountered the signs in use. Maybe the time for kinky sex was the wet season, not the dry. She'd find out when she got the permanent job here.

Gritting her teeth, Audra scanned her ID at the door, rocking on her feet as she waited to be told to go away or alert the guests that housekeeping was at the door.

The door hissed open. No one was home.

Audra hesitated on the threshold. Entering the house now, when she was off-duty and he hadn't called for maid service, smacked of an invasion of Jay's privacy. What if he was out for a night-time walk on the beach with someone and he brought her back here, only to find a maid he hadn't called for in his villa? Talk about killing the mood. She'd gone to so much trouble to help him, too.

Besides, who was she to ask for favours from someone as famous as Jay? He probably got asked for free tickets to his shows all the time and was sick of it. How would she feel if someone asked her to clean their house for free? A couple of concert tickets cost a month's worth of housecleaning.

Good thing Jay wasn't home.

Silently wishing him and his partner good night, Audra headed back to the staff accommodation to sleep. She'd have to be up early to get the best tickets before they sold out. Front row at one of his concerts was the closest she'd ever get to him, and she'd be satisfied with that, damn it. Even if she dreamed of more, who was she fooling? He'd never be hers.

TWENTY FOUR

"Why are you so late this morning? Been servicing that hot trainer again?"

Half the staff in the dining room seemed to be staring at her, having heard Penny's loud taunt. Audra wished her cheeks would cool. "There's nothing going on between Serge and me!" she hissed, seizing a bowl and filling it with far more yoghurt than she could eat.

"Servicing the lonely VIP instead? I hope he pays you extra for that."

Audra slammed her bowl down on the table. Yoghurt flew everywhere, including on Penny, but Audra didn't care. "I'm not sleeping with anyone on this island. No guests, no staff, no one! Enough already."

She felt sick. She wasn't sure she could eat anything now. Snatching up her yoghurt-splashed banana for later, Audra turned on her heel and left the dining room.

Penny's final taunt followed her. "No wonder she's so bloody grumpy. Frigid and frustrated." Muffled laughter wafted out the door, but Audra didn't turn to see who'd sniggered along with Penny.

Audra clenched her fists at her sides, wishing she'd done more than spill yoghurt on Penny. She wanted to punch the bitch, rip her hair out and enjoy seeing her lying lips bleed. It was like being in high school again. She shouldn't let the bitch get to her so much, but Penny reminded her of the snarky teenage girls she'd gone to school with.

She ran full tilt into a wall of muscle.

"Fancy running into you this morning!" Serge didn't seem fazed by the collision. In fact, he was grinning. "Did you think any more about my offer of servitude?" He peered at her face and his grin faded. "What's wrong?"

"Penny," Audra bit out. "She's telling everyone who'll listen that I've slept with you and the VIPs in the Pearl Villas. If Annette believes her, I'll lose my job."

Serge patted her shoulder awkwardly. "I came by last night to thank you again, but you were skyping with your sister, I think, so I didn't want to disturb you. I'll set her straight. You won't need to worry about her again." With a grim look in his eye, he marched toward the dining room.

Oh shit. Audra was torn between stopping him and watching Penny's embarrassment when he accused her of being the lying sack of shit she was. Penny wouldn't take her viciousness out on Serge, though — no, she'd wait for lunch and make Audra's day hell.

Audra quickened her steps away from Penny. If she managed to get all her morning duties done early, maybe she could be in and out at lunch before Penny made it to the staff dining room. Give the girl someone else to focus her anger on. Now for the big question: should she do the Pearls first, or let Jay and his guest sleep in while she dealt with the common areas?

Pearls last, she decided. There was less chance of running into Penny in the villas, so she'd leave them until last as the most pleasant part of her job. As long as Jay hadn't spread the chocolate sauce across the rug and the sofa, it could well be the highlight of her day.

She vacuumed and polished, emptied bins and restocked mini-bars, all the while humming songs from Jay's latest album. The ticket website had been playing the tunes the whole time she'd been on there, handing over almost a week's pay for her and Sam to see Jay sing and dance live onstage. It'd be worth it, though. It was Chaya's farewell tour, after all, and they'd be close enough to the stage to see Jay's face. And he'd be able to see hers, if he even noticed one among the thousands-strong crowd. It didn't matter. She'd seen him at his lonely worst. At the concert, she'd undoubtedly see him at his performance best.

When everything else was done and she'd paused to eat her breakfast banana, Audra straightened her uniform and marched around the lagoon to the villas.

Albina was easy; having cleaned and prepared it yesterday, all she had to do today was tidy the mess left by the IT guys and add the list of welcoming touches. Fresh milk, fresh flowers and the welcome fruit basket. Carrying the basket proved the greatest temptation as the scent of ripe guava taunted her every step. Audra glanced at the clock on her ID. Only an hour until lunch. She had to hold on until then and load up a bowl of fruit salad. That'd fix her fruit cravings.

Satisfied with Albina, Audra loaded her trolley with fresh towels and toiletries, and wheeled it to the bottom of the steps to Maxima. Now to see just how good a night Jay had had with his guest. Audra added an extra packet of cleaning cloths to the top of her stack of towels and took a deep breath.

One swipe and the door shot open, just like last night, and Audra exhaled in relief. Jay and his lady were already out, enjoying the island and all the activities it had to offer. Maybe they'd gone snorkelling or diving with Hana.

Audra headed for the bathroom first to set down the towels, but found yesterday's stack still sitting there, untouched, beside the bath oil. Evidently Jay hadn't needed the spa to seduce his songwriter. The rock star was smoother than she'd expected. What she'd give to run her tongue over some of his smooth skin as he did the same to her…

Pressing her fingers to her cheeks to cool her blush, Audra left the towels in the bathroom and headed for the kitchen. The fondue set would need to be washed for sure.

She was greeted by an immaculate kitchen, complete with the untouched fondue platter in the fridge. The note she'd left, telling him to page maid services through Reception if he needed assistance with it, had wicked up the moisture in the fridge, so the soggy paper stuck to the side of the bowl of strawberries. Strawberries that looked just as inviting as they had yesterday.

Audra firmly closed the door. She couldn't take them now any more than she could yesterday.

No spa and no strawberries, chocolate or champagne.

Maybe the massage oil, then?

Holding her breath, Audra tiptoed to the bedroom, expecting to see the disarray only a night of wild, passionate sex could bring. Yet she stopped dead in the doorway. The crisply made bed was just as she'd left it. A quick check confirmed that all the beds in Maxima were equally untouched. So much for her efforts, or Jay's guest. He hadn't returned to the villa at all.

A whisper of worry crept into her heart. Was he all right? Had he and his guest simply drunk too much and passed out on the beach instead of in the house? Or had he chosen to stay in town instead of returning to the island? Maybe he'd call the resort to have his things packed up and sent home to him, wherever home was, and he'd never return. She felt a twinge of disappointment at never seeing him again.

Audra lifted the phone and called Reception. She waited for Heloise to purr a greeting before she blurted out, "The guest in Maxima. Is he on the island?"

What if the sharks had gotten to him? Most of them weren't all that big, but they could still bite and if he'd fallen into the lagoon drunk, he might not have been able to crawl out again.

"You want me to check his ID?"

Audra wet her lips. "Yes. Check if he's on the island and where his ID was last recorded."

Audra heard Heloise's perfectly manicured nails click across the keyboard and wondered what colour they were today. "No, the last scan is yesterday morning, when he walked through the gate to the helipad. Nothing since then. He doesn't seem to be anywhere on the island." A pause.

"Is there a problem with Maxima?"

Audra shook her head violently, then realised Heloise couldn't see it through the phone. "No, just that his place looks like he hasn't been here since I cleaned yesterday, so I wondered if he'd checked out." She took a longer look around his bedroom. "Actually, it looks like all his luggage is still here, too. Thanks, Heloise." Audra ended the call, wondering why she felt so saddened. She forced herself to swallow down her disappointment at not seeing Jay. It wasn't as if she knew Jay very well and he was certainly a demanding guest. She should be happy he wasn't back yet.

Well, her workday just got easier. With her morning tasks complete, she had time for a coffee and perhaps even some cake before lunch. If she was lucky, the cooks would let her have the fruit salad early. She was starving. Telling herself that everything would work out for the best, she hurried to the staff dining room. Everything would be fine if she hadn't skipped breakfast. She wouldn't do that again.

TWENTY FIVE

Jason woke up handcuffed to the bed. He recognised the cold touch of steel around his wrist and reached out with his free hand for the sexy dominatrix who'd shackled him. His desire stirred instantly at the thought, but his fingers closed on nothing but cold cotton and air. Where was last night's chick?

He pried his eyes open and light lanced his retinas, so he forced them shut again. Fuck, who'd unleashed a jackhammer in his head? He needed a beer. No, a bourbon. Yesterday he'd had beer. He'd never drink the stuff again. Only bourbon and vodka in future.

A persistent beeping irritated him. Slow and steady, like a heartbeat.

Jason cracked one eye open, just wide enough to take in the room. He was lying in a single bed. A hospital bed, handcuffed to the railing. What the fuck? He tugged at the handcuffs, which looked a lot tougher than the ones he'd played with in the past. He might actually need a key to get out of these. And he'd better, soon, because he needed to piss like a…something big and flowing. With lots of water. A waterfall, maybe.

"Get me out of these fucking things!" he growled, jingling the chain.

"Mr Felix, you're awake!" An older man in police uniform strode into the hospital room. His tight smile didn't look as friendly as his voice sounded. He held out his hand. "Inspector Burgess."

No. That couldn't be right. He only did handcuffs for women, not men. Something didn't add up here and he intended to find out what. Jason held up his cuffed right hand. "I'd shake your hand, but it's a bit hard in these. How'd I end up here?"

A flash of white caught his eye and Jason peered at his hand. Both hands. Someone had stuck patches of gauze on them, as if he'd gotten hurt. One was stained brown like dried blood. Jason swallowed and looked away. Now he wanted to be sick, too.

"Mate, I gotta piss."

Burgess coughed irritably. "Nurse!" he called. "Some help here."

Jason perked up. A hot nurse would sure help his mood right now.

But the nurse who walked in looked like she'd been the matron at the hospital since Jason was born. Maybe even before that. Definitely not hot enough for him. She smiled broadly.

"Are you going to get me out of these? I can't get to the

bathroom," Jason grumbled.

Her eyes shone. "That's up to Inspector Burgess, but he's not here right now." Jason looked around wildly, but she was right – the bastard had sneaked out while he wasn't looking. "I can help you with that."

Ten excruciating minutes later, Jason had a story about an elderly matron with cold hands and an unhealthy obsession with male catheterisation that would forever cure him of any sexual fantasy involving nurses, hospitals and handcuffs. A story he never intended to tell anyone as long as he lived.

When Inspector What's-his-name returned, Jason had never been so happy in his life to see a police officer. "Mate, I think that nurse just molested me. You should arrest her."

The officer laughed mirthlessly. "Well, now. It's funny you should talk about arrests. My constable swears you hit her and tried to kill her."

Jason might not remember much about last night, but he sure as fuck hadn't wanted to hurt any women. "I don't hit girls." He squared his jaw. "Learned that one back in primary school. When I make girls scream, it's because they like what I do."

The police officer's expression didn't change. "Well, it seems there's a first time for everything. Constable Nelson says you were driving on the wrong side of the road, crashed into her patrol car and then rolled your vehicle. You're lucky to be alive, you know."

Jason wracked his brain. He vaguely remembered something about parachutes and freefall and numbers and tits. "Does she have hot tits?" he asked finally. If he could find the owner of the tits, maybe he'd remember more about her. Maybe.

"Mr Felix, what happened two nights ago? After you left Matso's?"

"Matso's? Nah, that was last night."

"You've been unconscious for more than thirty-six hours, Mr Felix. You left Matso's almost two days ago." A notepad and pen materialised in the cop's hands.

"That the name of the pub?"

The officer nodded.

"I left the pub because I wanted to go home. Back to the hotel, I mean. I have a house on the lagoon and staff on call." Tits. He remembered the tits. The perfect tits belonged to a hotel maid. Audrey. No, Audra. "Where is she?"

"Where is who, Mr Felix? Was there someone else with you in the car?"

Jason opened his mouth to describe the perfect globes he wanted to wrap his hands around, but he didn't think the cop would understand. "No, don't think so. She's waiting for me at the hotel." This didn't sound right, but it was good enough. "Shit, have I really been here two days? I need to get back. There's a girl – "

"First you need to tell me about the other night, Mr Felix. My constable arrested you for attempted murder and if you're as dangerous as she says, I'm not releasing you. Instead, I'll charge you. And it won't be the only charge, either. Dangerous driving. Reckless endangerment. Resisting arrest. Assaulting a police officer. Even rock stars aren't immune to the law. Especially not when it comes to bashing police officers." The Inspector regarded him coldly.

"So start talking. The bar staff and your friends at Matso's said you left, and no one else saw you until you met Constable Nelson. Let's start with what we both know. You were driving in your Landcruiser," he prompted.

"Driving. New…my new car. Right. I left the pub with a carton of mango beer because she likes that. I wanted to get back to the hotel. It was a really long drive. It got dark and the road just kept going. I couldn't find the hotel, so I just kept on driving, figuring I'd find something eventually. There were…someone attacked me." Jason squeezed his eyes shut, trying desperately to remember. "A cow. Big brown one. Bigger than me. Came right at the car, like it wanted to gore me through the windscreen. Would've killed me. So I swerved out of the way. There were lights…and a crash…and…blood. And an angel in blue with a sexy voice." Not Audra, though. "And then I woke up here."

The police officer nodded as he scribbled in the notebook, then reached for his phone. He waited a few seconds, then barked, "Get Constable Nelson up to the hospital. He's awake." He terminated the call.

"How'd I get here?" Jason asked.

The Inspector hesitated for a moment before he responded, "Don't you remember?" Jason shook his head. "Constable Nelson radioed for backup and an ambulance. You busted up her car pretty good. We'll be down a patrol car for a while until head office sorts out the expense claims for getting it towed back to Perth and whether it's worth repairing or if it's a complete write-off. That'll add damaging police property to your list of charges, too. Forgot about that. Anyway, the other patrol car was at another call in one of the remote communities, so it was a few hours before we got a team out there. The ambulance got to you faster. We think they set a new record – four hours for a round trip. Constable Nelson accompanied you in the ambulance and received first aid. No thanks to you."

Jason squirmed uncomfortably. "I didn't mean to hit the other car. I hadn't seen anyone else for miles and when that killer cow came at me, I only thought about getting away without dying. Didn't notice the lights until it was too late."

Silence swelled between them.

"When can I go back to my hotel?" Jason asked, hearing his voice sound depressingly forlorn. Damn it, he'd felt bad enough when he started driving. And when he woke up. Now, he'd almost killed a cop when he should be curled up in bed with Audra.

"When I say so, Mr Felix, and not before." The Inspector rose. "Ah, here she is."

"Is the bastard really awake?" a woman demanded. "Have you charged him with attempted murder yet? I want you to yank his licence so he'll never, ever drive again. If that crash didn't kill him, he'll be a danger to every officer and driver 'til the day he dies. Drunk as a ditchie, he was." An angry policewoman with a sexy voice that Jason remembered walked into the room. No, an off-duty police officer. Her shirt collar was unbuttoned, she wasn't wearing her name badge or officer number, her shirt was untucked and her tool belt was mercifully absent. Good thing, too, because her hands were reaching for something at her hip and clenching air. "The first words out of his mouth had better have been an apology or I'm going to give him a second bump on the head to match the first."

Jason reached for his hurting head and found the fist-sized swelling hidden in his hair. He couldn't even remember hitting it. Or had she done it? "I'm sorry." He was. She had a cut above one eye that looked about a day or two old and he was fairly sure he'd caused it, even if he couldn't remember.

"You better be. Have you charged him yet, Inspector?"

The Inspector coughed. "Well, see, we have a bit of a problem. He says he swerved to avoid what he says was a charging cow. Your dash camera shows a bull near that bend where you two met. Wouldn't be the first time there was a bull on the road. Looks to me like nothing more than an unfortunate car accident."

"He was drunk. The whole car reeked of it and so did he! After he crashed into me, he even had the gall to ask me for my number. No sober man does that."

Jason knew he needed to be the full-on rock star and charm the pants off this chick before someone thought to charge him properly. No one did rock star charm better than Jay Felix, even if he was lying in pain in a hospital bed. Jason gave her the full benefit of a slow, sexy grin. "I dunno. I thought you were an angel come to rescue me. And I didn't ask for your number. I said I'd give you mine when I got out of the car I was trapped in. Upside down, as I recall. All that blood rushing south at the sight of an angel like you..." He winked. "I read somewhere that when you're in a car accident, you have to exchange phone numbers. I've never been in one before, so it's all new to me."

With what looked like considerable effort, the girl turned away from Jason. "Where are the blood test results? As soon as I was released from Emergency, I had them do a blood alcohol screening. Other drugs, too. Who knows what he was tanked up on before he tried to kill me?"

Jason forced his grin to stay in place as he replied, "Mango beer. I'd been enjoying a few brews and a bit of good food with some lovely ladies at the pub. I liked it so much, I decided to bring more back with me to the hotel. Where I could drink responsibly, of course." Fuck. He'd been drinking since breakfast and a blood test would show that for sure. There went his driver's licence and the PR team would be after his hide. If the rest of the band didn't skin him alive first.

"Sure, we got the results back. It shows some residual alcohol in his blood, but not enough for him to be over the limit." The Inspector raised his eyebrows. "Mr Felix, under the circumstances, I'm going to let you off with a warning. Once the paperwork's sorted, and provided you don't pose a threat to my constable here without your car, I think we should all forget the whole incident. No charges, no reporters, no lawyers and no hard feelings."

Jason eyed the two police officers. No charges and no reporters would be a relief for him, but the Inspector was worried about his lawyers. So he bloody well should be. If he had no evidence against him, he could sue the police for this.

What would a rock star do?

Jason hitched up his grin and drawled, "Well, that sounds reasonable. If you bust me out of this place and help me get back to my hotel, I think we have a deal. Inspector – " He wracked his brain for man's name and dredged it up. " – Burgess," he finished triumphantly.

Burgess nodded. "Uncuff him."

Constable Nelson drew in a deep breath, making her boobs swell so Jason couldn't possibly look anywhere else. "Inspector."

"Now, constable."

Metal clinked as she produced the keys and set to work on Jason's restraints. "This isn't over," she hissed. "If I ever see you driving in my town again, I'll have the breathalyser out before you can blink. If you blow over the legal limit, I'll have you slapped with a drink-driving charge faster than you can take your keys out of the ignition. Take a good look at these handcuffs, because you'll be seeing them again." She held them up and jingled them ominously.

Jason wanted to rub his wrists, but he was in full rock god mode now. "Oh, I see them, Constable Nelson. But next time you use those on me, make sure you're wearing your sexiest underwear because you'll need to be at your best when you go to bed with me." He winked again. "I've never slept with a real policewoman before and first impressions stay with you forever, you know? I am pretty unforgettable, after all."

She turned bright red and couldn't seem to formulate a reply.

"Thanks for coming in, constable. You enjoy your days off." Inspector Burgess dismissed her. She nodded curtly and left. Burgess dropped his tone so it wouldn't be heard outside the room. "She's a good officer, Mr Felix. If she said you were drunk, you're a lucky son of a bitch you had time to sober up before she thought to breath or blood test you. Not to mention the blood transfusions you had while you were unconscious. Diluted your blood alcohol quite nicely, I'll bet. Next time, she won't make the same mistake.

And neither will I. You put one foot over the line of the law in my jurisdiction again and I'll have you in the lockup. You won't get a nice private room like this. Not even a pillow. And most of the guys we have in the lockup are in for drunk and disorderly, violent crimes. Looking for a fight and someone else to beat up. So you'll have a roommate from hell. And my first call will be to the press. All the money and lawyers in the country won't get you off. Are we clear?"

Jason nodded. He understood, all right. "But you're busting me out of here, right? No more nurses molesting me?"

Burgess flashed a feral smile. "Sure. As soon as we're done with the paperwork."

TWENTY SIX

Audra finished restocking the milk and coffee in Albina, trying to hide her shock at how much the executives had consumed in less than twenty-four hours. Between them, they'd consumed enough caffeine to stay awake into next week. What was wrong with these people?

Shaking her head, she turned her trolley toward Maxima. Empty Maxima, she already knew. She didn't want to go inside the lonely villa. Last night she'd seen the photos on social media of Jay drinking and enjoying himself with some of the tourists in town. He'd evidently decided the loneliness and isolation on Romance Island weren't for him and he'd stayed in town. Probably shacked up with half a dozen of the bikini-clad tourists from the photos. Always the rock star, up for a good time. It made the last day of her work week much easier. In exactly ten minutes' time, she'd end today's shift and start two, much-needed days off, during which she intended to finish her job application and submit it before the deadline on Friday. Only four days away. There was a weather station with her name on it waiting for her next year, she was certain of it. No more cleaning floors or dealing with unruly guests who invaded her erotic dreams. She swore nothing would make her miss this year's deadline. Nothing.

Her wristband beeped and she glanced at the display. URGENT CALL. RECEPTION.

The phone in Maxima was closer, so she swiped her ID and entered the villa. Picking up the phone, she punched in the number for Reception.

"Hel – "

"Heloise, it's Audra. You said it was urgent?"

"It is. He refuses to speak to anyone but you. Putting him through now."

Audra's heart sank. It had to be Tad. She hoped he hadn't hurt himself yet.

A male voice cleared his throat.

"Tad?" she began. "Tell me you haven't done anything stupid. Please."

A snort. "It's Jay, not Tad." Far more self-assured, too. Not to mention sexy. "Most girls don't forget me that easily. And stupid really depends on your perspective. Reckless, yes, but I'm a rock star. It comes with the territory." Jay's laughter was deep and infectious.

Her heart slid out of her throat and back into place as Audra's panic faded. "Mr Felix. What can I assist you with?"

If he said he wanted his things packed up and sent to town, she'd eat the strawberries herself. Yes, with the chocolate. She'd only had fondue once in her life and she'd make the most of this one. He'd never know.

"My recklessness has landed me in hospital and the matron will only release me if I'm kept under observation for another forty-eight hours. She's threatening to send a nurse with me. Can you talk to her? I don't want to spend another night in hospital. Save me, Audra."

He knew her name. Jay Felix, rock god who could have any woman he wanted, actually remembered her name. As for saving him…

"Audrey?" The voice belonged to an older woman, not Jay. "Audrey, your boyfriend here's been in a car accident."

Audra spluttered. "He's not my – "

The woman wasn't listening. "He lost a lot of blood and he might have a concussion. The doctor wants to keep him under observation for another two days, him being a high-profile patient and all. We want to make sure he's okay. But he says you'll stay with him the whole time, won't leave him alone for a minute."

That was taking twenty-four-hour, on-call maid service way too far. "Look, I – "

"Do you have any first aid training, Audrey?"

"Yes, but – "

The matron launched into a list of symptoms she needed to watch out for and continued with instructions on what to do if Jay showed any of them. Audra grabbed the notepaper and pen from the counter and started scribbling furiously. She'd have to rewrite the whole mess later for someone else to be able to understand it, because there was no way in hell she'd stay in Maxima with Jay Felix.

"Have you got all that, Audrey?" The woman paused for breath, then ploughed on, "If he loses consciousness, I want you to call the hospital immediately and ask for Helen. That's me. I'll talk you through what you need to do until the Flying Doctors arrive."

Audra found herself nodding and making affirmative noises. All she was agreeing to was ensuring that one of the hotel's VIP guests was well taken care of, she told herself. Not that she'd take care of him personally. No one worked forty-eight hours without cease. And tomorrow was her day off. She wouldn't give that up for anyone, not even Jay Felix. As for masquerading as his girlfriend…

Finally, the woman shut up and Jay came back on the line.

"Audra, you still there?" he asked.

"Yes."

"Thank you. I swear, I owe you huge for this. Whatever you want, just name it."

A rock god who owed her a favour. Audra sighed. If only he'd said that before she'd forked out for concert tickets to see his show. Ah, he probably didn't mean it, anyway. He'd forget the offer as easily as he forgot her name. Sooner, maybe.

"Can you get to the helipad? I'll have the pilot pick you up before he comes to get me. They're taking me to the airport in an ambulance and if you don't come, they'll send a nurse with me. I don't want a nurse. I want you."

Her stomach did a sort of flip-flop of excitement. It couldn't be because of his words. No, it was the thrill of new things. Audra had never been in a helicopter before. Staff usually took the carrier boat back to the pearl farm and caught a lift into town from there. Helicopters were for rich guests. "All right."

She was going to regret this, she was certain of it. But first, she'd enjoy the flight.

TWENTY SEVEN

Audra hurried to get her trolley back into the linen room. A stack of towels fell off, but she didn't have time to pick them up. She broke into a run, already twenty metres down the path before the door clicked shut on the mess she'd made. The helipad. Would the helicopter already be waiting for her?

Hospital. Her niggling worry had been right – Jay hadn't been enjoying himself on the mainland. He'd been lying unconscious in hospital, injured, just like Leon. And if the medical staff wanted him under observation…what state would he be in? Would he be able to walk? What if…

She pulled up short as she reached the gates to the helipad. The helicopter was nowhere in sight and she couldn't hear even the faint thumping of rotors that told her when one left the pearl farm. That meant she had at least five minutes, maybe even ten. Time to get out of her horrible work uniform and don civilian clothes, seeing as she was officially off-duty now. If he'd told the overbearing nurse that she was his girlfriend, she'd better dress the part. As if she owned the sort of designer labels a rock star's girlfriend would wear.

Oh wait – she had just the thing. Digging through her drawers, she unearthed the fake designer shirt and shorts Leon had brought back from Bali from his Leavers trip last year. The logos proclaimed them to be an expensive surf brand, but Leon had assured her they hadn't cost more than the price of a beer. The sound of throbbing blades told her she'd run out of time. Shoving her feet into her sneakers, she pelted down the path to the helipad. Just in time, too – the blades slowed as the pilot jumped out, scanning his surroundings for his passenger.

Audra waved and shouted, and she was rewarded with a double thumbs-up from the pilot as he leaned against his aircraft.

"I'd have waited for you, you know," he said, watching her double over to catch her breath.

"He said…he said he'd been in a car crash."

The pilot shrugged. "That the one who claimed he was a rock god? If he was capable of making phone calls, that means he's alive, right? Can't have been that bad a crash."

Her head whirling with thoughts of Leon, Audra stopped dead. "What do you mean?"

"I'm just a charter pilot. Royal Flying Doctor Service has its own helicopter for emergencies and so do the State Emergency Service. So it isn't an emergency. It's just a spoiled rich boy pulling your strings. And you came running, didn't you?" He laughed softly.

Audra shook her head. "I'm hotel staff. I just got pulled off my normal work to do nursing duties in overtime. One of my brothers was almost killed in a car accident last year."

The pilot's smile vanished. "In that case, I apologise. I hope your brother's okay. And cheer up. Your job includes some nice perks – getting flown out to meet the guests. This guest must be a pretty demanding one. I've never had to fly staff to the mainland before."

Audra smiled tentatively back. "I've never flown in a helicopter before, so that makes two of us."

"I get to pop your cherry and someone else is paying for it? How do you feel about taking the scenic route, if it's your first time?"

She blushed. "You're the pilot. As long as we get to the airport in one piece and then back here with my patient, or whatever he is, the flight route's up to you."

He stuck out a hand for her to shake. "I'm Shou, anyway."

"Shoe?"

"No, Shou. As in Japanese for soar."

Audra's smile broadened. "So you were born for your line of work, Shou. I might say the same. I'm Audra."

"Audra? Not Audrey?"

"Right."

"Audra means something to do with flying, too?"

"No, Audra means storm. I've just finished a degree in meteorology. I hoped to see a cyclone while I was up here, but only if I get to stay on through the wet season."

Shou passed her the tiny lifejacket belt. "You know how to use one of these?" At her head-shake, he launched into the fastest flight safety briefing she'd ever heard, finishing up with, "You can sit in the co-pilot's seat, if you want."

"But I don't know what I'm doing."

"Sit down, put your headphones on, and enjoy the view. That's all my co-pilots ever get to do. Nobody flies my baby but me."

Audra laughed, settled into her seat and secured her headphones snugly over her ears. Shou climbed into the pilot's seat beside her and started flipping switches. If she'd thought the rotor noise outside was bad, she hadn't counted on it being worse inside the helicopter. How could anyone even hear themselves think over the thumping blades?

"You'll get used to the noise," Shou's voice said in her ear. "And that's why you have a headset with a mike. So we can still talk. And no, I didn't read your mind. It's what every newbie says on their first trip." He lifted the helicopter smoothly, rising until the entire Buccaneer Archipelago lay sprawled below them. "Ever wonder why the resort's called Romance Island?" He pointed.

For the first time, Audra saw that the heart-shaped logo on all her uniforms was more than just a cute concept — it was a simplified picture of the island. Teal-blue water paled as it rose to form the heart-shaped cay enclosing an equally valentine-themed lagoon. The Pearl Villas clustered around the eastern bump, ending in Villa Penguin and its private jetty as the heart tapered to its point. What she hadn't seen in her night-time picnic with Serge was the triangular swimming platform at the end of the jetty, making it look like an arrow's point. The western bump housed the rest of the resort buildings and the wide loading jetty with its boat pens feathered up either side, much like the fletching on Cupid's arrow. "That can't be an accident. Was the island really that shape to start with?"

"The island, yes. The lagoon, no. They get a dredger in there every year to keep it that shape or it becomes more of a teardrop than a heart as it silts up. I have it on good authority that the architect who designed the resort drew the jetties that way as a joke, but the owner liked it so much he chose that design over the ones that were closer to his original specifications."

He pointed out the various sights along the way, naming each island and building with the ease of a tour guide, for that's what he was, flying tourists to and from the resort. There were two major pearl farms on the way, along with the fabled Cable Beach, bordered by more expensive resorts. Teal waters and creamy sand gave way to pindan red as they headed inland to the airport. The town seemed so small, surrounded by red desert as it huddled close to the coast.

"Beautiful," Audra breathed, sighing as they started their descent.

"Cheer up. As soon as we have your boy aboard, we'll be back in the air and you can see the whole trip in reverse." He skimmed over the tarmac, avoiding the other helicopters and choosing a spot near a building marked with Flying Doctor and ambulance signs. His landing was a barely perceptible bump; a far cry from the rough jet landing when she'd arrived in Broome.

No wonder rich people preferred helicopters to flying in commercial aircraft. If she ever won the lottery, Audra swore she'd set aside a little of the money to charter a helicopter every now and again. Ha, if she ever bought a ticket. She'd leave the gambling to her mother and save her money instead. And enjoy this amazing experience while it lasted. She'd be cleaning floors again, soon enough.

Shou cracked open the door. "Right, let's go inside and get your boy."

Reluctantly, Audra climbed out after him. Despite Shou's reassurances, dread still crept in. How badly was Jay injured? Just because he was conscious and capable of talking, it didn't mean he was okay. What if he was confined to a wheelchair?

TWENTY EIGHT

Jason let out a breath he hadn't known he was holding as the helicopter's landing skids touched the tarmac. He wanted to run out to meet it, but his rock star reputation was at stake here. She had to come to him. The pilot jumped down, offering a hand to someone inside the cockpit, hidden from him by the reflective glass.

Audra emerged slowly, smiling slightly as she made her cautious descent. Jason grinned. Yep, that was the only woman in his head since he left the pub. Thank fuck she hadn't worn that horrible, shapeless bag of a maid's uniform. Instead, her t-shirt revealed her curves without clinging to them and her shorts showed plenty of leg. He longed to have her legs wrapped around him, nothing else between them, but not with these onlookers. No, he performed best with an intimate audience. As soon as they were at the hotel, away from the matron and police, then he'd offer her the private performance of her life.

The airside door opened with a sucking sound as if the air-conditioned interior didn't want to allow any more hot bodies inside. Audra stepped through, pausing to let her eyes adjust to the dimly lit waiting room after the bright afternoon sun outside. Jason waited for her to notice him.

Audra blinked, then scanned the room. Her glance landed on him and her eyes widened. Her mouth rounded in shock and he thought she whispered something, but he couldn't read her lips. He looked down and realised what had made her blanch.

Ripping off the hospital gown, he shoved the wheelchair back and strode to meet her. Dismissing the raised voices behind him as white noise, he reached for Audra, crushing her against his chest in a desperate hug. "Get me out of here," he whispered, feeling her stiffen against him. She nodded and pulled away. Needing the contact, he seized her hand and brought it to his lips. "Thank you." He didn't want to let her go and she appeared to understand, allowing him to keep her hand in his.

"You're Audrey, the girl I talked to earlier?" The matron marched to Jason's side, not willing to surrender him that easily.

Audra's eyes hardened as she seemed to grow in stature. "Helen, I presume?" Her tone matched Madam Matron's authority, to Jason's delight. "You spoke, but didn't listen. My name is Audra and I'm here at Mr Felix's request. I understood he needed my help."

Jason squeezed her fingers and was relieved to feel her return the pressure.

"Do you have any medical training, Audra?" The

matron's eyes flashed. "I'm not sure if I can release him into your care if you don't. He must be under constant observation for at least the next forty-eight hours before we can be sure he's out of danger."

Jason felt an incredible urge to run screaming as far away from the predatory matron as possible. Couldn't anyone else see this was the start of a horror movie?

Audra shrugged. "First aid training, as I've already told you. I'm pretty good with a defibrillator, too."

The matron launched into a long list of things Audra had to watch out for. It was Jason's second time hearing the lecture, so his eyes glazed over only a few seconds in. He hoped Audra had a better memory than he did. Not to mention a longer attention span. He wondered whether she'd be as good in bed as in his fantasies. He couldn't wait to find out. He found his mind drifting back to the present at the sound of Audra's voice.

"Drowsiness, blackouts, pain, numbness, seizures, nausea, discharge, fever…all pretty standard. Believe me, I've been on medical watch before."

She had? Jason made a note to ask her about it. Or maybe she didn't want to talk about it. He definitely didn't want to talk about his accident. Mistaking the policewoman for an angel…

The matron opened her mouth to say something else, but Jason had had enough.

"Everyone done talking about my health as if my gorgeous body isn't standing here in front of you?" He waved a hand to indicate the perfect physical specimen under discussion. "Because I'm taking my fine arse back to my hotel."

Audra tried to withdraw her hand, but he tightened his fingers around hers. For all his bravado, he hurt like hell and all he wanted was to get the fuck out of there. And they weren't going to let him go without her. He heard her sigh and her hand relaxed again.

The pilot grinned and held the door open. Just as Jason stepped through, he heard the police inspector call, "Stay out of trouble now."

Every cell in Jason's body wanted to flip the cop the finger and tell him to get fucked, but he didn't have the energy. Instead, he hunched his shoulders and followed Audra and the pilot out to the helicopter. They paused at the door, but he just kept going, climbing into the cockpit and sinking into one of the seats before he slumped against the glass bubble between him and the world outside. "For fuck's sake, get me out of here."

Something landed in his lap as Audra took the seat beside him. "You need a lifejacket." She tapped the yellow pack fastened to a belt around her waist, then jerked her thumb at the pack in his lap.

He thought about not bothering, but she just sat there, looking expectantly at him until he finally gave in and clipped the belt around his bare abs. He grinned when he realised that her eyes had stayed on his muscles. "Like what you see? You can touch them, if you like."

Audra shook her head. "Those bruises must hurt like hell. You really took a beating. By the look of it, you're lucky to be alive. Were you even wearing a seatbelt?"

"Yes," he snapped. "Yes, I was wearing a seatbelt, and no, I wasn't speeding. A fucking huge cow came right at me out of nowhere and it was swerve or die. I like living. But I clipped another car and then rolled mine, so I got all banged up. Not in a good way, either. Woke up in hospital. Don't want to talk about it unless that matron's been arrested." He clamped his mouth shut.

"All right."

Her reply took him by surprise. Any other girl would be berating him for being stupid, asking more questions or cooing over his hurts. No wonder she was special enough for him to remember her name.

He reached for her hand again. "Thank you, Audra. Like I said, I owe you."

She nodded. "Shou? Can we lift off, please? Mr Felix needs rest and the sooner we get him back to the hotel, the better."

Fuck yeah.

TWENTY NINE

Audra settled Jay on one of the couches in the foyer. He'd found a pair of sunglasses in the helicopter and the mirrored lenses lent an air of mystery to the man as they hid his eyes and his soul from public view. He seemed to straighten from his exhausted slump as he noticed everyone's eyes on him. Well, if Audra didn't have other things to worry about, she'd certainly spare more than a glance at Jay Felix wearing nothing but a pair of board shorts, ripped abdominal muscles guiding the eye downward to a tempting trail of hair leading into those shorts, hinting at the impressive package they concealed. The last of the glowing evening light darkened shadows and gave a rosy glow to the ripples of muscle, making him look even more impressive, while hiding some of the bruising. She felt an overwhelming urge to lick something.

"I need to speak to my supervisor about my schedule,

Mr Felix. Maybe – " Audra scanned the foyer and thanked whatever deity favoured her as Hana walked in. " – Hana, could you walk with Mr Felix back to his villa? You don't need to wait for me. I'll see you back at Villa Maxima."

Hana flashed an impish smile and greeted Jay. "Welcome to Romance Island Resort, Mr Felix. Have you come for some snorkelling and diving? Heli-fishing? Once you've met some of the resort sealife, you'll never want to holiday anywhere else again."

Jay's mirrored lenses turned to Hana and Audra breathed a sigh of relief. She hurried out of Reception to the corridor of offices behind it. She prayed her luck would hold and it did – Annette still sat in her office.

Annette greeted her with a smile. "How'd it go? Everything taken care of?" When Audra stared in puzzlement, Annette explained, "Heloise told me one of the VIPs requested maid service on the mainland and sent a helicopter for you." She rubbed her hands together. "Nice work. He'll pay a premium for that. He even requested you by name, Heloise said. We'll have to keep you on in the wet season if the VIPs like you that much. How was your first helicopter flight?"

"Wonderful," Audra admitted. "I only wish it'd been for longer."

"See if you can persuade the guests to charter a helicopter for a day trip with catering. The price includes a member of staff to take care of the catering and you get first preference if you made the guest's booking." Annette winked. "So, is everything taken care of to your guest's satisfaction? I have you rostered for two days off, I think." She scanned the roster sheet and nodded.

Audra swallowed. "About that. The guest was hospitalised and released early on the condition that someone keep him under observation for two days. Forty-eight hours."

"Perfect, then. You'll have no other duties for the next two days, so he's all yours." Annette rose. "Are you coming to dinner now?"

Her job application. Scrubbing toilets for another year while her degree went to waste? Audra felt her whole life slipping through her fingers. "But…my days off…"

"Postpone them. After the two days playing nurse, then you can have your time off." Annette eyed her. "I expect flexibility in my permanent staff, especially those who have to cater to the whims of the VIPs in the Pearls."

Audra's heart sank and she nodded silently. The deadline was four days away – even if her days off were delayed, she'd still get the job application in on time. Next year, she'd be reading rain gauges, not cleaning rosters. All she had to do was last forty-eight hours as a self-proclaimed rock god's babysitter. How hard could it be?

THIRTY

Pressing her lips together to stop herself from swearing where guests could hear her, Audra hurried to the staff accommodation to collect some clothes for her stay in Maxima. Her first stop was the laundry room for fresh uniforms. She found Pamela struggling alone with the laundry trolleys and moved to help.

"Where's Penny?" Audra grunted as she shoved at an overloaded trolley. It looked like there was twice as much as last week.

"Shagging her chef, where else?" Pamela waved at Audra's trolley. "I caught them in here, going for it on a load of clean uniforms. I think I startled him, because he made a mess all over them. Spurted like a fountain."

Audra couldn't hide her horror. "You mean we'll be wearing cum-stained uniforms this week because of Penny?"

Pamela giggled. "Not you, you're in civvies for two days. Maybe Penny, but how's that different from normal? I found a couple that were still clean right down the bottom of the pile, so I have enough until we get these back. The rest are headed back to the mainland for a wash."

Now Audra understood why there was so much laundry. "Change of plans. Annette cancelled my days off because of some emergency in the Pearls. My two days off just became two days as a live-in maid. But if there aren't any uniforms..."

Pamela shrugged. "You could wash today's one. Oh, unless it's already in here..."

Audra nodded. "Yep, all mine are in here. Now covered in whatever Penny coaxed from the sous-chef. I'd rather work naked than in a dress that's been stained by that skanky bitch."

Pamela smothered her giggle. "That'd be tempting fate! Jay Felix from Chaya's staying at the Pearls – I just saw him walk up from Reception. I can remember swooning over him when I was in high school. Never thought I'd see him in the flesh...and what flesh! I've never wanted to lick a man so much in my life when he walked past. I know you can't, but...if you get a chance to get his autograph, can you ask for one for me, too?"

Audra nodded, all her breath taken with the effort of shoving the laundry trolleys down to the dock. It took them two trips, but Audra couldn't leave Pamela to do it all on her own.

"I'd offer you mine but..." Pamela gestured at her body. "They'd be way too big for you." Wiping the perspiration from her forehead, her eyes lit up. "I know! Do you still have the shirts from that volleyball tournament Hana ran at the start of the season? With the matching shorts?"

Volleyball? Slowly, Audra nodded. "Yeah, I do. Annette said to keep them for the next one, but we haven't had enough guests yet to form teams." The shorts were on the short side, but they were better than nothing. Not to mention better quality than anything Audra owned. She sighed. "You're a lifesaver. Thank you."

Pamela waved her away. "No, you just saved me from having to do the laundry alone. And possibly a murder charge from going to kill Penny afterwards."

Audra blinked, trying to hide her shock. Surely placid Pamela wasn't contemplating killing Penny? Not that Penny didn't deserve it…

"I hope you get to meet Jay," Pamela added.

Meet him? She'd be forced to watch his every move. Audra managed a smile and hurried back to her room to pack her things. She found two volleyball uniforms and decided they'd have to do. In a couple of hours, she'd be in her pyjamas, anyway. Good thing she'd already set fresh linen and towels in the guest rooms at Maxima, though she'd never thought in a million years that she'd be the one using them.

Hitching her bag over her shoulder, Audra wondered if Pamela was right: that maybe she should look at this as a fun assignment instead of unwanted work on her days off. How many girls got to spend two days with their high school heart-throb? Her sister Sam would kill to be where she was now. And she could never, ever breathe a word of it to Sam.

Her steps quickened as she rounded the lagoon. Two

days of watching Jay's hot body as he relaxed on the island. She'd done worse jobs. Just as long as she still had her job at the end of those two days…

THIRTY ONE

Jay reclined on one of the veranda deck chairs, his bruised abs in clear view as she trotted up the steps to Maxima. "You took your time," he greeted her.

Audra bit back an angry retort. "Your matron's orders were not to leave you alone for the next two days. I needed a change of clothes for tomorrow and the next day."

A grin spread across his face. "You mean you'll be taking care of me personally for the whole time? Not dividing me up in a roster with your underlings?"

Underlings? No one worked under her. Audra suppressed a snort. But a roster…why hadn't she thought of it? Too tired, perhaps. "I'm sorry, Mr Felix. You're right. I didn't think. You should have a more alert staff member with you the whole time. I'll talk to my boss and tell her – "

"NO!"

His outburst shocked her.

Him, too, by the look of things. "No," he repeated in a more normal tone. "I want you. Tired or…whatever. There's plenty of beds here. Take your pick. Even mine, if you want it." He winked.

Audra shifted uncomfortably. Trying not to be obvious, she glanced around to see if there was anyone within earshot who might've heard his offer. Probably not, but there could be someone on the beach, hidden behind the palm trees…

"I won't work you too hard, I promise." The look in his eyes said otherwise. "If your boss sends someone else, I'll send them right back. All I want is you."

Audra avoided his eyes. She knew that look – it adorned one of Sam's favourite posters. She hadn't realised it would heat her insides like she'd swallowed one of the chilli dumplings on the guest menu. No wonder Jay was the idol of millions. "Fine," she forced herself to say.

He chuckled. "I am, aren't I?"

Arrogant prick! She raised her gaze and found him staring at her. Deliberately baiting her.

Grudgingly, she replied, "A bit of discolouration and damage around the edges, but otherwise in reasonably good condition." Her glance lingered on his bruised torso and the white patches stuck to his hands.

He laughed louder still. "It'll be fun, Audra, I promise. I'm sure you've done worse jobs than me." His eyes glinted with innuendo.

Sighing, Audra swiped the door controls and led the way inside the villa.

"I meant it when I said you can sleep in my bed." He was right behind her.

"Mr Felix – "

"Jay."

"Jay, then. I've already told you this, but I'll say it again. I'll lose my job if I sleep with you."

"And will they let you keep your job if I die in some sort of medical complication while you're sleeping in another room instead of keeping watch over me like my guardian angel?"

Like Leon nearly had…

Tears sprang to her eyes. "I can't do this." Audra turned on her heel and bolted for the door.

Jay blocked her exit, spreading his arms to catch her. "Wait, Audra." He seemed to notice her tears. "Shit, I'm sorry. All right? I'm sorry." His arms closed around her and it felt surprisingly good.

If only she could stop crying. Shit. She was in Jay Felix's arms, dribbling tears and snot down his sculpted chest. This was so many levels of wrong.

"You can do this, because I need you to. You stepped up to that matron and made her release me. Saved me from her. I swear she was going to torture me again in the name of medicine the minute no one was watching. If you don't, I'm going back to hell in hospital with her. Save me from a fate worse than death, Audra."

She figured he was trying to be funny, but it wasn't working. She shook her head. "I'm sorry," she said softly, pulling away from him. Snot. Oh God. "I should help you clean that up."

"I vote for naked in the shower. Now."

For a moment, she wished she could.

"Mr Felix."

"I told you, it's Jay."

Audra took a deep, steadying breath. "Mr Jay Felix, I intend to keep my job. Which means I will not shower or sleep with you. And while you might find car crashes funny, I don't." Her voice died to a whisper. "I'm sorry."

His eyes hardened. "Honesty. I like that." His tone said otherwise. "I'll be honest, too. I'd like to spend a night in bed with you, making you lose control in ways you never believed possible. No, not a boast. A promise."

Shit. The words, the tone, the voice…Audra wondered if her underwear was going to melt. Not that she intended to let him know if it did.

"I left a perfectly good pub and a bunch of willing girls because the only one I wanted was you, Audra. Only along the way I got lost and crashed my car. So you came to me. I know what I want and I will get it."

No you won't, you arrogant prick, she thought tiredly. He had to be lying about trying to find her. He was supposed to be bringing guests back to the hotel. Someone to share the fondue with. And the strawberries…

"Tonight, I want dinner and you're going to join me. Then you're going to stay the night here in whatever fucking bed you like."

"I'm not having sex with you," Audra said slowly.

"Not tonight, no," Jay said, to her surprise. He flushed and glanced down. "Do you think I can get that matron arrested for assault? She said the thing was called a catheter but there's no way it's natural to shove something up a man's…"

"Jay, stop. Please." She fought down her laughter. "Truce. I'll have dinner with you as long as you don't talk about your – " She waved at waist level. " – tackle box."

He considered her for a moment. "Deal," he said finally. "Get room service. Order me a steak with all the trimmings and whatever you want."

THIRTY TWO

The only steak Audra could find on the menu was a surf and turf that came with garlic prawns, so she made an executive decision and ordered that.

"Just dinner for one? Anything else, miss?" the kitchen hand asked. "Dessert, maybe?"

For one? No, she needed to eat, too. "Um, hang on. Do you have any mango chicken?" she asked hopefully. It'd be wonderful to taste it when it wasn't burned.

"Can you hold for a moment, miss?"

"Sure."

A muffled discussion on the other end of the phone ensued, before the kitchen hand's voice returned. "No, miss. We don't seem to have any mango chicken tonight."

"Again? That's happening a lot lately."

"Yes, miss." He sounded as annoyed as she felt.

She shouldn't. She really shouldn't. But Penny had gone

too far. "It wouldn't have anything to do with the chef and the maid I saw earlier, banging in the laundry room?"

"The what?"

"I was walking past the laundry room and couldn't help but notice the couple. Her name was either Penny or baby, judging by the groaning of the man she was with. And he still had his chef's hat on."

Audra heard muffled swearing. "I'll have to tell that to my boss. I wouldn't know. Can I get you anything else instead? The threadfin salmon's good. I'm making it tonight and I'll make sure you get an extra big fillet."

She agreed and ended the call.

"So the staff can't sleep with guests because they're too busy banging each other? And you like to watch?"

Audra whirled around to find Jay reclining on the couch. "No," she said. "I didn't actually see them. Another girl did. But she's been meeting up with him during work time most days and the rest of us end up doing her job. She was supposed to be on laundry duty but instead of doing the washing she let the chef do her and they messed up all the clean laundry, so none of us have clean uniforms and now we have twice as much work to do. That's what took me so long to come up here from Reception. I shouldn't be telling you this. You'll think we're a dodgy, shagging bunch of –"

Jay shrugged. "Hey, rock star, remember? Most of the people I work with sleep around. Can't say I've ever done anyone in a hotel laundry, though. Something to put on my bucket list."

Selfish, arrogant, promiscuous prick. No thought of what the poor hotel staff would have to clean up after he'd had his way with whichever random girl, who'd only ever be a few minutes of his life – a tick of a box, and then she'd be gone. He wouldn't remember her name or anything else. Just that he'd achieved another conquest. So full of shit it was surprising it didn't come out of his ears.

"Audra. Hey, Audra!"

She focussed on the fridge, where Jay now stood with the door open. "What?"

"Can I get you a drink? I know you like the mango beer."

Audra shook her head. "No. You're not supposed to drink and I shouldn't, either. I'm supposed to be watching for slurred speech and all the rest, but I won't notice if we're having alcohol."

"No booze? You're no fun. What'll you do if I drink one anyway?" He upended a beer bottle into his mouth, grinning widely.

Audra marched forward and snatched it away from him, only to find the cap still firmly in place. "Do you want to die?" she asked, fighting to hold back tears.

"No. Not today." Jay sighed and grabbed two cans of soft drink. "If you ever breathe a word of this to anyone, I'll deny it. I haven't drunk this stuff since primary school." He returned to his seat on the sofa and cracked open both cans. "Come over here and join me in a drink, then. And you can tell me who died in a car crash to make you cry when I so much as mention it."

"Or what?"

"Or I'll grab a beer and drink that instead. Your call, weather girl."

He remembered. "Meteorologist," Audra corrected.

"Whatever. Sit. Talk. And when you're done, maybe I'll

know how not to make you cry again."

It sounded fair. Audra settled onto the sofa opposite him and sipped her can of lemonade. "He didn't die, but he came damn close," she began.

THIRTY THREE

Jason couldn't help laughing. "So let me get this straight. Your little brother's old bomb of a car had dodgy brakes, cracked cylinders and stalled more often than it started, but he still drove it, crashed it into a tree on his way to a party and just walked away, booze in hand, leaving the wrecked car in the middle of a roundabout, wrapped around a tree? And still went to the party like nothing had happened? Fuck, that sounds like something I'd do!" He thought he might have actually done something like that in high school, except he hadn't crashed the car, he'd just left the clunky old thing by the side of the road.

Audra managed a small smile. "Yeah, I guess it is funny when you put it like that. He was late, so the party was well underway by the time he got there. He just joined in drinking with the rest of them. The next morning, I came to pick him up like I'd promised, and he was passed out like most of them were. The thing is, he didn't wake up, and in the morning light, we could all see there was blood in his hair, but no one knew how he'd gotten hurt." She paused, as if debating whether to say something. She made her decision and continued, "I drove him to hospital. They pumped his stomach, said it was alcohol poisoning, slapped a dressing on his head and said he'd be fine. So I took him home and he went to bed to sleep it off. I heard strange sounds a few hours later and I found him having a fit on the kitchen floor." She passed a hand before her eyes. "It was frightening. Like he'd been electrocuted. All jerky and…shit." She grabbed a tissue and swiped at her eyes. "I took him back to hospital. We couldn't…couldn't afford an ambulance or health insurance to cover it. So I had to drag him into the car. When we got there, his lips were turning blue and I didn't know what to do. I just parked in the ambulance entry and…and…" She covered her streaming eyes with her hands and her shoulders shuddered with what Jason realised were sobs.

So much for a funny story. He'd made her cry again, too. Awkwardly, he shifted to the seat beside her. "I'm sorry," he began. "I'm sorry about your brother. How long ago did he…did he…"

"Today." Audra sniffled. "A year ago today."

Fuck. Making jokes on the anniversary of her brother's death. Well, wasn't he a fuckwit and a half.

"They kept him in hospital for weeks. He kept saying he wanted to come home, but they wanted to do one more scan…"

Wait – what? Dead people couldn't talk.

"Eventually, they had to discharge him. They couldn't

find anything wrong. But he couldn't drive and he didn't have a car and he couldn't go back to his apprenticeship. I had to stay home with him and keep an eye on him, watch him for…symptoms of concussion. Like I'm supposed to be doing for you, instead of telling you sob stories you don't need to hear." Audra turned her teary eyes on Jason and gave an enormous sniff. "It's still not too late for me to call my supervisor and say you want someone else. Someone who won't go to pieces."

She saved her brother's life. Why the fuck would he want anyone else watching out for him?

Jason shook his head. "Nah, I think I'll take you, thanks. You know what you're looking for. Just as long as you call the Flying Doctors and don't try to drive me to the hospital. And guard me from that matron. She wants to get her hands on my dick."

Audra clapped her hands over her mouth. "I almost spat out my drink. Did you just say she wants your – "

"Dick. Cock. Penis. Say the word and I'll show you, in case you need to see it."

Audra opened her mouth and Jason grinned in anticipation.

"Room service," the recorded Englishwoman's voice announced over the intercom.

"Fuck," Jason swore. He stomped to the door and yanked the trolley inside, to the surprise of the kitchen hand wheeling it. "Go away." Jason made shooing motions at the kid. He wheeled the trolley into the lounge room to find Audra cheerfully setting the dining table with cutlery. If it weren't for her reddened eyes, he'd swear he'd imagined her tears.

"You said steak, so I hope this is okay." Audra set a plate on the table, piled high with huge prawns. "The steak's under the prawns." Her own plate held a slab of fish surrounded by a jungle of salad. "Thank you for this. The food in the staff dining room isn't this nice. Definitely no salmon unless the chef's burned it." Audra dropped onto a chair and transferred a forkful of greenery into her mouth.

Jason took a seat behind his steak. It did look good, he had to admit. A million times better than hospital food, for sure. He grasped the steak knife and swore.

"What?" Audra's wide eyes were on him.

"Nothing." Carefully, he kept his face blank, but the more his fingers tightened around the knife, the more the gashes on his hand hurt. Gritting his teeth, he clumsily cut himself a bite of steak and shoved it into his mouth. At least it tasted all right. He started slicing another piece.

"I can help you with that."

He met Audra's eyes and lowered his gaze quickly to his plate. Did she think he didn't have the guts to tackle his own steak? It was just a bit of pain. Not like he was a baby. There were just cuts on his hand. Cuts covered by gauze. And one that was now bleeding...

He forced himself to look away, his stomach rebelling even at that tiny spot of red. Fuck. Stay conscious, don't throw up. Fuck. He was going to, whether he wanted to or not. "Not hungry. Going to go...to the..." he mumbled, shoving away from the table. He stumbled for the bathroom and barely made it before he vomited violently. He stayed on his knees for a while, until he was sure he wasn't going to bring any more up. Fuck, what would she think of him?

He flushed away the mess, rinsed his mouth, then brushed his teeth to get rid of the taste of bile. Reluctantly, he dragged himself back to the dining room.

Audra glanced up from her almost empty plate. "Are you all right? Can I help?"

"No." Jason felt his body swaying and forced himself to stay still. "Tired. Going to bed."

Audra looked uncertain. "Do you…do you really need me to sit by you while you sleep? To keep watch?"

What, and have her see if he threw up again? "No. The nurses didn't stay in my room in the hospital. Just…I'll leave the door open. So you can hear if I need your help." Fuck. What if he had a fit like her brother? He wasn't ready to die. "Don't let me die."

"I won't." Sincerity seemed to gleam in her eyes. Of course he believed her.

"Thank you." Jason stumbled to bed, praying to any deity who'd listen to let him wake up again. He needed to thank this girl in true rock star style and he needed a body to do it. Not to mention hers.

THIRTY FOUR

Audra finished her dinner, then tidied away all the dishes and left the trolley outside. Now what? She didn't want to watch any of the pay-per-view movies at Jay's expense. If she'd brought her laptop, she could've worked on her job application, but her computer was on the other side of the island and she didn't dare leave Jay to go get it. Whatever he said, he wasn't okay and she had no intention of letting him get as close to death as Leon had. She knew first aid now, and could resuscitate with the best of them.

Figuring she could kill a few minutes in the bathroom, she decided to brush her teeth. Audra made lazy circles with her toothbrush as she scanned the room, looking for something to do. There wasn't a frog in sight, not even in the enormous spa bath. She wondered what it was like to bathe in a tub so huge. Talk about luxury. Even getting the shower for more than five minutes at home had been a miracle. Here, Jay had a tub big enough for her to swim in and she'd have it all to herself. If he was asleep, surely he wouldn't mind if she took a bath. Surely...

Five minutes later, Audra gave in, grabbing a bathrobe from one of the guestrooms to cover herself as she padded across the tiled floor to the decadent bath. She reached for the hotel shower gel, then thought better of it and grabbed the rose bath mixture that came in the honeymoon pack. If Jay hadn't brought a female friend back, no one else would use it. And he couldn't get his stitches wet. In went the bath oil, rose petals and all, before Audra turned on the taps. She climbed in before the water was ankle deep, settling with a contented sigh.

The water level rose, covering her legs and her belly until only her breasts floated on the surface between the rose petals, like the buoys at the pearl farm that signified pearl-bearing oysters below. Audra snorted. If that wasn't the worst euphemism for her lady parts she'd ever heard. She wished she'd thought to bring a book. Tomorrow, she promised herself. Tomorrow she could visit the hotel library and pick out a few books so she could snigger at their references to glistening pearls. She could offer to get Jay some reading material, too. There were plenty more rock star books.

A dragging sound made her turn to find the source. To her horror, Jay shuffled into the bathroom and headed for the toilet.

Not again!

Trying to keep quiet, hoping he hadn't seen her, Audra brought her knees up to her chest and wrapped her arms around them, trying to hide her breasts from sight. The rose petals carpeting the surface hid everything else, or at least she hoped they did.

She closed her eyes so she wouldn't see Jay's fire hose again. Once was definitely enough. Especially as she couldn't touch it.

"You know, those have got to be the most perfect pair of tits I've ever seen. It should be a crime to cover those up."

Audra cracked open one eye to find Jay's reflection staring at her. She clutched her knees tightly. "Damn it, Jay!"

He laughed and turned to face her. "No, I mean it. I've seen a lot of tits and yours deserve to be worshipped. I'm volunteering, here and now."

Audra snatched up the soap and threw it. The bar smacked into his eyebrow before it tumbled to the floor.

"Ow! Alright, I'll go, but I wasn't kidding. I'll be dreaming about your tits tonight."

Audra wanted to swear at him some more, but knew she shouldn't. Even if this was the most mortifying situation she'd ever gotten mixed up in. "I'm sorry, now you're bleeding and it's my fault. Turn around so I can get out and I'll help you."

"I'm what?" Jay whirled and squinted at himself in the mirror.

Audra rose to a crouch, her arms folded across her breasts, and lifted one leg out of the bath. Movement caught her eye and she saw Jay topple. "NO!" She threw herself at him and they both tumbled to the floor in a tangle of wet limbs. His face ended up mashed into the breasts he'd been making fun of, but he didn't make another joke.

Instead, his weight settled on her limply as she realised he'd blacked out.

She could hear his breathing, much to her relief, so she heaved him off her and onto his side. She shoved his arm and leg out to stop him from rolling over onto his belly, and left him in the recovery position while she hunted for some clothes. Belting her bathrobe around her, she knelt beside Jay on the wet tiles. "Jay? Mr Felix? Please be okay. Please."

He didn't respond, and she reached for his ID to tap an emergency signal. But Jay's wrists were bare – he didn't have an ID on either arm. Swearing softly, Audra pulled up her sleeve to activate her own ID, but she only touched bare skin. She'd taken her ID off in the guest room, just as she did before she used the staff showers, because the staff IDs weren't waterproof. Shit. What to do? Should she leave him to call for help, or stay with him and hope he woke up?

Audra reached up to the basin and grabbed a face washer. She ran it under the cold tap for a few seconds, then turned the water off and brought the dripping flannel to Jay's face. "Please, wake up," she begged, stroking the wet cloth across his eyes and cheeks. "Jay, wake up, damn it! You have ten seconds or I call the Flying Doctors!"

Something warm touched her chest, tracing her cleavage. "Mm, angel tits."

Audra slapped his hand away. "Jay, don't!" She pulled her bathrobe closed and tightened the belt. "I need to get you back to hospital. You fainted."

"You hit me."

"It was an accident!"

"Fucking wasn't," Jay mumbled. "Pass like that, you

should play AFL. Do they take women with hot tits on football teams?"

Audra wet her lips. "I'm sorry, okay? I'm not used to strange men walking in on me when I'm naked in the bathroom. Give me a minute to get dressed and I'll call for a helicopter to take you back to hospital."

"No, I'm fine. Really." Jay seemed to struggle with the words. "I…fuck. Don't laugh. I can't stand the sight of blood. I throw up and sometimes I pass out. You can't tell anyone, all right?"

"Only if you don't tell anyone you saw me naked. And forget everything you saw."

Jay laughed weakly. "I'm not going to forget that in a hurry. But sure, I won't tell anyone." He climbed shakily to his feet and walked toward the door.

Audra crumpled against the side of the bath in relief.

"Let me just say one thing."

She lifted her eyes to his face.

"You really do have awesome tits."

He staggered out and Audra wanted to sink through the floor. But there was probably a knot of frogs waiting for her under the house, angry at being evicted from the spa. Jay was better company than the frogs. At least his hands were warm.

Jay Felix admired her breasts. Another crazy first.

"Thank you," she said softly, hoping he didn't hear.

THIRTY FIVE

It took Audra almost a full minute to remember why she'd slept in one of the Villa Maxima bedrooms and not her own room in the staff accommodation. Between the blockout curtains and luxurious bed, she could definitely get used to this. Maybe being Jay's babysitter might be bearable after all. Just as long as he didn't remember last night's debacle on the bathroom floor.

If only she could've thrown caution to the wind and given in to his advances. Let those warm hands continue caressing her breasts, then more skin on skin until…

Audra drew a shaky breath and laughed quietly at herself. The reality was very different to her teenage fantasies, but somehow in her dreams last night the two had morphed into a tangled memory. One she had to forget if she wanted to keep her job. One night with a rock god wasn't worth losing her livelihood.

She dressed quickly, not wanting to be caught out again, and smoothed her hair with her hairbrush. There. A consummate professional, who never thought of...

The way his body had moulded to hers, slick with water as they lay on the floor together, and the strength of hard muscle as she'd moved him, letting her hands linger on a body she never thought she'd get to touch.

Get a grip, she told herself. Having sexy thoughts about a guest who needed no encouragement would only make her job harder.

Mm. Harder.

Audra stalked to the kitchen and made herself some coffee. Her stomach grumbled a protest that breakfast wasn't forthcoming, but she ignored it. Normally, she'd be in the staff dining room by now, trying not to strangle Penny. She'd have to wait for Jay this morning. Speaking of Jay, she should check on him.

Carrying her coffee, she tiptoed to the darkened doorway to his room. Light snoring told her he was very much alive and still asleep. She returned to the kitchen and decided to raid the fridge. The strawberries were calling her name and her self-control was so busy battling lusty thoughts about the rock star in the bed only a few metres away that the fruit won. They wouldn't last much past today, anyway, Audra counselled herself as she set the bowl on the bench.

Slowly, she lifted the largest one to her lips and bit into the sweet flesh.

"Fuck, that's huge! Makes me think of you putting other big things into your mouth."

Audra choked. "Mr Felix!" she mumbled.

Jay lifted a hand to stop her. "You're not fucking freezing me out again with the Mr Felix shit. You know my weakness and I've seen the secret you're hiding under that shirt. Been dreaming about them all night. Tonight I'll probably be dreaming about your mouth, too. It's the twenty-first century, not the eighteenth, and you're going to call me Jay. Just Jay." He eyed the strawberries. "Is that all there is for breakfast? I need protein."

"There's the buffet up at the resort restaurant," Audra began.

"What, Jay Felix eat in public while every girl in the place recognises me and interrupts to get my autograph? Fuck that. Order something for me from room service. Lots of protein, not too many carbs." His voice lost its edge. "Get something else for yourself, too. Even those huge strawberries aren't enough for breakfast. Now, I'm going to have a shower. Where are the gloves from the hospital?"

Audra pointed at the bag and Jay upended it. Gloves, dressing packs and sachets of antiseptic wipes cascaded onto the coffee table.

"If you like, I can change the dressings for you when you get out," Audra said softly. "Then you won't have to see any blood."

Jay nodded curtly. He strode toward the bathroom and stopped. "It goes without saying, but I'm going to be naked in the shower. If…if something happens like it did last night, are you going to come help me?" His tone held a note of panic that vanished as he continued, "You're not going to go to pieces because you see the size of my cock, are you?"

She hadn't the first time, but she wasn't going to tell him about that. Or the frog that had felt her up in his bathtub…

Audra fought to maintain her composure. "I'm sure I'll manage. If I have any trouble, I'll just tell myself it's a large bratwurst." She continued before he could comment, "Please try not to fall or pass out, Jay. You're heavier than me."

He grinned. "So that means you prefer to be on top, too? Good. That's what you were in my dreams. Your tits bounce better that way, too." Whistling and swinging the gloves, he vanished into the bathroom.

Only when she heard the sound of the shower flowing did she allow herself to laugh, glad he couldn't see her blush. Evidently they both had similar dreams, but she swore that's all they'd ever be.

THIRTY SIX

Jay sat on the sofa with his eyes closed, extending his hands toward Audra. She shook her head and guided them onto her knees. For a moment, she wished she'd chosen to do this at the dining table, but Jay kept his hands courteous. As long as he didn't grope her, she could manage.

For all her first aid training, she'd never had to practise it much on real wounds, but the principle was the same. Off came the old dressings, with the peculiar ripping sound that made both of them grit their teeth at the thought of hair being pulled. Not that Jay's hands were hairy. His long, smooth fingers curved over Audra's as she pressed down each new dressing, careful not to touch the cuts or the stitches holding them shut.

"What did you do?" she asked.

"You mean aside from crash my car?"

"I mean to your hands. Why are they all cut up?"

"Broken glass. From the smashed windows. And the beer."

Beer? He'd been drinking and driving? "You were drunk?" Audra asked carefully.

"Maybe. Dunno. But the beer in the car wasn't for me. It was for you. A present." He sucked in a breath and winced. "I'll have to get you some more. I wonder if they deliver."

Audra laughed. "A present for me? I don't believe you."

Jay shrugged. "Don't believe me, then. But I've been completely honest with you."

"Jay, I'm just a random member of staff at the hotel where you're staying. Why would you even remember my name, let alone buy me presents?"

Even with his eyes closed, his grin was sexy. "Audra, your name was the mantra I chanted the whole way back from the pub. The bottles in the back were the same as the one you'd wrapped your lips around the night before and I couldn't get the image out of my head. Do you know what I did in town?"

Audra set his bandaged hand back in his lap and lifted the other one. "That's the day they announced Chaya's farewell tour, and you were all over social media because you had drinks with some tourists in the pub."

He laughed. "So you even got the news out here. Those girls wanted me. They always do. And they made no secret of it. I could've had any one of them, or all at once."

"So why didn't you?" Audra challenged before she could stop herself.

"Is that what you'd have told me? If you'd been there in the pub with me, and I'd said, 'Audra, do you think I should fuck these girls senseless until my cock's sated and all my frustration at the band's breakup is gone?' Would you have told me to go for it and bonk my brains out?"

She bit her lip. "That's what you usually do, or at least that's what the news always says. I'm sure you didn't need anyone's advice. If that's what you wanted to do, why didn't you?"

"I was going to," he admitted. "And then one of them mentioned the band breaking up. Looked at me all accusing, like it was my fault and I could fix it. Those bitches were angry at me for something that's not even my fucking fault!"

"So Jay Felix doesn't do hate fucks? That's why you didn't bring them back here?" Audra swallowed. "Reception called me and said to prepare your villa for guests. I assumed you were looking for romance, so I tried to help. The fondue in your fridge, the rose petal stuff in the spa, the champagne, the candles…What changed your mind?"

His eyes opened and bored into hers. "You. All those voices yammering at me and all I could think of was your quiet sympathy. Someone who saw me as a person and not the rock god they feel is their personal property."

Audra snorted. "If they think a rock star's their personal property, they're delusional. Maybe one day you'll be someone's, but I hope for your sake it'll be a girl you love and care for, someone who'll give you her heart as she treasures yours. When I was a teenager, I remember thinking like they did, and maybe occasionally I dreamed…but I woke up. Someone like you will never settle for someone like me."

"I keep telling you, but you're not listening. I want you,

Audra. In my bed. In my arms. Wrapped around me with nothing between us. Fuck everyone else. I want you."

Audra dragged her hands out of his grasp. "But that's it, isn't it? You have fucked everyone else, except me. I'm just a challenge. One night and you'll forget me, never to think of me again, but that night will cost me my job. My self-respect. If you have any respect for me, you'll quit with the sex talk and let me do my job. Until you leave me in peace to go back to your rock star life."

"It wouldn't be like that, I swear." Jay swallowed. "Fine. Give me two days. You're supposed to be watching me all day anyway, and tomorrow, too, so you're stuck with me. Give me two days to demonstrate you're more to me than a night's conquest."

"Sure." She still wouldn't sleep with him, she swore. But she could admit she'd been wrong about him. And it'd make the next two days a lot easier. At least, she hoped so.

THIRTY SEVEN

Jay threw down his fork. "So, what do you want to do today?"

Audra swallowed her mouthful of muesli. "What do you mean? I'm supposed to tag along with you. I should clean the bathroom, too. After the mess last night..."

Jay waved as if he could sweep it all away. "Not your problem. I'm not staying cooped up inside. I had enough of that in hospital. Let someone else clean the damn house. Come with me to a secret beach I found at the south end of the island. You have to scramble a bit and you'd have to watch the tides because it looks like it might be cut off from the rest of the island at high tide, but it's worth it."

"But you shouldn't swim. Doctor's orders. You'll get your stitches wet."

"We won't. Last time I just took a book with me. I've read the ones you gave me, though. Is there anything else?"

Audra permitted herself a small smile. "Oh, plenty of books. I'll take you to the resort library and show you. You can pick your own then."

Jay nodded. "Sure. Can we get lunch sent down to us?"

"Can we get a room service trolley to your secret beach?"

Jay eyed the breakfast trolley doubtfully. "Don't think so. It'd probably get bogged and if it doesn't, it won't handle the rocks too well."

"Catering make up picnic baskets for day trips. People take them heli-fishing or sightseeing when they're out on a charter flight. I can pick up one of the menus on the way to the library and we can order one, if you like."

"A picnic for two, yeah? You're joining me for lunch."

"If you insist."

After stacking the breakfast dishes on the trolley, Audra found Jay pacing around the lounge room.

"Get your shoes on and let's go."

Audra balked at the note of impatience in his voice, but let it go. She'd seen the bruises hidden under his shirt and she was fairly sure she was responsible for a few fresh ones last night. He was allowed to be grumpy from the pain. She nodded, then watched in amusement as he shoved a cap on his head and put on an enormous pair of mirrored sunglasses. "You're trying to hide from people? I thought you loved the attention."

His mouth set in a grim line. "Not today."

"It's harder to smile when you're in pain. I understand."

Jay flashed a smile. "And that's why I want to spend today with you. You're the only one who does. So show me this library of yours."

Audra let Jay set the pace at a leisurely stroll and walked beside him instead of hurrying like she normally did when she was working. A pair of rainbow-coloured birds she'd never seen before flew across the path to a palm tree, where another pair screeched at the uninvited guests.

"Bloody lorikeets," Jay said. "We used to get them all the time at home. Drove me nuts early in the morning."

"Where did you grow up?"

"Perth, of course, but I had this old place in Cottesloe and they used to screech in the trees by the beach over the road. Working gigs late at night, then coming home and being woken up a couple hours later by those feathered pests almost made me want to take up shooting."

Privately, she thought they were pretty and she'd have welcomed their chirping over the neighbours screaming as they beat the shit out of each other at all hours of the day and night. Her parents might've been poor but she had nothing to complain about; with five children, it was a miracle they'd never tried to kill one another.

They walked in silence until they reached the fork where the path branched off to the staff accommodation and kitchens. "I should get a catering menu for you. I'll be right back," Audra said.

She darted down the path at her usual pace, slipped through the screen door to Catering and stopped dead. Backed up against the wall was a chef with his eyes raised to heaven as a kneeling girl deep-throated whatever she'd found in his unzipped pants. Audra squinted at the girl's worn sneakers and recognised them as Penny's. That made the chef Patel. If they knew she'd reported them yesterday... Silently, slowly, Audra retreated the way she'd come until her backside met something that shouldn't have been there. Shit. Luckily, the chef emitted a groan that drowned out the sound of her squeak. She squeezed past Jay, shaking her head, but he grinned and started forward.

"Oh, sorry, I didn't realise this place had an onsite brothel. I thought this was the kitchen," Jay boomed and Audra clapped both hands over her mouth so she wouldn't burst out laughing. The sounds of choking, coughing and frantic zipping only made it worse. "I hope you didn't pay too much for that one. She didn't even swallow. I'd ask for my money back, if I was you." He raised his voice. "OI! Where's the service here?"

"I can help you," a shaky male voice said. Patel, Audra presumed. She heard the squeak of running sneakers and ducked behind a linen trolley, hoping Penny didn't see her as the girl rushed past, the front of her uniform streaked with fluid that Audra could only presume had come from Patel.

"Oh, so this is the kitchen! And the call girls come to you, to service you on shift. Shit, that's a nice perk of the job. Wish I could get a blowjob while I'm working."

Audra snorted. If the stories were true, Jay had enjoyed more such perks than Patel would in his lifetime.

Jay ordered a picnic basket, which the chef promised would be delivered to his villa in an hour. Jay waved and thanked him, then marched outside, shooing Audra ahead of him.

"Library," Jay managed to say as he fought down the same laughter that threatened to make Audra lose control.

They made it to the library before Jay fell to his knees on the floor and laughed so hard that tears streamed down his face. "Fuck, Audra, your colleagues are worse than roadies with groupies! Did you see that bloke? If he can get a blowjob, no wonder this place has rules about staff sleeping with guests. That chick would fuck anything with a boner."

Audra agreed, but didn't dare say so. Anyone could be listening outside the door and Penny hated her enough already.

Instead, she swallowed and headed for the bookshelves. "What do you want to read? There's plenty more rock star books." She grabbed the three nearest and held up the bouquet of shirtless men. "Pick your pleasure."

"I'm not into naked men," Jay said, wincing as he clambered to his feet. "Shit, that one looks like me. I should send a copy to my agent and get him to look into it."

"I doubt you can copyright even your sculpted six-pack," Audra said, lifting a couple more off the shelf. "What about these?"

Jay pulled off his glasses and grinned at her. "I knew you'd noticed! They're sexy, right?"

"That's why they're on the cover of so many books here, I imagine."

"What's with the shelf markers? I've never seen bookstores with labels like this." Jay scanned the shelves and pointed as he read, "Rock stars. Billionaires. Motorcycle clubs. Kilts. Seriously? Cowboys. Mail-order brides? Fuck, who gets a bride by mail order?" He grabbed one off the shelf.

"They're historical romances. When Australia and America were settled, it was mostly men, and they got lonely, so they put ads in newspapers and things for brides and were pen-pals for a while before they finally met." Audra didn't want to admit it, but she'd had a thing for mail-order bride romances when she'd first arrived and she'd read every one on the library shelf.

"Sounds like it's still a thing. This one's an email-order bride," Jay remarked, reading the back of the book in his hand.

"Seriously?" Audra snatched it from him. Sure enough, he was right. "I haven't read this one."

Jay snorted. "Be my guest. I don't want it. There's something you'll never read. The rock star's email-order bride." He eyed the pile of books Audra hadn't put back. "I should check out this one, just to see if he's anything like me."

Exactly like him, and yet completely different, Audra thought, recognising the book as one she'd read. No fictional rock star compared to the complex reality of Jay Felix and she was okay with that.

"Right, got your book? Let's go back to the house and get our stuff for the beach. We should have lunch delivered in fifteen minutes or so, and then I can whisk you away to my secret spot." Jay winked and beckoned. Shaking her head, Audra followed him home.

THIRTY EIGHT

"Got your bathers on?"

"If you're not going in, then neither am I," Audra said. "It's my job to keep an eye on you, and if I'm underwater while you're on shore, I'm not doing my job."

"And here I was hoping to see those perfect tits again." Jay sighed. "You're cruel. I'm going topless. You should, too."

Audra frowned at him. "It's not the same. And you promised you wouldn't talk about it. That you'd try to forget about last night."

"I said I wouldn't tell anyone about it. Judging by your blush, you remember it as well as I do. Better, maybe, because you were conscious for all of it."

The blush heating her cheeks crept lower, warming her throat and reminding her of how hot his hands had been as they traced the curve of her breasts last night. Shoving the memory out of her mind, Audra draped the towels over her shoulder, hiding the curves in question. "We going or what?"

"Sure." Jay hefted the picnic basket and led the way outside. They passed the other villas — Pinctada, Albina, Margaritifera, Akoya and Penguin, the southernmost house — before the paved path gave way to a combination of crushed rock and beach sand, marbled into swirls of rust and cream.

"I wish I had a camera to capture this," Audra breathed, staring at the ground. No one would believe the spectacular artwork nature had wrought in this place.

"Capture this?" Jay's voice was sharp and unpleasant. "Your day with the rock star?"

Audra glanced up in surprise. "No. Everything isn't about you. I was talking about the rocks under my feet. The colours and the patterns..." She traced a curlicue with her toes.

She wouldn't need a photo to remember her time with Jay, even if she had a camera and was allowed to take one. Not just a day, but the whole week of working with him.

"Don't you have a camera on your phone?"

On her cheap prepaid one that didn't work up here? Audra shook her head. He wouldn't understand and she didn't want his pity.

"I'm sorry. I thought..." Jay didn't seem able to articulate his thoughts, so he changed tack. "Never mind. I'll get you a camera next time I'm in town. I want a photo to remember the girl who saved my life and won't let me thank her properly for it."

Audra snorted. "I didn't save your life. Saved you a few

bruises, maybe."

"Give yourself some credit. How many girls would've done what you did for me last night?"

Audra managed a smile. "Millions all over the world, I'm sure. The world would be a darker place without Jay Felix and the way his voice can creep into your heart and make you feel things that haunt you for days. That first song of yours, *Necessary Evil*, the way it blends darkness and light, about how you have to endure and what matters through all the evil is the end..." She trailed off as she found him staring at her. "What? I was having a hard time in high school when I first heard that song, and it stuck in my head. It was as if you'd seen into my soul when you wrote it. And it...it helped."

"I didn't write it. The band's songwriter did when she was...still recovering." Jay strode forward, picking up the pace so Audra had to break into a jog to catch up. When she did, she wasn't sure she'd wanted to, his face looked so dark and forbidding.

No talking about evil, then, necessary or otherwise, she told herself, saving her breath for the hike. She needed it, too – not long after, the path ended as red rocks rose up and blocked the way.

"Come on, this way." Jay shoved through the pandanus and skirted the rock. Audra followed, using the towels to push the spiky leaves aside so they wouldn't scratch her legs. His warm hand grabbed hers and tugged. "Up here."

The boulder was cracked down the middle, the shattered pieces forming a rough set of steps that were just close enough for her to climb, with occasional assistance from Jay.

"Take a look at this." He held out his hand and she climbed up beside him. "Highest spot on the island." He slid an arm around her waist and extended his other arm to point. "That's one of the mining islands, I think. Occasionally you can see the trucks on their way into the pit. The resort's over on the other side of the lagoon, but you can't see this rock from there because it's just under the palm tree canopy. On a clear day like today, you can see clear to the mainland and the pearl farm."

Audra's gaze followed his pointing finger and she spotted the carrier boat crossing the aqua-blue expanse between the farm and Romance Island. "Look, there's the boat with our laundry. Fresh uniforms for me and probably more supplies for the kitchen. Today's the day to order fresh lobster or oysters because the oysters would've only been out of the ocean for a day, maybe less."

"I only have oysters if I have a big, hot night planned. Have you changed your mind, Audra?"

She shrugged out of his embrace and shook her head. "Some people eat oysters because they enjoy them. The world doesn't revolve around sex, you know."

"Sure it does."

"Which way off this rock?"

"This way." Jay lifted the picnic basket and led the way to a cleft in the rock. "You have to jump." He backed up a couple of steps and leaped, the basket swinging from his hand as if it weighed nothing.

Audra sidled up to the edge and looked down. Dark water roiled at least ten metres below. "No. This is crazy."

"I'm a rock star. Crazy's part of the deal. But this is actually pretty tame. Look, give me your hand. You could almost step across, but it's just easier to jump. I won't let you fall."

She wanted to believe him. "Jay…"

"Count of three, right? Give me the towels and your bag. I'll put them over here so all you have to worry about is yourself. And I'll catch you, so you don't need to worry."

Audra handed over her things, dreading watching them fall to the water below, but Jay didn't drop them.

"Now your turn." He held out his hand.

It's just like Point Peron when she was a kid. Her brothers would jump but a girl couldn't possibly…ha, she'd showed them. Point Peron was only a couple of metres into shallow water, though. Not a ten-metre drop with rocks and sharks in the water. Wouldn't be a problem if she didn't fall. Just like Point Peron. As long as she didn't look down…

Audra shook her head, backing up a few steps as she'd seen Jay do. Every bit of her body screamed at her to keep retreating until she returned to the villas, but Audra was determined. Just like Point Peron.

"One, two…"

She didn't wait for three. She broke into a sprint and leaped, smacking into Jay as she hit the other side. His own fault for getting in the way. Warm arms surrounded her and her eyes snapped open. "Let go of me."

With what looked like reluctance, Jay released her and gestured toward her belongings. "Not far now."

Audra nodded and shouldered her bag and the towels. Jay squeezed between two rocks and even Audra found it a tight fit, though not for long. The rocks hid a perfect white beach beside the lagoon, curving invitingly around a rock pool. Lagoon water splashed over the side of the pool, and

Audra caught a glimpse of purple coral before the rippled surface hid it from sight.

"Next time we come here, we should bring snorkelling gear."

Audra found herself agreeing with him, but then reality hit her. There wouldn't be a next time. By tomorrow evening, Jay wouldn't need a babysitter and she'd be back in her room, focussed on her job application. Her future lay far from here and even further away from him. She spread a towel out at one end of the beach and laid the other one in the shade of a palm tree at the other end. Several metres of sand separated them, and an ocean of life and experience, too. "Do you want your book?" Audra dug out the library books and held out his.

Jay grabbed it and tapped the title. "Sure. If nothing else, I want to find out how it's possible to steal a tattoo."

Audra knew the title was the band's name in the book, but she didn't bother telling him. Let him find out for himself. Throwing herself down on the shaded towel, she cracked open her own paperback and settled into a fantasy that didn't involve rock stars.

THIRTY NINE

A shell landed on her page. Audra brushed it off, looking for the source.

Jay stood beside her. She had to twist around to squint up at him. "What?"

"Didn't you hear me calling you?"

Audra shook her head. She'd been engrossed in her book. Too engrossed, she realised, when she should have been keeping an eye on Jay. "Sorry."

"I'm having a drink. Want me to get you one?" He didn't wait for an answer. Instead, he dragged the basket over beside her towel and settled in the sand next to her. No, not the sand – he'd shifted his towel over already. Within arm's reach of her. So much for separation distance. "Okay, morning tea is…iced coffee and cake." He pulled out a thermos and cups, then reached into the basket for the cakes. Peering into the box, he added, "They look like tarts.

Wonder if they were made by the blowjob chef or his tart?"

Audra laughed. "Penny told me she trained to be a chef, but I think she gave that up around the time she poisoned her housemate. I hope neither of them made our food." She took the tart and bit into it. "Well, it tastes all right and it isn't burned. Patel tends to burn stuff when he's preoccupied with Penny. Sometimes he burns the guest dishes and they make it to the staff dining room instead of the restaurant buffet."

Jay stared at her. "They make the staff eat burned food?"

"No! They don't make us eat anything, but our dining room has a buffet, so sometimes we get stuff that's a little overcooked or singed around the edges. Anything that's deemed not fit for guests. Patel's speciality is mango chicken. Even when he burns it, it's good. That's why I haven't reported him and Penny before – because that's the dish that usually suffers, and it's my favourite."

"You like your mango. Chicken and beer," Jay said, stretching out on his side, facing her. He twisted the squeaky cap of the thermos until it popped open. He poured, then waited until Audra had her mouth full of iced coffee before he added, "But you don't like me."

She swallowed. "Of course I like you, Jay. I like all hotel guests who don't make me clean blood off the ceiling or chocolate out of the carpet."

His eyes widened. "Blood on the ceiling? How the fuck did someone get blood up there? Now I know I could never do your job. I don't even want to ask..."

Audra shrugged. Telling him the story about the bloodbath in the gym beat confessing that she liked him a lot more than she was willing to admit. So she told him about Serge's surprise, warming to her tale as Jay laughed in all the right places.

When she was done, he lay back, staring up at the sky, and said, "So that's why you don't like me. You're dating the personal trainer."

"No. Serge and I aren't like that at all. We're just friends. His family, they – " Audra swallowed. Serge's secrets weren't hers to tell. "He's someone to talk to who understands, that's all." She drained her iced coffee and threw the cup on the sand.

"I bet he'll listen to you talk about almost anything if he gets to stare at your tits while you're talking." His eyes hardened. "I bet he's thinking of fucking you all night and doesn't hear a word you say."

Her fingers itched to pick up the cup and slam it into his sneering face. "Screw you, Jay. That's the last time I tell you anything. You turn everything into a suggestion about sex. I'm here to do my job and make sure you don't have brain damage, but it's damn hard to work that out when you keep saying stupid things like that. Do your millions of fangirls care that you're an arsehole?" She bit her lip, trying to stem the flow, but since she'd started, she might as well finish. In for a penny, in for a pound. "They don't care, do they? They think you're allowed to be because you're a rock star. Well, news flash, arsehole. If you're having trouble finding a girl for more than a passing fuck, that's why. Maybe your band breaking up is a good thing, because you'll have to learn a few manners and a bit of respect or the only sex you'll get is what you pay for." Breathing hard, she lay on her towel, staring fixedly at the palm frond above. He was going to report her and she'd lose her job, because the whole tirade would be recorded on her ID for all the world to hear...

"You don't like me because you think I'm an arsehole. Figures. I'm not, you know." Jay didn't sound pissed off at all.

"Yes, you are. And you're delusional if you don't think so."

"If I were as bad as you say, I'd have fucked you already. Kissed you senseless, sucked those nipples raw as I fondled those perfect tits until you spread your legs and begged me to fuck you. I want to. I've told you that. An arsehole wouldn't listen when you say no. He'd take what he wants and to hell with the consequences. If I had no respect for you, I'd take you now."

Audra shot to her feet. "If you touch me, I'm going to—"

Jay didn't move. He just kept staring at the sky. "Like I said, you don't like me. Go on, get it all off that gorgeous chest. It looks sexy as sin when it's heaving in fury."

"I used to like you," she hissed. "Loved your music and the band. I had posters of you in my room. Shit, I even bought tickets to your last concert. Spent half my paycheck on them. But you know what? I'm putting them on eBay when I get home. A dickhead like you isn't getting another cent of my hard-earned money."

"Sell 'em. I don't care. I'll give you VIP ones with backstage passes instead. You should've said you wanted to go."

Audra's mouth gaped, but she couldn't seem to form words. Finally, she found one that framed the tangle of questions in her head. "Why?"

"Because whatever you think of me, I like you, Audra. And I want to see you again when you're not working or angry at me."

Delusional. Not going to happen.

Audra dragged her towel to the other end of the beach and did her best to ignore everything Jay said for the rest of the day. It was her job to keep him alive. Beating him to death with a palm frond would make her lose her job as readily as sleeping with him, so she forced herself to resist. Some parts of her job were so much harder than the others.

FORTY

Audra lost count of the number of times she checked the time on her wristband. Counting down the seconds until her forty-eight-hour stint in hell was over. She'd read two books and said exactly twelve words to Jay in that time, but now she had five minutes left and she'd be free. She drummed her fingers on the kitchen counter, counting down the seconds until she could leave Maxima and Jay.

The crack and fizz of a bottle opening startled her. "We made it. Want a beer to celebrate?" Jay grinned as he held out the drink.

Audra almost didn't take it, then changed her mind and snatched it out of his hand. Five minutes and he could die for all she cared. No, four minutes and thirty seconds.

"Upset that I didn't die on your watch?" he asked cheerfully, taking a deep draught of his own beer.

She shook her head.

"Right. Because you'd have had to clean up the mess."

She met his eyes. "I'm not the arsehole here. I care when people are hurt or if they die. I worried when you weren't back that first night, gave up my days off to be here for you when the resort couldn't spare anyone else, and I would've done my damnedest to save you if you'd collapsed. Even though you threatened me with sexual assault. I have it all recorded on this." She tapped her ID. "Every damn word."

Jay's hand closed over her wrist. "No you don't. I remember my briefing when the manager took me on a tour of the resort, because I was thinking of buying the place. Those things only record when you're close to a guest's ID." He held out his bare arms. "Mine must've gotten lost when I crashed my car, or they cut it off in hospital. So you can relax. No one'll ever know what you called me and I won't say anything, except to thank you for taking such good care of me. I owe you a thank you gift, too. I'll get one on my next trip into town. Want to drop any hints, like your bra size, maybe?"

Audra recoiled in horror. "Keep your gifts, arsehole. I'll stop by Reception and have them send you a new ID. I won't put any other staff in danger now I know what you are. A bullying, manipulative – "

"Hey! I only said I could have done it. Not that I would, or that I ever have. For the fucking record, I've never slept with a girl who wasn't willing. Enthusiastic, even. I don't get off on forcing women. If you say no when you really want to say yes, it's not my fucking fault. That's your choice."

Audra pressed her lips together. She wanted to spit some more insults at him, but grudgingly she admitted the truth. He hadn't threatened her – hadn't even touched her.

And she didn't think he would, either.

"Tell me one thing, though," he continued. "Now you know your boss will never know your answer. If you wouldn't lose your job for it, and were free to do as you pleased, and I asked you to spend the night with me…dinner and drinks and the offer of mind-blowing sex if, and only if, you want it, any and every way you desire. Would you do it?"

"No," she spat. Her heart twisted uneasily at the blatant lie.

"Then I have nothing more to say, except thank you for your care and…your honesty."

Audra met his eyes, only centimetres from her own, and her resolve wavered.

Something warm touched her lips, tracing the top one and then the bottom. His thumb, she realised, closing her eyes as she took a deep breath to shout at him to take his hands off her.

"Aw, fuck it," she heard him say.

Warm breath wafting over her lips gave her a moment's warning that she didn't heed. His lips tickled hers as they brushed lightly over them. She inhaled sharply, tasting the sweetness of mango beer as he sealed her mouth with a kiss. Gentle at first, then more firmly as he drew in a breath. His tongue caressed hers, enticing her to taste and be tasted. And then they were entwined more closely than when they'd tangled on the bathroom floor two nights ago, but eagerly, willingly. Audra's hands ached to hold him, pull him closer, so she could take as much as she gave.

No. She'd end up giving more. Her job, her life, her dreams…for one night with this arsehole?

YES, her heart screamed.

Traitor.

Audra wrenched away from Jay.

"Stay for dinner. And a drink," Jay panted. Triumph flashed in his eyes. "I knew you liked me."

"I've been nothing but professional, Mr Felix," Audra said coldly, summoning every half-learned lesson from her high school acting classes to make her sound believable. "I've merely done my job and no thanks are necessary. I like you no more or less than any of my other guests. And now that I'm off duty, my time is my own and I won't be spending it with you."

Even as her heart screamed at her to take it all back and tell him the truth, Audra turned on her heel, grabbed her bag of belongings, and strode out of Maxima and Jay's life.

FORTY ONE

As soon as she was out of sight of the Pearls, Audra slowed her pace to match her exhaustion. She'd barely slept, jumping at every noise as she half expected Jay to make good on his threat. Bluff. Whatever it was he'd said on the beach. It wasn't until his kiss…assault…tonight that she'd admit to herself that it wasn't him she didn't trust, but herself. She wanted him. It didn't make any difference, though. She needed a job more than she needed a night of hot sex. And that's all it would ever be, she reminded herself. Jay Felix was a man whore of the first degree.

But he wanted her…

Just because she refused him. She was a challenge, that's all, and he'd grow bored and move on after she gave in. Every girl wanted him. He was her high school crush, like a million other girls, she was certain. If she stayed away long enough, he'd forget about her completely and never trouble her again.

She'd kissed Jay Felix. If she had a bucket list, that would've been on it. Not sex, just a kiss. And he'd even initiated it.

"Oh, look, the slut's back."

Audra raised her head to peer blearily at Penny.

"Did the VIPs send you back for a refund because fucking you's like doing a blow-up doll?"

Audra wanted to punch the bitch, but she was too tired to even lift her arm. She had to get a new ID for Jay, then she could go into her room, lock the door and sleep for the next twelve hours. Tomorrow, she had a job application to write to get her the hell out of here.

"Or are you picking up more lube because you've run out, trying to get him to fuck your tight arse?"

The door to Reception closed, shutting out Penny's taunts. Audra trudged to Dennis' office, where she found him reclining in his chair as far back as it would go, his feet up on the desk.

"I need a new ID for the guest in Maxima," she announced. "He says he lost his somewhere on the mainland. Whatever he did with it, he needs a new one. He can't open his mouth without suggesting sex."

Dennis raised one eyebrow. "Did you give it to him?"

Audra laughed dully. "What? A well-deserved slap or a kick to the balls? No. He deserved both, though. Sex? Not a hope in hell."

"Do I need to download the recordings from your ID?"

She shrugged. "No need. He didn't have one, so nothing got recorded. He knew about the voice recordings, too, though I didn't think guests were made aware of that.

Maybe he lost his on purpose. He sure said a few things he wouldn't want to come up in court."

Dennis nodded. "Just making sure. I'll call Reception and get them to issue a new one for him. Maybe we should chain it around his neck like a collar."

Audra managed a weak smile. "Collaring the VIPs. Sounds like a service we can offer those whose tastes run that way. You should mention it to Hana. She's the activities coordinator."

"Maybe I will." Dennis waved her away. "You look like I feel. Go grab some grub and then get to bed."

Audra gave him a limp salute and headed off.

Annette's voice rang out, "Audra? Is that you? Can you come in here for a moment, please?"

Audra swore under her breath and hitched her smile back up. "Yeah, it's me. What can I help with?"

"It's the Pearls. I just got a call from there."

Audra crossed her fingers behind her back.

"The VIP in Maxima was so impressed by you that he wants a live-in maid for the rest of his stay. For the next fortnight. He specifically requested you."

"I'll kill him," Audra blurted out, bunching her hands into fists.

Annette's jaw dropped. "You'll what?"

Audra took a deep breath and forced herself to relax. She had to keep a cool head and present this in the right light. Her job depended on it. "I've just worked a full week, including extra hours and being on call, before I worked fifty-five hours straight, without a break, with this guest. That's more than a week's work in two days. Not even mine shift workers do that. And he's a demanding one. I'm so tired that I'm scared I'll say or do the wrong thing right now. Give me a couple days' rest and maybe I can return to the Pearls, if I'm still needed, but right now…I'm an occupational health risk to guests and staff alike."

Annette seemed to consider her words carefully. "Jackie's back next week and she can take over from you then. Can't you just see out this week?"

Heloise knocked on the door. "You needed a new guest ID?" She handed the wristband to Audra, who fumbled and dropped it on the floor.

Audra slid to the floor after it, cracking her head on the desk. "Fuck." It took her a moment to add, "Sorry. Like I said, so tired I have no filter between my brain and my mouth. Right now, I'm not sure I'd even notice if I called one of the VIPs a demanding arsehole instead of just thinking it."

"But who can I send? Penny just came to me to say Pamela's been taken sick with a sudden attack of gastro."

Penny poisoned her, Audra was sure of it. Audra had heard Penny talk about the housemate who tried to steal her boyfriend and how she'd slipped poison into the girl's food. Somehow, Pamela had managed to piss her off, too. What if it was because she'd caught Penny banging the chef in the laundry?

"Send Penny," Audra suggested. "She's been dying to work in the Pearls ever since you gave them to me."

She shouldn't wish Penny on Jay or vice versa, but right now, Audra didn't care. They were both adults who could fend for themselves. And if they managed to kill each other, she wouldn't complain. As long as they let her sleep and she got her job application in on time.

Annette nodded. "Sure. I'll send her right over with that new ID band so she can introduce herself."

Then Penny wouldn't be in the staff dining room when Audra got there. If she hurried, maybe she could avoid the bitch altogether.

"Can I go?"

Annette didn't even lift her eyes. "Sure, hon." She dismissed her with a flick of her wrist. Audra had never felt more grateful to the woman.

FORTY TWO

"There," Audra breathed, pleased at the result. Her curriculum vitae had matching headings and made her sound like an ideal employee who'd do anything, go anywhere and still be sunny. She'd proofread her selection criteria responses so many times that the words blurred on the page, but she was certain there were no mistakes. The Bureau of Meteorology HAD to take her as a graduate for next year's intake.

Just as long as she submitted the application in time. She had twenty-six hours until the deadline.

Part of her wanted to take the extra time to perfect her application, but Audra had seen the satellite uplink knocked out before. It took a week to get the repair guy out. A week she didn't have.

No time like the present.

Audra switched on her laptop's wi-fi connection, waiting

for the uplink to go live. She closed her eyes and counted to ten. Her future was about to take off, she knew it.

The laptop beeped and an error message popped up on the screen. It couldn't find the wi-fi network. Audra swore and told it to look again. Three times the error popped up and three times she jabbed the cursor at the button, commanding it to retry.

Fuck.

Audra closed her laptop and tucked it under her arm. Carefully opening the door to her room, she peered out at the veranda. It was deserted. She slipped out and hurried to the IT office where she found Cam and Seb, the two computer experts, playing poker.

"The wi-fi's down," she announced.

"No, it's not."

"I can't connect in the staff accommodation."

"Nah, there wouldn't be much of a signal there."

Audra wanted to slap him. Both of them. "It's usually fine. What's wrong with it now?"

"Nothing. The router's out at one of the villas on the other side of the lagoon. Loses a lot of signal strength."

"But I need it."

"You could just plug your PC in to one of the ports here. What's so urgent, anyway?" Seb asked.

"It's personal," Audra snapped.

Cam perked up. "Video call with your boyfriend back home?"

"Maybe."

"Well, if it's privacy you want, you could just go sit on one of the villa verandas. What's the name of the one where the executives are staying?"

"Albina?" Audra suggested.

"That's it. Pick the one next door and sit on the veranda. All the privacy you could want," Cam assured her.

Seb coughed.

"Thanks, guys." Audra left.

As the door closed behind her, she caught the hissed words, "D'you think she'll flash him her tits?" followed by, "Shhh! What's her IP again? And don't move the mouse this time or she'll know!"

Great. Jay wasn't alone in having an obsession for her boobs. For the first time, she wished she worked in a ski resort where her winter clothes would be so bulky no one knew she had breasts. If she didn't get this graduate job, maybe that's what she'd try for next.

What was she saying? Of course she'd get this job. She just had to apply for it.

Straightening her spine, Audra strode confidently toward the Pearls. She'd sit on the Pinctada veranda and send her hopes for the future winging across the water to the east coast office that had the power to grant dreams. It was time for hers to come true.

FORTY THREE

"Come on, baby, you can do better than that!" Jay's laughing voice taunted.

Audra's steps slowed. She didn't want to run into him on the narrow path. Hugging her laptop to her chest, she prayed he'd ignore her. After all, it sounded like he had someone else to occupy his attention now.

She rounded the corner to find the path mercifully free of rock stars.

He groaned, the sound coming from her right, where the thinning jungle gave way to the lagoon. "Five minutes more, baby, and you'll set a new record."

The path to Pinctada passed the lagoon and Audra couldn't seem to stop herself from taking those extra steps to see what she both dreaded and hoped for. Jay stood knee-deep in the lagoon, buck naked, while a girl in a maid's uniform deep-throated him. His eyes widened as he spotted

Audra and the girl inhaling his dick choked, spraying fluid everywhere. Audra hoped it was vomit, seeing as that's what she wanted to do.

"It's not what it looks like," he protested weakly.

Audra forced herself to shrug, as if she didn't care and couldn't feel bile rising up in the back of her throat. "It looks like you're getting a record-breaking blowjob from an expert. Aren't you going to make the most of it, or are you just going to blow her off like you do everyone else? Don't stop on account of me." Audra averted her eyes and hurried away, struggling not to be sick.

Silence hung in the air for a few seconds before Jay shakily proclaimed, "I knew you couldn't beat the record. Your arse is mine!" He didn't sound half as happy as he had before Audra's appearance.

Behind her, she heard Penny's giggle, followed by a splash and a shriek. "Ooh, Jay…yes, yes!"

Audra was going so fast she almost slammed into the group of executives from Albina. She apologised and moved aside to let them pass.

For a moment, she considered warning them about the R-rated scene around the bend, but thought the better of it. Penny would take what was coming to her. Damn it, Audra had never blown a guy in her life, but for a moment there, she'd been jealous of Penny. Not for choking on his cock, but because she'd had her hands on his abs as if they were hers to stroke. Audra wanted to break every one of those splayed fingers for touching what she couldn't have and the other girl had no right to.

Meanwhile, the Albina executives had discovered the porn show in the lagoon.

"Oh my God!"

"Are they having anal sex?"

"Nah, just doing it doggy style, I think."

"Is that Jay Felix?"

"I can't believe they're allowed to do that here, where anyone could see them!"

Audra swallowed and resumed walking, reaching Pinctada and falling to her knees on the veranda. Waking her laptop, she waited for the wi-fi to link up and almost cheered when it connected. The email was ready to go, so all she had to do was hit SEND. Which she did.

A few seconds later, she was rewarded with the Bureau's automatic response that her application had been received.

Audra shut the laptop down and set it carefully beside her. Now all she had to do was wait and hope.

Tomorrow. Tomorrow she'd start hoping. Right now, all she could think about was Penny digging her claws into Jay. He'd forgotten her already, just as she'd expected. What she hadn't expected was how much it would hurt.

Why was life so unfair? A week ago, all she'd wanted was to get the job of her dreams and her life would be perfect. Now, she couldn't seem to summon any enthusiasm for the job. Her thoughts weren't of storm clouds and heatwaves, tides and tempests, but the heat of a man's hard body against hers. She wanted Jay. Who preferred Penny.

Audra hugged her knees to her chest, laid her head on her arms and cried her heart out.

FORTY FOUR

Later that evening, after watching the Albina guests leave in the thumping helicopter, Audra lay on her bed with her laptop, waiting for the wi-fi to connect. She'd seen the IT guys carrying all the gear back from Albina, so she figured everything would be back to normal. Sure enough, this time the connection worked on the first try. Her email chimed, telling her she had a message from Sam, wanting a video call.

Audra didn't hesitate. Waiting only long enough for the webpage to open, she initiated the call.

"Did you get them? Did you? They're sold out everywhere!"

The Chaya tickets. Which, despite her threat, she hadn't sold. And she couldn't. Even if she hated Jay, she couldn't do that to her sister.

Audra summoned a smile. "Yeah. Happy birthday, I

guess."

Sam's happy scream set Audra's teeth on edge, but she didn't complain. She'd rarely seen Sam so happy. Sam's voice slowed into intelligible speech again and Audra realised she was talking to someone off-screen.

"Who else is home?" Audra asked.

"Just Ben," she said, then frowned. "He says he needs to talk to you."

The room blurred as Sam twisted the webcam to face Ben.

"Hi," he said, mirroring Sam's frown. "Your car rego's overdue. And the insurance, too."

Audra blinked, then remembered. "I gave you the money for that before I left. In cash, remember?" It was the last money she'd had at the time – she hadn't even had a couple of dollars for a bottle of water at the airport.

"What? Oh, so that's what that was for. I used it to replace my tools. They got stolen off Joe's ute when we were at lunch a week after you left." Ben shrugged. "I'll have to owe you."

Audra wanted to reach through the screen and throttle him. "That was more than a thousand dollars, Ben! Money to pay those bills that I gave you because I trusted you!"

Ben's eyes dropped to his lap. "Yeah but...I forgot, and when I found the money, it was like a miracle. Joe was going to take another apprentice instead if I didn't replace those tools. I'll pay you back, honest."

No, he wouldn't, because he'd never have the money, Audra thought but didn't say. Instead, she sighed. "You better. So I have to find another grand so you can pay the bills?"

Ben hunched his shoulders. "Um, probably more than that. Y'see, there's fines for paying late and for driving unlicensed and the car'll need to go over the pits for inspection, so there's inspection fees, too."

Audra felt all her savings slip away. "How much?"

"Leon says about three grand. No, wait, four including the rego and insurance."

"Four thousand dollars? My car's not worth that! What the hell for?"

Ben mumbled something that Audra didn't catch, so she asked him to repeat it. Her older brother pressed his lips together as if he didn't want to.

Sam shoved his shoulder and the room blurred again as she turned the camera back to her own face. "If he won't tell you, I will. All the taillights are gone and the blinkers, too. The hatch on the back doesn't close properly on account of it being bent out of shape, so you'll need a new one of those, too. Leon said that's why the police declared it not roadworthy any more. Even if you replace the lights, exhaust fumes will creep into the car unless you can shut it."

"Leon? He's not supposed to be driving," Audra began ominously.

"Nah, he got doctor's approval a fortnight ago, but he didn't have a car, so he borrowed yours." Sam grinned gleefully. "You should've seen him hit the letterbox on his first drive. One minute it's there, the next, SMASH. Bricks and dust everywhere. I never liked that letterbox."

"Leon. Our brother, Leon, who crashed his car and nearly killed himself, has been driving my uninsured and unlicensed car for a fortnight?!"

"Four weeks, actually," Sam volunteered. "He has a new girlfriend and he couldn't take her on a date on the bus, so he borrowed your car."

"BEN! I trusted you!" Audra bellowed.

A firm knock sounded at her door.

"I'm busy!" she called.

The knocking resumed.

Swearing, Audra told Sam, "I have to go. I get paid in a couple of days. I'll sort something out." She terminated the call, crossed the room in two strides and yanked open the door. "What?"

Serge folded his arms. "You all right?"

"Fine." Audra waved at the laptop. "Family problems."

"I heard. Actually, I think everyone on this side of the lagoon heard. If you need someone to talk to, you know I'm here."

Did his gaze drop to her chest, or was she imagining it? Jay couldn't be right. He couldn't be. Serge wasn't interested in her boobs or any part of her body. "Thanks, but I'm not sure there's much to say. What do you do when you want to kill your family?"

Serge grinned. "Work out. It's why I got into fitness, I guess." His smile faltered. "If you want, I have tomorrow morning free. I could give you a training session. Help you work off all that frustration."

She wished with all her being that she could take Penny's advice and take him to bed, eyeing the bulging biceps that showed at their best when he had his arms folded like that. She had frustration on all sides tonight.

Shit. Take advice from Penny, the bitch who gave blow jobs to every dick she saw and called HER a slut? The girl who was probably wrapped around Jay right now? Fuck no. Just the thought of that made her want to hit something.

"Yeah. Sure. Tomorrow," Audra said finally.

"It's a date." Serge sauntered off.

A date? Well, maybe. Tomorrow, she'd see. Right now, she just wanted to go to bed and sleep before anything else happened. Tomorrow couldn't be worse than today.

FORTY FIVE

"So, you all set for this morning's session?" Serge greeted Audra as she set her breakfast on the table beside him.

She waved at her gym clothes. "As ready as I'll ever be. You know, you don't need to do this. I feel bad taking your time for free when you could be helping paid clients."

"Actually, you're doing me a favour. I need to get my hours up before I can take my next assessment. I'm ten hours short and if you want, they're all yours."

Ten hours? She'd never spent more than an hour in a gym and it'd been years since she'd done that. "Let's see how I go today first."

"Go for a high-protein, low-carbohydrate breakfast. Not too much fruit and sugar." He jerked his chin at Audra's bowl of mango yoghurt and muesli.

Audra opened her mouth to mutiny.

"Whew, that man has the stamina of a stud bull!" Penny

stage-whispered as she plopped a plate of pancakes on the table. To Audra's horror, the girl slid into the seat beside her.

"What are you doing here?" Audra demanded.

Penny shrugged. "A girl's gotta eat. Can't live on cum alone." She winked as she rolled up a pancake and deep-throated it, much to the fascination of the IT guys at the next table.

Audra shoved her bowl away, feeling too nauseous to eat another bite. Not only had Penny seduced Jay and had sex with him in front of multiple witnesses, but the bitch hadn't even gotten fired for it. What the hell was wrong with the world?

"He fucked me all night. So big and hard and powerful...I'm going to have trouble walking all week. Not that I'll need to. As soon as I've eaten, it's back to bed for me." Penny looked gleeful. "I figure two more days of this and he won't want to let me go. He'll take me with him when he leaves the resort and I'll get to go to all his concerts free as a VIP myself." She sniffed. "Next time we're here, maybe you'll be my maid."

Over her rotting corpse. Audra jumped to her feet.

Two heavy hands landed on her shoulders. "Come on."

Audra allowed Serge to herd her out the door and in the direction of the gym. It wasn't until they reached the gym doors that she unclenched her fists, not sure whether to thank him or shout at him for interfering.

"I have the wraps, gloves and punching bag ready to go," Serge said, opening the door. He gave an extravagant bow. "After last night, I figured you'd want to hit things pretty hard."

He helped her wrap the bindings around her knuckles, then pull on the boxing gloves. Audra almost laughed. She felt like one of the boxing kangaroos they sold in the gift shop, a souvenir they'd started stocking after tourists talked about the fights between the young bucks that often happened on the road just outside of town. "You going to get me a strap-on tail like the gift shop toys, too?" she grumbled.

Serge stared at her in shock. "A…what?"

Audra sighed. "Never mind. Can I hit something yet?"

"Sure." He lined her up and gestured for her to punch the bag.

Audra swung her arm, imagining her fist colliding with Penny's chin. First one side, then the other, smacking into the…leather? PVC? Audra shrugged, not caring as long as the sound was satisfying. And it was.

"Wait. You want to make the blows unexpected, signalling as little as you can to your opponent, while making them as powerful as possible. Here, start by guarding your chest and your face. The power comes from your shoulder, flowing right through your arm, not from your wrist." Serge demonstrated, then helped her shift her arms to more of a boxer's stance. "Now, jab." He shadowboxed beside her, matching her blows, though only hers landed on the bag. "Good. Now let's see some repetitions. Try thirty and keep pace with me. One, two, three, four…"

Audra drove her fists into the bag on his count, feeling it sway slightly as she hit it harder. If it were Penny, she'd be breaking her ribs through her flat chest. She deserved it for making Audra's heart ache for Jay when she shouldn't have any feelings for him at all. Wouldn't, if Penny hadn't deliberately tried to make her jealous.

Goddamn it! Why did Penny get to have her way with Jay and still keep her job? If Audra knew she could've gotten away with it, maybe she'd have given in to Jay. Let him do all the things he'd said he would. That the tabloids — and the fangirls who said they'd slept with him — claimed he was brilliant at. Instead, the fickle bastard was with that conniving bitch and she wanted to pound her fist through the wall in frustration at the very thought of them together.

"Hey, hey! I said thirty! Stop for a break!" Serge grabbed her wrists and Audra relaxed. "Wow, you must be more pissed at your brother than I thought."

"My brother?" No, her brother wasn't banging Penny, and she didn't much care if he did.

"It was your brother who wrecked your car, right? I admit I was trying not to eavesdrop, but you were shouting so loud..."

Ben and Leon. Right. "One of them's been driving my car without a licence and he wrecked it, while the other took my money for registration and insurance and didn't pay them, so now I have to pay a huge fine as well as pay for repairs." Audra slammed both fists into the bag. "That's all my savings!"

"Make them pay for it. Their mess, after all."

"My car and they don't have the money. So I have to pay for it or lose my car."

Serge shrugged again. "So lose it. Is it worth less than you'll have to pay?"

Audra nodded.

"So stuff it. You don't use your car up here, and when

you get your amazing job at some weather station in paradise, you'll have a work car. Keep your savings and tell them to fix your car by the time you get back. Not like you're in any hurry. They're your older brothers, aren't they? Grown men, anyway. They don't need you to take care of them. Let them sort it out."

"Not Leon. He's younger than me. And Ben…he got a girl pregnant in high school and all his money goes to child support. I can't, Serge. You don't understand."

"No, I don't. You've got the right to live your own life. You don't owe them. They owe you. If you don't leave them to themselves, they'll drag you down, Audra. Don't let them drag you under. You're so much better than that. You work so hard. You deserve to rise above…all that." Serge turned his head away and swiped a hand across his face, as if he was wiping away tell-tale moisture from his eyes. "I'll go get the sparring pads from the storeroom. You're going to pretend I'm your brother — both of them, if you want — and you're going to beat some sense into them." He nodded at the punching bag. "You do another thirty on that one while you're waiting."

Audra lined herself up and raised her gloved fists.

Wham.

That's for crashing your car and going missing.

Wham.

That's for drinking yourself into a stupor and not telling anyone about the accident.

Wham.

That's for not telling me and scaring the shit out of me when you almost died.

Wham.

That's for my taillights, Leon, and this —

Wham.

— is for the letterbox.

Wham.

And for giving him the keys, Ben, you traitor…

This set of thirty felt effortless, but she was sweating when she was done. Wiping her streaming forehead, Audra pulled off one of her gloves and reached for her water bottle. As she sucked down the cool liquid, she heard the squeak of the door.

Serge was back. She was ready for the next set. Leon first, then she'd go back to Ben's misdemeanours.

Claws dug into her shoulder, tearing through her shirt and trying to spin her around.

"It's your fault, you fucking bitch! You're just jealous!" Penny screeched, dragging on Audra's shoulder with all her weight so Audra almost keeled over backwards. "Just because you're too frigid for a rock star like Jay Felix to even look twice at you, you reported me for giving him what he wanted. You're the one who should've lost her job, not me, for being so fucking useless!"

Audra flailed to maintain her balance and clocked Penny on the side of her head with the water bottle.

The girl's eyes seemed to ignite. "YOU'LL DIE FOR THAT, BITCH!" She grabbed both Audra's shoulders and forced her to turn around. Claws reached for Audra's eyes.

This is for sleeping with Jay and making my job a living hell.

Audra slammed her gloved fist into Penny's face, knocking the girl off her feet. Blood spurted from Penny's nose as fear filled her eyes.

Audra's breakfast welled up in her throat, threatening to escape, but she fought it down. She pulled off the bloodied glove and let it drop to the floor. She was done training and she needed to find the safety officer to report Penny's injury. She didn't trust herself to give the girl first aid without smothering her.

The gym door squeaked and Serge stood on the threshold, grinning, with his arms full of vinyl pads. His smile slid into a look of horror. "No!"

Yes, Audra thought. Even nice girls snap under pressure and the bitch had it coming. Besides, she hit first, so it was only self-defence. But this time, she wouldn't be cleaning that bitch's mess off the gym floor. She refused to take any more shit from –

Something slammed into the back of Audra's head and reality was sucked away like the retreating tide.

FORTY SIX

Audra woke with the worst hangover in the history of hangovers. I'm never drinking again, she thought groggily. No more alcohol, ever. Especially the kind of drink that was so potent you couldn't even remember drinking it the following morning.

"Audra?" Pamela asked softly.

A tentative hand patted hers. "If I say I'm not, will this headache go bother someone else?" Audra grumbled.

Nervous laughter. "I doubt it. How are you feeling?"

"Like that bitch hit me with one of the mining trucks from the next island over." With effort, Audra pried her eyes open and blinked painfully in the light filtering through her flimsy blinds. "I should've hit her harder so she stayed down." Even as the words left her mouth, Audra regretted them. The feel of Penny's face crunching under her fist was enough to make her throw up. She'd never hit anyone so

214

hard in her life and never wanted to again.

"I think Serge did it for you. He got arrested."

"What?" Audra sat up and her head exploded with a burst of light and unbearable pain. She slumped back onto the pillows. "He wasn't even there. The police should've taken me instead."

"You mean you broke her arm? No wonder she knocked you out, then."

Audra winced. She couldn't remember any broken bones. Unless you counted Penny's nose, but wasn't that cartilage, like sharks? "I punched her in the face."

Pamela grinned. "I've wanted someone to do that for a long time. I wish I'd seen it. But if you didn't break her arm, it must've been Serge. And they were fighting. I was in Reception with Hana and Heloise when we heard screaming. Dennis came running out of his office and Hana and I followed. When we got to the gym, Penny and Serge were grappling on the floor and she was shouting all sorts of things at him. Dennis and Annette took Penny to the first aid room and that's when I saw her arm was bent all wrong. She was still screaming, too. They called the Flying Doctors, I guess, because the rescue helicopter came to get her. Hana went to help, so that left just me and Serge. He had claw marks all over his face and his shirt was ripped like he'd been attacked by a dropbear or something."

Audra managed a faint smile. There weren't any dropbears in Western Australia.

"I didn't even see you until he pulled you out from between the weights benches. You'd been lying there unconscious on the carpet through all of it, I guess. He lifted you up like something from one of the covers of a romance novel, all those muscles bulging through the rips in his shirt, and carried you in here. He told me to stay with you until you woke up and then he left. When the helicopter came back, there were police in it and they took Serge away in handcuffs." Pamela scanned Audra's body. "They should've taken you to the hospital on the mainland, too. I'll go tell Dennis you're awake and to call them back."

"No. I'm not going to any hospital while Penny's in it. Tell him to get the security footage for the gym. That'll show what Penny did." And what Serge had done while she was unconscious, Audra thought uneasily. He shouldn't have gotten involved. He'd never get his personal training qualifications if he was in prison on an assault charge. Didn't he have to get police clearance to do his job? He'd lose everything.

"Are you sure?"

Audra lifted her hand to the spot on her head that throbbed the worst. She touched a tender lump that unleashed a fresh burst of agony. Her head hurt too much to talk, let alone think. "Yeah. I'm fine," she lied. "I probably need a bit of extra sleep, anyway. Go tell Dennis to check the tapes and he'll see that Penny started it."

"If you're sure." Pamela rose and opened the door. "I still have half the rooms to clean. Lucky we're not full. If I go now, I might get them all done by dinnertime."

Audra nodded encouragingly, but that made her head ring again, so she stopped. The moment the door closed behind Pamela, her smile vanished and she let out a groan of pain. She didn't want to move ever again.

FORTY SEVEN

Urgent beeping startled Audra out of her doze. Thank heaven the pain in her head had lessened. Or was that because there was less light in the room? It looked like night-time outside, but that could mean anything. 7pm or 5am looked the same out here: pitch-dark and sparkling with stars. She glanced at her wristband. Oh, lovely: 1am.

Her stomach grumbled, reminding her that she'd missed not just lunch but dinner, too, and there'd be nothing until the staff dining room opened at six.

Would that bloody beeping stop already?

It took her a moment to realise the source was her ID. She touched the display and up flashed the last two words she wanted to see:

MAXIMA URGENT

It would beep until she scanned her wristband at Maxima's door or the summons got diverted to someone else. Audra rolled out of bed, wincing, but managed to make it to her feet. She was still fully dressed, so she slipped a pair of thongs onto her feet and shuffled to the main building, where the night porter, Dan, occupied the Reception desk.

"I'm not responsible for the Pearls any more," Audra told him, pointing at her ID. "You have to send someone else."

Dan glanced at her flashing display. "No can do. You're the most senior of the Housekeeping staff on the island. Annette left with an injured girl and put you in charge."

Annette hadn't known she was unconscious, Audra realised.

"You have to send someone else," Audra repeated, not willing to tell this man she barely knew about what had happened in the gym.

"You send someone else. You're the boss. But you better send someone quickly, because the guest in Maxima calls every hour to ask why a maid hasn't turned up yet. Been trying to get maid service since noon, he says, so now he's one angry bastard." As if on cue, the Reception phone shrilled. "That'd be him. I'll tell him you're sending someone right over, yeah?"

Audra nodded mutely, her brain struggling to find a solution. With Penny, Jackie and Annette on the mainland, that left her and Pamela. Pamela had already worked both hers and Penny's jobs today. It wouldn't be fair to send her to deal with an irate idiot. Audra would have to go.

She headed outside, breathing deeply to let the cool, night air settle her pounding head. At least, hoping it would. She'd explain the staffing situation to Jay and tell him that someone would see to his request in the morning. For all his rock star reputation, Jay was a reasonable man.

Every light was on in Maxima, illuminating the jungle around it and the path outside, too. The door stood open, as if Jay was waiting for her. Audra stepped over the threshold and almost tripped on a drift of linen that blended with the white floor tiles. It wasn't the only pile, either – a trail of white led from the front door to the bathroom, where the remainder had been piled into the spa. Broken glass littered the mess like pieces of brittle on top of a cake. Well, except for the corked top of a champagne bottle. The rest of the bottle was smashed into pieces and, judging by the smell, the contents had been poured over the linen. Audra inhaled deeply, smelling more than champagne. Yep, the multicoloured glass confirmed it – it looked like he'd smashed the whole contents of the fridge in here.

For a moment, she hoped he'd bled to death from cutting himself, but she banished that thought. She wanted him alive so she could kill him for making this mess, but first she had to find him. Hurrying out of the bathroom, she slipped on a damp patch and caught the doorjamb to stop herself from falling flat on her face. Glancing down, she recoiled at what looked like a pool of blood. No, it couldn't be.

The pool tapered to a trail that led back into the living area, so Audra followed it. Along the floor she couldn't be sure if it was blood or not, but when the meandering line crept up the wall, she doubted it. Blood wasn't that thick or that red. This looked more like ketchup.

The trail climbed up to the ceiling, and Audra couldn't

look away as she followed it to its inevitable end. Audra let rip with every swear word she knew until she ran out of breath, then sucked in more air to repeat them.

"Go on, read it," Jay slurred. He lifted a beer to his lips and flashed a lazy grin.

Audra squinted at the ketchup letters smeared across the ceiling.

"All the world's a stage, and all the men and…what's that word?" Audra pointed at spot where the ketchup splatter obscured whatever the drunken dickhead had tried to spell out on the ceiling.

Jay looked irritated. "Women. It's women. Shit, fine. I'll read it to you." He cleared his throat dramatically.

"All the world's a stage,

And all the men and women merely players;

They have their exits and their entrances,

And one man in his time plays many parts…"

He held out his arm, the one with words tattooed down it. "It explains everything."

Audra repeated his words, tracing first the ketchup letters on the ceiling that continued down the wall until the sauce had run out, judging by the empty bottle on the floor. Jay was a bloody artist, all right – he'd dragged the lounge room rug up to the wall for the final, brown lettered lines, probably because the white weave made them stand out better than the terracotta floor tiles. Beside the last word was the empty fondue pot. Chocolate. The arsehole had smothered the rug in chocolate just to spite her.

Breathe, she told herself. Her head was pounding with fury and not pain, now, her heartbeat hammering in her ears. After Penny, she was going to demolish this dickhead.

"Why in God's name did you trash the place?"

"To get your attention. I missed you. It worked, too." He blew her a kiss and drained his beer.

"You wrote Shakespeare on the ceiling with ketchup because you missed me? Haven't you heard of giving a girl chocolates? Oh wait – yes, you have. When you ran out of ketchup, you finished the quote in chocolate on the carpet. What kind of crazy man does that?" Audra felt tears building, but she blinked them away. He didn't deserve to see her cry.

"The kind you kept waiting all day and half the night to see you. If you'd come earlier, I'd have poured you champagne instead of smashing the bottle. As for the chocolate..." He winked.

She was going to kill him if he didn't get out of here now. She ripped off her ID. "Take this. It'll get you into the villa next door. You can't stay here. It's not fit for human habitation. Go. Take it and go!" She threw the wristband at Jay and he caught it. Maybe he wasn't as drunk as he looked, though that only made this worse. If he'd done this sober... "I'll get you fresh towels in a moment, once I'm done assessing the damage here."

Jay rose and sauntered out of the house.

Audra waited until she couldn't hear his footsteps any more, then counted to ten. On eight, she dropped to her knees on the narrow, unsoiled section of the rug and burst into tears. Had Penny put him up to this? One final blow to make her life hell?

"Nope. You're coming with me."

Before Audra could protest, Jay lifted her up, slung her over his shoulder in a fireman's lift and carried her out of the villa.

FORTY EIGHT

Audra wanted to shout at him, but all the blood rushing to her head as he held her partially upside down brought back her headache with a vengeance. She bit down hard on her lip to stop herself from screaming. Or maybe she should, not that anyone would hear her out here. Jay had threatened her with sexual assault before – who knew if he'd actually do it. As soon as he set her down, she'd bolt, faster than this drunken idiot could run, and she'd vanish into the dark before he could follow her. Just as soon as the world stopped spinning and got its colours back.

She fell on something soft and breathed a sigh of relief, trying to focus on what she knew was Jay's face in front of her.

"Wow, you have a black eye. I've never seen a chick with a black eye. Have you been fighting over me?" He grinned like it was one big joke.

"What?" Audra couldn't remember Penny landing a blow to her face. When had Penny managed that? While she was unconscious? Audra scrambled to her feet and stumbled for the bathroom. Shit. The bruise blooming on her face was going to be spectacular tomorrow. If Penny had laid into her while she'd been unconscious, no wonder Serge had joined in. The girl was so crazy he'd have had to break her arm to stop her, most likely. Shit. What a mess. And all because of Jay. Who'd just appeared in the bathroom doorway.

"It's your fault," Audra snapped, turning on him. "If you hadn't seduced that bitch yesterday and made her suck your dick in front of half the hotel, she wouldn't have lost her job and taken it out on me. You want to know why no one answered your oh-so-urgent call? It's because you fucked, as you so eloquently put it, the maid who was assigned to your villa, and she got fired. Then she tried to bash me to death with the gym equipment, and attacked anyone who came between her and her prey. Most of the senior staff are on the mainland, either in the police station or the hospital emergency department, while I was just left to lie there because somehow no one saw me on the gym floor when they broke up the fight between the psychopath and the personal trainer. So you want to know why I didn't come earlier? It's because your bitch-whore knocked me out and I was unconscious. I could've died. But hey, I'm not some rich rock star, so when someone like me might have a concussion, there's no hospital staff trying to seduce me. There's no police officer standing at my side to protect me. No helicopter on stand-by to take me to a fancy hotel to recuperate. There's no twenty-four-hour, on-call first aid officer watching over me to make sure I'm all right. Or even hand me a couple of paracetamol. Instead, I get paged to some arsehole's house, where he's decided to emulate Pro Hart and smear the contents of his fridge all over the ceiling so he can make fun of me while he watches me clean up the mess he's made. Well, fuck you, Jay Felix. You may be a rock star, but you're a failure as a human being."

With considerable satisfaction, Audra noted that she'd shocked Jay into silence. Well, that was a first.

"Now get out of my way." She elbowed her way past him.

"Where are you going?"

Audra didn't turn around. "To clean up the arsehole's house. If I'm lucky, I might've finished dealing with half the mess you've made by lunchtime tomorrow."

His strong arms caught her round the waist. "No, you're not."

Audra brought her foot up and kicked behind her. She heard a grunt and he let go. "I'd rather clean chocolate off the carpet than stay here and get raped by you, caveman."

"Audra, wait. Please. I'm not thinking. Too much to drink. I shouldn't've..."

"Fuck you, Jay." She kept walking, trotting up the stairs to Maxima as if every step didn't make her head pound. She lifted her arm to scan her ID, but nothing happened. Her wrist was bare.

Jay had her ID. Gritting her teeth, Audra returned to Pinctada, where she had to knock on the door. "Give it back!" she shouted.

The door slid open. "It's inside."

Of course it was. "So go get it for me."

"No." He sounded sad. "You're injured, Audra. You said it yourself. Someone should be taking care of you. I can't let you clean that house."

"You think I'd let you touch me? Watch me while I sleep?" she demanded. "I told you already, I'd rather – "

"Clean than get raped. Yeah, me, too. And everyone else in the world, I imagine." To his credit, he didn't crack a smile. "I bought the hotel, Audra. The owners accepted my offer this morning. I wanted you to share a bottle of champagne with me to celebrate. And I wanted to explain what you saw yesterday. It's not what you think."

Audra lowered her voice. "What I saw yesterday made me physically sick. You called her a prostitute the day before when you saw her giving the chef a blowjob, then yesterday you were happily thrusting down her throat. Like you keep saying, you're a rock star and that's what rock stars do. And like I keep saying, there are better men than rock stars."

"She begged me for it. Said she could give me the best blowjob I'd ever had and that you'd sent her over to give it to me. Bloody awful is what it was. Then when I saw you…" He swallowed. "My first thought was to stop, but you looked like you didn't care. She'd said you'd sent her and you said to keep going…so then I wanted to make sure you knew I appreciated your gift and I…"

Audra held up her hands. "Stop. Seriously, stop. Seeing it was bad enough. I don't want to hear all the gory details. Just give me my ID."

He shook his head. "I can't. It'd be criminal negligence if I let an injured staff member keep working. Not after you took such good care of me, Audra. Let me return the favour. And I promise…I promise to keep my pants on, unless you say otherwise."

The pounding in her head was starting to leach colour out of her vision. Audra rubbed her temples, trying to dislodge the pain. "In your dreams, Jay."

"Oh, you'd love my dreams. But not tonight, I think." He moved aside to allow her to slip past him into the house. "Pick a bedroom. Unless you want a drink first? I think I saw some booze in this fridge. Ice for that shiner, too."

"I should be doing that. You called for maid service and I answered." Audra dragged her feet toward the kitchen, but Jay got there first.

"I didn't call you to clean or serve. I called you to come have a drink with me. Now, what's your poison? There's no champagne here, but there is some of that mango beer you like."

"I really shouldn't."

"Yeah, you really should. There's about as much alcohol in one of these as a light beer or a midstrength. I think there might be a couple of cans of soft drink, if you want." Jay noticed Audra's wrinkled nose. "Mango beer it is, then."

Audra grudgingly accepted the opened bottle from him and sipped the frothing sweetness. What she'd give to be able to afford one of these every night. Maybe next year, when she got her weather station posting. If she got it. Shit, with the luck she'd had today, maybe they'd lost her application. That didn't bear thinking about. She needed to think about something else entirely. Work. Jay. Sharks. No, not sharks. Shit, the whole lot made her head hurt. Didn't alcohol help dull pain? She should just drink the beer and let him talk.

"So what made a rock star choose to buy a hotel? And this one, of all places?" she asked carefully, keeping her eyes on her beer as she took another sip. If she focussed on her drink, she wouldn't smash the bottle in his face like he deserved.

Jay grinned. "Oh, that's easy. I bought this place because of you."

Audra choked.

FORTY NINE

"Here, some ice for that eye." Jay crossed the room and pressed the ice-filled tea-towel to her face. Before Audra could stop him, his other hand reached around the back of her head and touched the tender spot where Penny had tried to bash her head in.

Audra let out a wordless cry as the pain blinded her.

Jay pulled back, taking the ice with him. "Fuck, I'm sorry. She really did a number on you, didn't she? Here, lie on the couch and put this under your head."

Audra tried to stifle a sob as she let Jay help her. Alarm bells screamed in her head, but she hurt too much to react to them. She forced her eyes open, fixing her gaze on Jay's tear-blurred face. Was this when he tried to take advantage of her?

Apparently not, because he returned to the kitchen. A minute later, he was back with a second icy tea-towel.

Audra accepted it gratefully and set it to soothing her eye.

Jay retreated to a seat out of her line of sight. "It's funny. My sister and I came here to view the place with the intention of buying it, but she said she didn't want to. I stay here for a couple of weeks, and buy the damn thing myself. I'll have to sell my place at Surfer's on the Gold Coast, I think. Either that or my place in Sydney, but I want to hold on to the Sydney one, just in case I don't retire. Depends, really. I heard this tour's concerts are almost all sold out already, which means they'll pay well. Maybe I can keep the Gold Coast apartment. Get a tenant in there or something. Don't know…"

Audra's attention drifted as Jay talked about money and investments the likes of which she could only dream about. Buying a whole island? Owning multiple houses that no one lived in? She couldn't even manage to hold on to her own car. But she couldn't afford to lose it – even if it did cost all her savings to make it roadworthy again. If she didn't get the job up here or if the Bureau of Meteorology turned her down again, she'd need a car to get places. No public transport served her parents' area – too dangerous. Not to mention dangerous for her if she came home after dark, which she would if she had to go back to waitressing. Damn Ben and Leon.

"Is your head hurting too much? Want me to shut up?"

"What?" Audra lifted her head so she could see Jay. "No, it's all right. I just…it's been a really bad day." She flopped back down on the ice pack with a moan of relief.

"I could improve it for you." Jay shifted so he stood above her, grinning. His voice took on the underwear-melting tone that shouldn't have worked on her, but it did.

"Make you forget everything else except one perfect moment."

She squinted at him. "This is about sex again, isn't it? So much for promising to keep your pants on." Audra took a deep breath, and for what felt like the hundredth time, began, "I'll lose my job if I – "

His finger touched her lips. "Sleep with a guest? Yeah, but I'm not a guest any more. More like the landlord of this place. And even if I wasn't, no one will ever know. There's only us out here."

"My wristband's recording every word you say, Jay."

Jay laughed softly. "Not tonight. Where I've hidden it, it won't hear a thing. Does anyone know you're here?"

"The night porter does."

"Do you think the night porter will hear you scream from the other side of the lagoon?"

Audra was done playing. This was getting way too creepy. "Yeah, he will. I'll make sure of it. You're freaking me out here, Jay. I'm not one of your fangirls and I don't want to sleep with you. I took a hell of a beating today and I hurt. So I'm going back to bed now. I'll send someone out here to clean your villa in the morning." She winced as she stood up. "Thanks for the beer and the first aid and the Shakespeare, even if it was on the wall. It's been surreal."

"Fuck, Audra. Why do you always take what I say the wrong way? If a rock star makes you scream, it's a good thing. 'Cause you're enjoying yourself?" His eyes seemed to beg her to understand. "No one's ever seduced you properly, have they? Fine. I want you to ride my tongue, Audra. I want to thrust my fingers into your pussy and make you come so I can taste it. And when you do, I want to hear you scream. For joy. Pleasure. What do the blokes in your romance books say? I want to taste you. Well, I do."

Audra managed a shaky laugh. "Sex isn't like in books, Jay. The only time girls scream is if they're faking it like Penny or if it's rape. Real sex? A bit of grunting, a lot of mess and that's about it. Life isn't a romance novel and no one comes twice in a night." Not even once, most times.

"Rock star sex is all that and more, Audra. Twice?" Jay stepped closer, close enough to kiss. Even his eyes seemed to draw her in. "I'll make you lose count before I even take off my pants. We'll still be going at dawn. Trust me, Audra. I'll make your body sing better than I can."

Her knickers weren't just melting — she was afraid they were going to burst into flame. If she didn't take them off first. Every word seemed to warm her insides like melted chocolate. A tiny voice inside told her he was seducing her. Of course he was. And she wanted him to, damn it. "Jay," she breathed.

His eyes seemed to glow. "I bought this place so that you'd be free to make your own choices. Not constrained by someone else's stupid rules. Free to do what you want. I know what I want. Do you?"

Hell yes. She threw her arms around his neck and kissed him, feeling his hands slide around her back to pull her closer. Only then did he open his mouth, enticing her tongue inside. Like the big bad wolf in a fairy tale, or was it some sort of pig? She didn't care. His tongue caressed hers, an erotic dance that more than hinted at what he wanted to do later. No, not later. Now. He was hard and ready, all she'd have to do is reach down, unzip his pants and…

No. Then it'd be over in five minutes. He'd talked about

dawn and that was hours away. Time to call his bluff.

"I want you to make me scream for joy," she ventured, feeling ridiculous.

"You will." He kissed her throat, his lips lingering for just a moment. "And…fuck. Everything's in the other villa." He closed his eyes, as if in pain. From the look of his straining pants zipper, he probably was. "I'll be right back. Please, don't go anywhere."

When he let her go, Audra's knees folded and she barely made it back to the couch. Not that she cared. Jay would be back soon and there'd be no space for anything in her head but him.

FIFTY

Cold fear settled into her heart as Audra waited alone in Pinctada, and it wasn't just from the ice numbing her hurts. Giving in to Jay was a mistake which could cost her everything she'd worked for. She'd lose her job, just like Penny. Shit, sleeping with him made her no better than Penny. And he'd already fucked Penny. He only said he'd bought the hotel – he could be lying to get her to sleep with him. If he was lying about that, then he was probably lying about his prowess, too. He'd turn out to be like the only other boy she'd been with, just a quick fumble in the dark in less time than it took to stuff him into a condom. Oral sex was a fantasy only found in books. No man she'd ever met wanted his mouth anywhere near a girl's lady parts. Jay wouldn't, either. He was as full of shit as any other man.

She needed to get her ID and head back to bed. Alone. Now, where had Jay hidden it? It wouldn't hear them, he'd said, which meant under or inside something. Shit…what if he'd stuffed it between the couch cushions? It would have recorded everything.

Audra ripped the cushions off the modular sofa, sweeping them all onto the floor, but there was no sign of her ID. She ducked down to check under the couch, but it wasn't there, either.

Jay's laugh echoed off the tiles as he entered the house. "Look all you like, but you won't find it there. Are you trying to trash this place like I did next door? Go ahead." He set the heart-shaped box on the bench. "You said you put this in my bedroom for romancing my guest. The only woman I want to romance is you, so I hope you picked the ones you like. There sure are a lot of them." He flipped open the lid and pulled out a strip of foil packets. "Studded for those who like it rough. Ribbed for extra pleasure. Chocolate for extra sweetness…"

Audra snorted with laughter. "You made that up. A chocolate condom? It'd melt."

Jay held it up. "Chocolate flavoured, it says. We can open it up and see."

Audra pressed her lips together and swallowed hard. "We shouldn't. I shouldn't be here. I should go…"

"Really?" Jay's eyes burned with frightening intensity. "Then let me give you a goodbye kiss."

He didn't hesitate this time. Audra found herself yanked hard against him as his tongue seduced her lips apart. With every stroke of his tongue, he licked away her resistance and coaxed the spark of desire inside her into a roaring bushfire that devoured all her good intentions.

"What do you want, Audra?"

The moan that came out of her mouth didn't sound like hers. "You."

Jay chuckled. "That's the best news I've heard all day." He fished something out of his pocket and slapped it on the table. "That says I'll give you the best orgasm you ever had and you'll beg for more."

Audra's gaze followed his pointing finger and what she saw sliced through her lust like a shark fin gliding across the lagoon. She'd never seen as much cash as the stack of fifties sitting on the bench. "How much is that?" she said faintly.

"Five grand."

Enough to pay for the repairs to her car and buy her the basic DSLR camera she'd seen at the electronics shop in town without touching her savings. But… "Jay, I'm not a prostitute. You can't pay me for sex."

He caressed her face. "You're not and I'm not. Fuck. No, that's a bet. You're still not sure and I get that. You don't think I can give you what you're asking for. That money says I can and I will."

"I can't match that. I don't have that kind of money, Jay." A hysterical giggle escaped her. "If that's how much it is to hire you for a night, I can't afford you."

He silenced her with another searing kiss. "If I can't deliver, you take the money. But if I can, and I know I will…I don't want your money. I've already told you what I want." His hand cupped her breast through her shirt. "When you scream for more, I won't give it to you until you've let me worship these properly. I want all your clothes off, so I can taste your tits next."

"Deal," she whispered, not believing she was agreeing to this. But she had to.

"Fuck, yes!" he groaned. "You won't regret this, I swear. Ohh, Audra." He swept her up in his arms and strode across the living room to the master bedroom. He set her in the middle of the bed and grabbed a pillow. To her surprise, he slid it under her backside.

"What…why?"

Audra closed her eyes as he leaned in to kiss her again, this time slow with smouldering passion.

"For a better angle. You'll see. Or maybe not, but you'll feel it." His hands slid down the back of her pants, cupping her arse cheeks. "These have to go." He slid his hands down the backs of her thighs, dragging her shorts and underwear until they garnished her ankles.

With shaking hands, Audra reached down to free them and toss the clothes to the floor. Naked to the waist, she turned her eyes to Jay. "You're still dressed."

But as she watched, he shed his shirt so he mirrored her. Taking her hand, he placed it on his rippled abdominal muscles. "This is all I take off until you're naked. I want to hear you scream, Audra. No holding back."

She gasped as he slid a finger inside her – something no one else had ever done.

"There's the pearl," he whispered, touching another finger to her clitoris. Magic button, more like.

Audra almost choked. "No one calls it that outside of books."

"I do." His finger circled slowly, teasing her. "Pearls show a woman's beauty and make her radiant. When I stroke this pearl – " He pressed harder. " – you're not just the most beautiful woman in the world. You're the most incredible woman in heaven, too."

He bent and she felt the rasp of his tongue across sensitised skin. "And the sweetest."

His tongue danced with her, more intimately than before. Swirling her into a storm of sensation as his finger seemed to swell inside her. One, two? No, three, surely. Filling her and thrusting, thrusting for all the world like the fire hose he kept in his pants.

She wanted it. She wanted him. Every inch of him as he explored every inch of her.

"Jay, Jay…" She spread her legs wider, giving him unlimited access to all of her. Anything to keep his fingers moving and his tongue…his tongue…stirring a storm into a cyclone centred on one point. Not a pearl. An eye that wasn't a calm centre at all. Because that's where Jay's tongue sparked her nerves, setting off a lightning strike that ignited her like a forked discharge lighting up the sky.

She sucked in a breath of charged air, sensing it was her last before she detonated.

"Say it, Audra. I can feel you tensing. Scream for me."

Selfish bastard. I'm doing this for me. She bit down on her lip to smother the scream that wanted to escape. Her body convulsed in an orgasm so powerful it blinded her, but she didn't make a sound. Vision returned and she blinked to find his eyes boring into hers, even from between her thighs.

"Didn't you enjoy it?" he asked, grinning as if he knew the answer. Or he thought he did.

"No," Audra replied, forcing her voice to sound normal and not breathless from the ecstasy she hadn't entirely returned to Earth from.

"No?" He ran his tongue over her…pearl again.

Audra sat up, scissoring her legs closed to stop him from tempting her any more. "No. No, I don't want more." Yes, she did. Every cell in her body was screaming for it. She couldn't let him know that, though. Lust didn't rule her life. Her head did, and her head said to find her pants and get the hell out of there with her money and her ID.

She yanked on her knickers, then her shorts, not caring that her skin was burning for more of his touch. Burning so much maybe her pants would combust…

"Thanks for showing me what you can do. I'll send someone to clean up the mess tomorrow so you can move back into your villa." Audra didn't recognise her own matter-of-fact voice. She was a raging storm of emotion right now, yet she sounded like she was discussing the hotel's annual report.

She had to get out of there before he could touch her or even meet her gaze, because he'd know she was lying with every fibre of her being. Audra marched to the kitchen and pocketed the money. Now all she needed was her ID…where had he put it?

How had he known what drinks were in the fridge? Or that there was ice in the… Audra wrenched at the freezer door and threw it open. There on the top shelf sat her ID. She grabbed it and bolted for the front door, hoping she'd be out of sight before he could see her cry.

She made it to the lagoon before her tears blurred her vision so much she had to stop. But she couldn't – what if he caught up with her? Heedless of her surroundings, Audra sprinted back to her room and locked the door. She threw herself on the bed and cried herself to sleep as a new day dawned.

FIFTY ONE

"Audra, are you okay?"

Audra made a noise in her throat that she hoped Pamela took as agreement. She was asleep, damn it, or at least she wanted to be.

"Serge is back and he wants to see you. I said he has to wait until you're awake and dressed, but he's getting a bit impatient."

God save her from demanding men and their lack of patience.

"Audra, the police want a statement from you. And they need to photograph your injuries." Serge's voice sounded hesitant. "They need it as evidence to charge Penny."

Penny? But sleeping with Jay wasn't a crime. Audra climbed out of bed and stumbled toward the door. Why did her head throb again?

Oh. Penny had attacked her in the gym. Maybe she'd get

prison time out of it. She could only hope.

Audra peered at her reflection in the tiny mirror and winced. That black eye on her otherwise wan face made her look like her parents' neighbour's pit bull, Patch. If only people would give her as wide a berth as they did that menacing-looking dog. Something yellow caught her eye and she turned to scan the room. Why was there a stack of fifties on the desk? Were those real?

Her memories came flooding back. Ecstasy with Jay before she'd lied to him, taken his money and run back to her room. She couldn't let Pamela and Serge see it – she didn't even want to look at it. She should never have taken it. Grabbing an envelope off the desk, she stuffed the money inside and threw the innocuous white packet onto the laminate surface, making it look far cleaner than the dirty money it was.

"Okay, I'm coming," she called, pulling on clothes as she heard a muffled conversation between Pamela and Serge. "Right." Audra threw open the door, only to find Serge standing outside alone. "Where's Pamela gone?"

Serge shrugged. "Something about the big conference thing here tomorrow. She has to get all the rooms ready. The hotel's going to be packed all week." His shoulders lifted as he straightened. "They've booked morning and evening relax sessions with the gym, so even I'll be kept busy."

Audra rubbed her eyes. Right. She'd forgotten. "That's good." She reached for her toiletry bag. "Let me just brush my teeth and freshen up, then I'll be right with you."

Five minutes later, she strode at Serge's side toward the main building. To her surprise, he took her to Dennis' office. It wasn't Dennis' domain this morning, though — a police officer sat in the seat of power, with Dennis perched uncomfortably in one of the guest chairs off to the side.

"You must be Audra Zoo…how do you pronounce it?"

Audra chose the chair beside Dennis. "Audra Zujute."

The police officer coughed. "An unusual name."

"Yes." She gazed at him impassively. She was used to police raiding the houses in her parents' neighbourhood, or on rare occasions coming to break up her neighbours' domestic disputes. Looking guilty or obeying her instinct to run only made things worse.

"Miss…can I call you Audra?" Without waiting for a response, he continued, "I'm Inspector Burgess. Investigating yesterday's incident here at the hotel. We've already seen the surveillance tapes, but we'd like to hear your account of the events of yesterday."

"You mean when my colleague went crazy and attacked me while I was working out in the gym?"

Inspector Burgess coughed. "Your colleague says you and the personal trainer attacked her."

"Is that supposed to scare me?" Audra snorted. "If you've seen the surveillance tapes, officer, then you've seen what happened. Penny lost her job and for some reason blamed me. She grabbed me from behind and I defended myself. When she was down, I walked away, but she attacked me again. Things…got a bit dark after that, because I woke up in my own bed several hours later." She waved her hand at her face. "Looking like this."

Inspector Burgess lifted a compact camera and Audra felt an uncharacteristic twinge of envy. Maybe, if she got the permanent job here, she'd treat herself to a camera. The smallest, cheapest digital camera in the electronics store, probably, but it was a start.

"May I take some pictures of your injuries for evidence? Those bruises will fade, you see."

He thought she was an idiot. Someone so stupid that she didn't even know bruises faded. Audra clamped her mouth shut as the officer snapped a few photos of her face, then stood behind her and photographed the back of her head, or at least that's what she thought he was focussing on. He could've been taking close-up shots of her backside, for all she knew.

"Thank you. How's Mr Felix?" the inspector asked, sinking onto his chair.

"Mr Felix?" Audra couldn't seem to close her mouth. How did he know?

"Mr Felix. You're the hotel staff member who came in the helicopter to collect him. The hospital surrendered him into your care. I hope he's in good health?"

She forced herself to smile. "Yes, I believe so. Good enough that he doesn't need a constant nurse, anyhow." But probably angry as hell at her for walking out on him last night. Oh, please don't let the officer pay him a visit today. Or search her room for the money…

"Good." Inspector Burgess' smile seemed as insincere as hers.

"Well, if that's all you want to know…I have work to do. A whole conference of people arrive tomorrow and we're down a staff member, so that means more work for me." Audra rose and headed out the door.

She marched to the laundry room without breaking stride, but once the door closed behind her, her breath whooshed out of her in a huge sigh of relief. She'd never trust the police, not after having grown up where she had.

"Come for your uniforms?"

Audra whirled around and found herself facing Jackie. "When did you get back?"

"This morning with a boatload of laundry and boxes for some conference. Good thing, too, seeing as we're one down. How'd you like the Pearls?"

Jay. Jay and his talk of pearls as he drove her to the peak of the best orgasm she'd ever had. She'd remember last night for the rest of her life.

Jackie smirked. "Dealing with VIPs isn't all it's cracked up to be. How many did you want to kill?"

Audra forced out a laugh. "They make me prefer the hotel. Normal guests are more…normal."

"Good, because the Pearls are mine again, now I'm back. I need the money. My oldest has it in his head that he wants to learn to be a pilot and flying lessons don't come cheap." Jackie nodded at the plastic-wrapped uniforms. "What size are you?"

"Small, please," Audra murmured, taking the stack of dresses from Jackie. "I better go hang these up and start work."

"You do that."

Audra stepped onto the veranda, then turned around to say, "Jackie? I really missed you. It's good to have you back."

The older woman laughed, ending in her characteristic smoker's cough. "Yeah, yeah." But she smiled, so Audra suspected she appreciated it.

Audra hurried back to her room. She shoved everything

to the back of her desk and heard the sound of things falling behind it, but right now she didn't care. She dumped her work clothes in the space she'd created. Audra seized the topmost dress, stripped off her civilian clothes, and clothed herself in anonymity once more. Resolving to make sure none of the conference attendees felt the need to know her name, she hurried off to help Pamela with preparations. The more they managed to do before the guests arrived, the less exhausting the event would be. Ah, who was she kidding? Big events had everyone running around like headless chickens. But being kept too busy to think was exactly what she needed right now.

FIFTY TWO

Audra reached across the table just in time to stop Pamela falling face-first onto her plate. She wasn't any less exhausted, but the almost empty cup of coffee in front of her would help keep her eyes open for another hour or two, at least. "Go to bed. Your pillow's got to be more comfortable than that curry and rice."

Pamela blinked blearily and managed a tiny smile. "How are you still awake?"

Audra raised her cup and Pamela laughed. Audra explained, "I haven't spoken to my family all week. I'm going to call them before I go to sleep. If I don't, they might send a search party up here to look for me." They wouldn't, of course. Not that they wouldn't worry, but the most they'd be able to afford would be a call to the police to report her missing.

"I'm going to sleep through that. See you tomorrow."

Pamela rose and staggered out of the dining room.

Audra waved, then concentrated on finishing her meal before she headed back to her room. She set her laptop on the desk and slumped onto the chair behind it. She considered checking her email first, but she knew her family were waiting for her call. Email could wait until afterwards.

The call initiated and she listened to the trill of it telling them that she was still alive.

"Audra? Hey, sis." The dark screen showed a dim picture of Leon.

"Hi Leon. How are you?" The question was more than simple politeness.

He screwed his face up. "All right, I guess. Well, not really. Leteesha says she's going to dump me if I don't pull my finger out."

Out of what? Who? "Leon, I don't understand."

"If I don't get my car fixed. Your car. I sort of told her it was mine. So when are you going to send the money? I'm going to lose my girlfriend, sis, so you better hurry up. I can't lose Leteesha. All the other blokes are jealous 'cause she can go all night and she can do this thing where she relaxes her throat and…shit, I've never been with a girl who could do that."

Leteesha sounded a lot like Penny. "Leon, it's a lot of money. If you need my car so urgently, maybe you should pay for the damage you caused."

"It's not my fault," he whined. "Dad parked his car on the driveway and I had to reverse round it on the lawn. The letterbox was too low to see. You should get a reversing camera on the back of it or something. I got a mate who says he can do it for under a grand, but you gotta send the money. You're up at that big, fancy resort while we're stuck here at home. And it's your car!"

Audra sighed. She was too tired to argue. "How much will it cost to fix?"

"Five grand."

"Ben said it was only four, including the registration and insurance he should've already paid!"

"Five with new tyres. One of the guys up the road noticed the plates are gone, so he nicked the tyres. Won't give 'em back. Says it's going to the wreckers so he's just helping make the car lighter."

"The car's not worth five thousand dollars! It was barely worth two!" she protested.

"C'mon, sis. Leteesha's the first girl to even look at me since my accident. She says she doesn't mind if I have fits and shit. As long as I can drive her to the dole office and to her dealer, she'll fuck me any way I want."

Lovely. "So Leteesha's into drugs, is she?"

"Just a bit. They make her hotter in bed, but it takes a lot, so I have to pay for 'em if she's using her supply for sex." Leon peered at the screen. "C'mon, sis. They pay you heaps up there at the resort. We're family and it's your car. Cough up."

"I'm a maid, not the manager!" Audra hissed. "Why can't you pay for it? You're the one who crashed it!"

"I told you. I'm back on the dole again 'cause I lost my job and I got a girlfriend now. She has needs." He sounded absurdly proud about this. "C'mon, sis. All the boys at high school and round here wanted you. You could've had anyone. Why don't you ask some of the celebrities at your resort? Bet there are a few who'd pay five grand for you to spend the night with 'em."

Like Jay. Audra fought back tears. Her brother wanted her to prostitute herself to pay for his skanky girlfriend's drugs and repair her car so he could trash it again. She'd heard enough. "Did you just suggest I have sex with strangers for money so you can keep some crack whore in your bed? Leon, fix the car yourself or get fucked. I'm not sending you a single cent. Ever. I work my arse off here every damn day so I can live my own life, not pay for your drugs or sex or some girl you picked up. Grow up and take some responsibility for yourself. When I come home, I want my car fixed. Or cough up the two grand it's worth so I sign it over to you. In cash. Maybe you should sell your body to strangers for it. I heard gigolos are in demand at the old people's home." She slammed her laptop shut and shoved it across the desk until it hit the wall. Now the tears started. "Fuck."

Too late. She'd already done what she swore she'd never do: have sex with a stranger for cash. Sure, Jay was no stranger, but she wouldn't have done it if it weren't for the money. Money her brother didn't deserve and would never get. Money she didn't want because it branded her a prostitute. "FUCK!"

She'd take the money to Maxima in the morning and give it back to Jay. She had to, or she'd be no better than Penny. Worse, even. She wouldn't be able to live with herself if that's what she'd become.

FIFTY THREE

The thought of that envelope of dirty money burned in her mind all night, not letting her sleep. At 5am, Audra finally gave in and switched on the light. She'd find the envelope, write a note to Jay and slip it under the door to Maxima. Or drop it on the doormat, seeing as a wad of cash that thick might not fit under the door. Now, she just needed to remember where she'd put it...

Audra searched the desk, but came up with nothing except empty envelopes. Had she put it somewhere safe and forgotten? It'd been an exhausting week, after all. She checked the cupboard, then her suitcase, her heart sinking further with every moment that passed without finding the money. But she had to. She needed to find it to return it to Jay, or she'd always know she was tainted. No one else knew about it but her, so it had to be here. She repeated her search, shaking out all her clothes before putting them back.

Still nothing.

Now more than a little frantic, she peered under the furniture, wondering if it'd ended up on the floor. Under the bed? Nope. The rubbish bin! Maybe she'd accidentally thrown it out. Pawing through the tissues and other waste brought her failure home to her like nothing else. Rooting through rubbish in search for absolution for her actions. As if Jay would forgive her, or she needed him to. No, she wouldn't ever forgive herself.

Eventually, she realised there weren't any envelopes or money in the bin and her hands were as soiled as the rest of her, if not more. She should go and wash. Rising stiffly, she stumbled along the boardwalk to the communal staff bathrooms. She was mercifully alone with her thoughts as she scrubbed her hands with soap. Over and over again, but never feeling clean. It wasn't the feeling of crumpled-up tissues in her hands she was trying to wash away. It was the feel of his hard muscles under her fingers as he placed her hand on his belly. The deep purr of his voice telling her he wanted to hear her scream. She hadn't even given him that satisfaction. Even for a prostitute, she'd been a disappointment. He should be banging down her door, asking for a refund. And she owed it to him, her accusing reflection insisted.

What she really wanted was to go back to that night with Jay and forget about the money. To surrender to him utterly for just one night, for that was all it would have been, but one blissful night. A memory she'd treasure for the rest of her life. Now…even the memory of his touch was tainted.

He'd bought the hotel, she remembered with a jolt. How could she face him, after what she'd done? She couldn't work here during the wet season. She'd run into him again on this tiny island and every time would be a stab to her heart, knowing that she'd lied to him out of sheer greed. She'd done it for her family, but that didn't excuse her. How in hell could she tell him she'd taken his money over the pleasure he'd promised so her brother could supply drugs to his crack whore? Real classy.

She needed a job in meteorology, somewhere far from here. It was probably too early, but maybe there'd be news about her job application. She'd forgotten to check her email last night, so she should probably rectify that before breakfast. It wasn't like sleep would return to her any time soon. Better to keep her mind busy.

When she settled in front of her laptop, Audra forced herself to breathe deeply. There wouldn't be any good news yet, but she had to hold on to hope now. She scanned through a week's worth of messages, deleting all the advertising until she found one from Leon dated yesterday, telling her to hurry up and send the money already. She stabbed her finger at the touchpad, feeling more than a little satisfaction at deleting that particular message. The remaining ones on the screen moved up and she spotted one she hadn't before – with the tantalising subject line:

GRADUATE OFFICER APPLICATION

She held her breath as the message downloaded from the server, revealing what was probably just an automatic response, telling her she hadn't been successful or when to give up hope if she hadn't heard from them. But as she started reading, she discovered it was more than a polite rejection letter. They wanted her for an interview in – Audra gulped – three days' time. She thought she had a day off then. But she had to contact them to arrange a time…

Her fingers ticked frantically over the keyboard, apologising for being out of phone and email contact, but she'd be available for an interview any time that day. Phone or video call, she added, as she worked at a remote site and travel was difficult to arrange around her present roster. As if she could afford to fly to Melbourne for a job interview.

If she found Jay's money and chose not to return it, she could, a nasty voice in her head taunted. Oh, it was her own voice, she knew, the same one that seemed fixed on reminding her at every moment that she was a whore for taking the money in the first place. Should've taken the incredible sex for what it was…

A tentative knock sounded at the door.

"Yes?" Audra squeaked, then cleared her throat and added in a more normal tone, "Who is it?" She sent the email and turned her eyes to the door.

"It's me," said Serge. "I wanted to see how you are this morning. Especially after last night."

Audra rose and cracked open the door. "You heard my video call, huh?"

He shrugged. "I've been wondering what the going rate is for gigolos who service residents at the retirement home. If it pays better than personal training, I'll have to keep it in mind."

Much-needed laughter bubbled up in her throat. "I can just imagine all those little old ladies dying to get their hands on you!"

"Dying's probably the right word. If I give the old girls a heart attack, they might not pay me. Hmm, maybe I should stick to what I'm good at." His expression softened. "No matter how bad you feel about what you said, you did the right thing. You deserve to live your own life. Good on you for telling them now instead of when you're on a much bigger salary. Imagine how much crack you'd be buying for your brother's girlfriend when you're not making beds. Is your brother really dating a crack whore? I didn't think they were allowed to date."

She managed a smile. "I doubt it. It's probably just pot. Weed. Or is it ice, the one that makes people stay up all night? Whatever. Not my problem now." She took a deep breath. "About the job I applied for. I…heard back from them today."

"And? When's the interview?"

Audra laughed. "Spoil my news, why don't you? In three days. I thought they weren't interviewing for months, but I guess I was wrong. They even sent the interview questions so I can adequately prepare, or at least that's what it says. How do you prepare for an interview?"

"Oh, you just get someone to ask them and you make up responses. Practice, I guess. Must be an important job if they think you need to prepare for the questions."

"Can you help me with them?" she blurted out, then wished she hadn't. She never asked for favours, because then she'd never be disappointed. Like she'd told her brother, she had to stand on her own two feet and not rely on someone else to support her. "Oh, never mind. I shouldn't have asked."

"I wouldn't know whether to predict sunshine or rain tomorrow, if that's what you're asking, but if you want me to put on my best drill-sergeant voice that I keep for boot camps and hit you with all the hard questions, I'm your man." Serge winked. "Hey, I still owe you for helping me clean up carnage. Friends help friends dispose of bodies, as well as land their dream jobs. What sort of paradise are they planning on sending you to?"

"I don't know yet," she admitted. "We don't get assigned a weather station until we've definitely got the job and there's some training we're supposed to do first, so maybe not even then."

"Tell me when. Any evening this week. We'll take some beers down to the Penguin jetty, I'll interrogate you until you break and then we'll both drink to dreams."

"Tonight, then, or maybe tomorrow, depending on how much mess those conference delegates left behind," Audra said. "There's boxes everywhere in one of the seminar rooms where they put all the conference materials together. I heard they were supposed to take everything with them when they left, but I guess someone wasn't listening. I hope the boxes are all empty."

"It's a date." Serge headed off, whistling.

A date. But whores didn't date. She had to find that money, so she could be a normal person again. One who hadn't sold her body and her soul — if she even had one. Who knew?

FIFTY FOUR

Audra lifted what felt like the millionth box and she'd lost count of the number of times she'd cursed the conference organisers. They'd bought boxes full of conference programmes that weren't any use to anyone now. Whole forests of trees had been felled for no reason. Now they'd be recycled into cheap toilet paper, or that's what she'd heard. All the hotel's waste paper and cardboard was sold to some recycling company. They'd have a shipload from this bunch.

"Oh, not another one!" Pamela's expression was thunderous as she shifted the box carefully off the top of the stack. The one beneath it tipped dangerously and Audra opened her mouth to issue a warning. Too late. It fell over, scattering round, blue things all over the floor.

Audra reached down to examine one that came to rest beside her foot. "A bloody box of stress balls." She threw it at the wall and it bounced off. "Actually, that helped. Maybe we should keep these."

"You can pick them all up, then," Pamela grumbled. It took a lot to piss Pamela off, but Audra wasn't surprised at the girl's grumpiness today. They'd both heard Annette tell Audra to come by later that afternoon to fill in the paperwork for the permanent, year-round position. Audra hadn't realised that Pamela wanted the position, too, until she'd caught sight of the girl's sour expression. Now Audra wanted to apologise for her success.

Pamela wasn't Penny. She was just as capable a cleaner as herself, Audra knew, and if she had another job to go to, she'd happily leave the place to Pamela. Pamela's family lived in one of the small communities between the resort and Broome, so this was more home to her than it would ever be for Audra.

"Sure. These ones are all full of papers, so we should get one of the porters to bring a trolley to deal with them. Too heavy for us."

"I'll go get one," Pamela offered.

Audra nodded and took Pamela's place by the stack of boxes. Beneath the box full of balls was a much smaller one, which explained why the ball-box had overbalanced so easily. Stupid way to stack boxes, really, she thought as she lifted the little one. It was sealed with packing tape and addressed to…her. Well, Audra from Housekeeping, which was close enough. Not the conference people at all. It must have come on the boat with all the conference gear and accidentally gotten lost amid all the other stuff. The conference people probably hadn't even noticed.

It couldn't be from her family. They'd have used her full

name and they'd have put a return address, even if they had sent something. This didn't have any postage marks or even a postcode on it. She pulled her multi-tool out of her pocket and selected a blade. Audra made short work of the tape holding it shut, but then she paused. Who'd sent her something?

She'd never know unless she looked inside the box. Swallowing, Audra flipped aside the box flaps to reveal a shapeless package shrouded in bubble wrap. Her hands shook as she cut the tape this time. There was a folded sheet of paper in the modern mummy wrappings, which had to hold the answers she sought. She focussed on that, trying to ignore the box with it until she knew more. Finally, she freed the paper and unfolded it with trembling fingers. It was a receipt from the electronics store in town. A receipt for the expensive DSLR camera she'd ogled in the window but known she'd never be able to afford. That meant in the box was…she swallowed and unwrapped it. Oh, it was the camera, all right. Twin lens kit, memory cards and all. She'd wanted a decent camera since studying photography at high school, but she'd never been able to afford it. Shit, she still couldn't afford this. It was worth as much as her car. If she'd doubted that, she had the receipt in front of her to confirm it. A receipt dated the previous week, the day she'd submitted her job application.

Only one person could have bought this. Jay.

Audra didn't deserve gifts from him. Not after what she'd done.

If she couldn't return the money, at least she could give this back to him. Numbly, she wrapped the coveted camera back in its bubbly shroud and entombed it in the box. She rose and marched out of the building, forcing herself to take the path to Villa Maxima. At least it was Maxima and not Pinctada. She wasn't sure she could bring herself to set foot inside Pinctada after her hurried departure last time. Once again, she thanked whatever powers that be that had allowed Jackie to return and care for the VIPs like she couldn't any more.

For a moment, Audra hesitated at the villa door, but she knew she couldn't keep the camera. Resolutely, she swiped her ID. The display beeped an error:

UNAUTHORISED.
GUEST NOT PRESENT.
CONTACT RECEPTION.

Someone had revoked her access to the villas. Probably a good thing. And if Jay wasn't home, she wouldn't have to face him. Setting the box carefully on the doormat, Audra turned and bolted back to the function centre, hoping Pamela hadn't missed her yet.

FIFTY FIVE

Audra beat Pamela and the porter to the seminar room by less than a minute, she figured, glancing at her wristband as the porter loaded the boxes onto his trolley. No one need ever know about the camera or her unscheduled excursion to the villas.

She worked in silence for most of the day, turning the function rooms from a shambles into the uncluttered spaces they normally were. Good thing they'd dealt with the guests' rooms the previous day, because it was dinnertime before she cleared away the last load of boxes.

Serge was waiting for her outside the staff dining room, carrying a familiar package in his arms. "Looks like you've really impressed the VIPs, Audra. Jackie said this was yours."

Reluctantly, Audra took the box.

"She said he wouldn't use any packing tape, either. VIPs

have their own strange ideas. I mean, who'd close a box with half the first aid kit?" Serge laughed.

She glanced down and realised that he was right. Jay had sealed it with some of the adhesive dressings from the hospital, then used a red marker to scrawl her name across them. The letters bled into the gauze, making it look gorier than it truly was. She wondered if even the illusion of bloodstained bandages had made Jay dizzy. Audra dropped the box on a table, and returned to sit beside it when she'd loaded her plate.

Serge slid into the seat beside her. "So what's in it?"

Something she didn't deserve, Audra thought but didn't say.

Jackie appeared beside the table, a look of grim determination on her face. "I'm under orders to make sure you don't try to return it. He said he'd pay for some of my son's flying lessons if I agreed. Don't you mess this up for me. Now, open it. We're all dying to know what it is."

One of the chefs appeared with a box cutter that she handed to Audra with a flourish. Now she was attracting a crowd – every staff member in the room was staring at her.

"All right." She sliced through the dressings and peered into the box. The folded receipt was on top, now with a message scrawled on the back:

Audra

Thanks for not letting me die.

Jay

She pulled out the well-wrapped camera and almost

snorted as she realised he'd imprisoned two mango beers in the bubble wrap, bracketing the camera.

"If you try and take it back, I'll sit on you," Jackie announced. "Flying lessons don't come cheap."

Laughter surrounded Audra on all sides. She knew she was beaten. If only for Jackie and her son, she'd be forced to keep this outrageously expensive gift.

More than ever, she needed to find the money and return it to Jay. If she didn't, she'd have to take it out of her savings. No, she couldn't do that, but she did have to tell him. He deserved to know the truth.

Serge reached over her and snagged the beer. "I'll put them in the fridge for later, if you like. I'm up for tonight, if you are." He winked.

More laughter erupted, but it wasn't as loud as before, because people started to drift away, returning to their dinner and whatever had occupied their attention before. Uneasily, she wolfed down her food so she could leave and stash the camera away where she wouldn't have to look at it any more. Damn Jay for finding a way to make her feel worse.

As she scraped the last forkful of lettuce into her mouth, Serge snatched her plate and carried it to the washing-up racks. "Time for that interrogation," he said when he returned, rubbing his hands together.

Half an hour later, clutching a printout from the gym office computer, Serge walked beside her on the path to the Penguin jetty. "It's the only place on the island where we definitely won't have anyone listening," he insisted and Audra knew he was right. After all, they'd been sitting on the Penguin jetty when he'd told her his big secret and, to the best of her knowledge, no one else knew it. Shit, even Jay had thought she had a relationship with the personal trainer. As if any woman could tempt a man who preferred men.

She found her gaze drawn to the windows of Maxima as they walked past. Jay sat on the sofa with what looked like a bottle of bourbon in his hand, or something amber, anyway. Audra swore she'd take her room apart to find the money on her day off. It had to be there.

"You like him, don't you?"

Audra met Serge's eyes and then dropped her gaze. "Maybe," she said finally.

"He's a good-looking bloke, Jay Felix. Just my type, if I was his."

Audra sighed. "I wish he was, Serge. But he's a boobs man – or tits, as he calls them. He's made it abundantly clear that he's definitely into women and not men."

"I bet he is. Don't let them rule your life, Audra."

She stared at him. "What? My boobs?"

Serge burst out laughing. "Those, too, but I meant the hotel management. He's no better than you are. In fact, he probably has no idea that behind those boobs is an amazing woman he has no hope of winning. You and your new camera will be winging their way to paradise and a new job soon enough, and he'll have missed out."

"You're the only one who's even guessed. Most people think you and I are an item. Please, don't say anything."

"Keep my mouth shut for three more days? Sure. Well, unless Jay Felix's super-sexy gay doppelganger visits the island. Then you're on your own."

Audra nodded. "That's fair."

He wrapped a hand around her arm. "I mean it, though. The day you quit, go up to his house and ask him to have a drink with you."

Audra tugged her arm free. "I can't. I…just can't. Please, can we talk about something else?"

Serge pointed at the jetty that extended past Villa Penguin. "Get on that jetty, woman, and we can start the interrogation."

FIFTY SIX

"What do you think is the biggest disadvantage of working at an isolated location?" Serge demanded.

Audra took a long, slow pull from her beer and lay back on the jetty. Now that she was finishing up her second beer, the timbers didn't feel so hard. "It attracts those with a sense of adventure who will never be satisfied with a normal job. Having to rely on your own skills and experience, often without access or even open communication channels to your superior, and defend your decisions later. Working in places most people would kill to visit, let alone live in. Knowing that if you make a mistake, the risks are higher because it's harder for help to reach you, and hence weighing your decisions carefully. You know you're doing a job that someone has to, but you miss those you love back home. Email and phones and video calling can only go so far to alleviate how much you miss being able to touch them.

"Here at Romance Island Resort, I've seen all of that. I took the job because the location was somewhere I'd never been and the isolation allowed me to save money because there was nowhere for me to spend it, except on alcohol. It's hard to find the enthusiasm for more than one or two quiet drinks in the evening because you're still at work, being judged by your colleagues, and if you get drunk you could put everyone in danger. An ambulance took four hours to reach a car accident and take the injured driver to hospital. He could have died in that time and he was lucky to live. I found myself practicing first aid skills I only knew from theory and courses, then later having to assume a level of responsibility I hadn't expected.

"I have no partner and no children, but I still have family and my absence affects them, too, because where they might have relied on me in the past, now they have to rely on themselves and each other. But in my experience, meeting the challenges of working in an isolated location like a remote island resort makes you more resilient and better able to meet even greater challenges in the future. Even if you don't have a sense of adventure to start with, you soon develop one. It's hard not to. At the end of the work day, just standing out in the dark and looking up at the millions of stars in the sky...it's like no city job anywhere."

"Hmm." Serge frowned at the paper in his hand, holding his phone over it to illuminate the words. "What would you do if one of your colleagues took the last mango beer and refused to share it with you?"

Audra sat up. "I don't believe that's on the list."

"Answer the question!" Serge barked.

"If he was both a colleague and a friend who'd paid for the beers, and I'd already drunk half of them, I'd probably wish he'd share it with me. But I wouldn't say so because I've probably drunk more than I should have, anyway." Audra drained her beer. "Do I get the job?"

"I'd hire you, and I'd send you to one of those adventurous places before looking for a transfer for myself. You make working in the arse-end of nowhere sound exciting."

Audra laughed. "This isn't the backside of anything. This is paradise."

"That's the beer talking for sure. Cleaning toilets is paradise? Weren't you ready to kill some VIP the other day?" he teased.

"Cleaning toilets in paradise. There's a difference. You know I got the permanent position? Annette told me today. All I have to do is fill out the paperwork and I'll have a job until the graduate one starts next year."

Serge cracked open the beer and raised it. "Congratulations." He passed it to her and waited until she had her mouth full before he added, "Adam's had to let me go. The day of your job interview's my last day."

"Oh no!" Romance Island wouldn't be the same without Serge and his easy humour.

"It's only a week early. No big deal, really. The resort's pretty low on bookings next week, so that's it." He retrieved his beer and drank deeply.

"Will you have enough hours to get your certification?"

He shook his head. "My brother's got me a job at one of the wineries near home, so I'll work there through the summer and see if I can do those hours at one of the local gyms. I'll get there. We're all working toward our dreams, but you'll get there first. I know it. And now you have a camera, you can send me pictures of paradise, here or wherever you get sent, via email."

"I still have to do the interview. They might hate me," she admitted.

"Nah. Just repeat what you said to me, especially the bit about adventure. They'll give you anything you ask for after that."

"Even the last beer?"

Serge handed it over. "Even the last beer."

FIFTY SEVEN

"…Like no city job anywhere," Audra finished, then swallowed nervously. "I wish I could show you what I mean, but it won't be dark here for hours yet."

On the laptop screen in front of her, Scott grinned. "I have a fair idea. One of my first postings was to the Cocos Keeling Islands. Talk about paradise. If you ever get the chance to work out there, take it and go."

Audra gave the manager of the graduate programme her best nervous smile. "If the Bureau gives me a job, I'll take whatever posting I'm offered."

He leaned forward. "Would you really?"

"Of course. The adventure bug bit me out here, I think, though I thought it was a midge at the time. At low tide in the mangroves, there are millions of them…"

"What about Antarctica?" Scott interrupted.

Audra paused to consider her answer. "I would say

Antarctica is probably the most adventurous and isolated workplace I could think of," she ventured.

"Good. Antarctica's usually somewhere we don't send staff until they have a few years' experience at one of the remote stations, not to mention a year's training here in Melbourne, but you come highly recommended and one of your references, a Professor – "

"You've called Peter already? I thought you didn't contact references until after the interview." Audra's blood ran cold. Her research supervisor hadn't smiled once at her during her entire honours year, while constantly telling her that her work needed to be better. Never good enough...

"We've been trying to contact you all week, but your mobile phone goes straight through to your voicemail."

"I...I thought I mentioned that there was no mobile access up here."

"We didn't know that until we got your email three days ago."

"Ah." She realised she'd interrupted him. "Sorry, please continue."

Paper crackled and the edge of a white page appeared in Scott's hands. "It says your honours thesis was on analysis of storm intensity in relation to climate change. Did you do all the analysis yourself?"

Audra felt stung. "Of course."

"We're short a junior meteorologist for this summer's Antarctic field expedition to Dome Argus. We need a meteorologist who's better with numbers than most and your research supervisor said you were one of the most mathematically gifted students he'd ever taught. He was quite angry that you didn't continue to do your PhD. The staff member who was allocated to go didn't pass her medical. Would you consider yourself physically fit, Audra? Capable of meeting all the requirements?"

Now she smiled. "I've been working with the personal trainer in the gym here at the resort and that's when I'm not fighting linen trolleys twice my size and weight. I…probably, yes."

"You're our first preference for the spot, but the ship leaves Tasmania in eight weeks and you won't be able to go until you've done at least four weeks of training at the Australian Antarctic Division facility here in Australia. You can start the graduate training programme next year with your colleagues in March, when the *Aurora Australis* brings the summer staff home. How soon can you start?"

Not work here for the wet season? Trade tropical seas for the icy Southern Ocean? "The dry season ends at the end of this week. I could start next week, but I don't have the right winter clothes or anything."

Scott waved her concerns away. "The AAD provide all your gear, and your space allocation for personal belongings will be pretty limited, or so I've heard. I've never been to the Antarctic stations." He nodded, as if a decision had been reached. "I'll send through the paperwork. It should be in your inbox…now. We only need you to sign the contract. Once we get that, I'll get my PA to book your flights. I'm looking forward to meeting you."

The call terminated before Audra could protest or say goodbye.

What had just happened? She'd expected to feel relieved after the interview, not more stressed than ever. How could she go to Antarctica? Or tell Annette that, after working her arse off to get the permanent position, she no longer wanted it because she was taking a job at the South Pole? Not to mention her family. If they couldn't contact her, who would sort out their problems for them?

There was still the problem of Jay, too. She'd searched every inch of her room twice and still not found the money. More and more, she'd started thinking that she'd need to take the cash out of her savings and give it to him. If she took this crazy, cold job, she'd earn it back soon enough. In the first month, maybe. Cold comfort, but she didn't deserve any better.

A soft tap started at her door. "Audra? How did it go?"

She slammed the laptop shut and rose to let Serge in. "Good, I guess."

He held up a six-pack of beer. "I guess you won't know for a while yet, but let's celebrate anyway. My last day on the island and to your future job in paradise."

"Antarctica," she blurted out. "They want to send me to Antarctica. This summer. In eight weeks. He sent through the contract, too." It sounded even crazier coming out her mouth than Scott's.

Serge laughed softly. "Seriously? That is awesome. So in eight weeks, you'll be sending me pictures of penguins. I want to see one of you standing next to an emperor penguin. And you have to tell me what they smell like when you email the photo. I hear they stink." He grabbed her hand. "Come on. The tide's out so we can drink on the beach. I'll fight off crabs, sharks and any VIPs who think they can steal you from me. I should've let you buy the beer. You'll be earning triple what you get here, at least."

"Graduates don't get paid that much," she protested.

"One of my mates is a plumber and he took a job at one of the Antarctic research stations because...well, because. He said the pay from six months out there is enough for you to holiday for the next year. Danger money, extra pay for the isolation, all your accommodation, food and clothing included, plus overtime because you have to do shift work and it pays extra." He edged toward her laptop. "Here, let me show you." He opened it, waited for the computer to come out of hibernation, then typed until he brought up the AAD website. "See?"

Audra saw. It was more than anyone in her family had ever earned, even when her father had worked on a minesite. When she got home, she'd be able to pay for a brand new car in cash. Her stomach twisted. It was too much, too far, too...

"You're thinking of turning it down, aren't you?" Serge asked.

She lifted her shocked gaze to meet his. "No, I just..."

"I'll tie you up and fill out the forms for you if you're even thinking about refusing. This is it. Adventure. You living your own life. Your own freedom. This is a dream job, the sort that people fantasise about but never get. Do you know how few people get to visit Antarctica? You're going to get paid to go to the South Pole."

"It's too much for me." Her voice sounded terribly small and forlorn.

"Fuck that kind of thinking. It's what you deserve, Audra. Nothing's too much for you. You've taken shit from the dregs of the Earth in people like Penny and you've put up with arseholes at the top like the VIPs in the Pearls, when you have every right to be right up there with them.

Swear to me you'll take that job."

"It's not that simple, Serge."

He reclined on her bed with his arms folded behind his head. "It is. I'm not leaving until you sign that contract and email it off."

She swallowed. Could she do this? "What if I refuse?"

He grinned. "Then I'm going to the Pearls and I'm going to tell Jay Felix that you've had a crush on his fine arse since high school. Then I'm going to drag him to your room here and…"

"NO!" Audra shouted, then forced her voice back down to normal. "You can't. Please."

"Sign. And you have to build me a snowman as tall as you are and take a photo of you beside it."

"You're crazy." So was she, Audra thought, as she opened the email containing her contract. All she had to do was fill out a few lines, add her digital signature and it was done. "It's sent. Serge, what have I done? I've just agreed to go to the ends of the Earth."

He leaped off the bed and peered over her shoulder at the email. When he seemed satisfied, he cupped her cheeks and turned her head so he stared into her eyes. "Not an end, sweetheart. A beginning. You've just started the life you deserve."

Realisation settled heavily on her shoulders. "I need to tell Annette. My family, too. I'll need to pack."

"Tomorrow," Serge said gently. "My boat leaves this afternoon and you're about to be whisked away to your dream destination. We are going to celebrate with beer." He tapped the six-pack. "And I liberated a picnic lunch from the kitchen, complete with fresh mangoes and ice cream, so we're going for a picnic on the beach. I'm your fairy godfather and I insist." He flexed his muscles.

With her mind whirling and her stomach churning, Audra lost the ability to resist. "Okay. A beach picnic with beer it is."

FIFTY EIGHT

"I can't believe you're going and I'm staying," Pamela said, sinking onto Audra's bare mattress.

Audra shrugged, then zipped her bag shut. Every moment on the island since she'd accepted the Antarctic job offer had seemed like a dream. "It's all a bit fast for me, too. Don't tell anyone, but I'm going to miss this place." She surveyed the tiny room that had been the most luxurious accommodation she'd ever stayed in. A space of her own, if only for a short time. "And you deserve to stay. When I was doing light duty at the villas, dealing with all the VIP requests, you were pulling double shifts cleaning the rooms here while Penny sneaked off for sex with her chef." She waved at the desk. "Are you sure you don't want me to tidy up in here before I go? I don't want to make extra work for you."

It was Pamela's turn to shrug. "I'll clean all the empty

staff rooms at the end of the week. Annette has a cyclone-ready checklist for the wet season, she said. I can't believe you'll miss the storms. You'll have to come back up some time in another wet season. You're welcome at my place, any time."

Audra thanked her and gave her a hug. "Don't let the VIPs give you trouble, or the resort's new owner, either. Have you applied to that nursing school yet?"

Pamela smiled shyly. "I applied this morning. I didn't know you could do most of the study here and just go up to the university for the practical placements. With this new job, I'll be able to afford the flights to Darwin and I can study at night when there's nothing else to do."

Audra forced her smile to stay in place, though she felt tears brewing. She hated goodbyes. "Take care, Pamela." She hefted her backpack onto her shoulder and grabbed the handle of her duffle bag. Without looking back, she wheeled the duffle down the veranda and toward the dock. A few more steps carried her to the door to Reception; she almost made it before the downpour started.

Heloise stood at the Reception desk, frowning at the rain. "I always look forward to the first storm, but when it comes, I want the dry season back."

"Not even meteorologists can control the weather. We have trouble enough predicting it," Audra replied, dropping her bag on the floor. She held out her ID. "I won't be needing this any more." She peered out the door toward the dock. "It's raining so heavily I can't even see the boat."

"The boat's not coming." Dennis strode into the foyer. "Baz just radioed to say the storm's blown in earlier than expected. The swell's too dangerous. The forecast's for clear conditions on Sunday, but it won't be calm before Monday at least."

Audra's jaw dropped. "But…my accommodation's in town. I don't work here any more."

Dennis jerked his head at Heloise. "Give her one of the rooms in the main hotel. Ocean view, so she can see the boat coming. And book her a full meal package in the guests' restaurant." He held up a hand to stem Audra's protest. "Free of charge. It's not your fault you're stranded. Baz should've brought the boat over earlier. Your flight home doesn't leave until Monday evening, right?"

"Right. But I had a few days planned in Broome for…sightseeing…" She'd intended to go to the bank and arrange to have a cheque written for Jay. It would be open on Monday, too. Cutting it close, though.

"Better sightseeing here. You can make use of this." Dennis tapped the camera bag that now contained Jay's gift. The bag wasn't new – it'd been in the lost property box, snared in a nest of phone charger cables – but it was the perfect size for her camera and the extra lens.

"Maybe I will. I guess if I have a whole weekend to kill…" First, she'd go back to her old room and clean it properly. Pamela shouldn't have to clean up her mess.

Heloise passed her a guest wristband. The waterproof kind that didn't beep, display urgent messages or record her conversations. "Room 123. I can send the porter up with your bags, if you like."

Audra shrugged her backpack off her shoulder. "Yeah. That'd be nice. Thank you."

A flash of lightning illuminated the skylight, drawing Audra's eye. She'd never photographed a thunderstorm before. "Actually, I might go and see if I can get some pictures now." Leaving everything but her camera bag with the porter, she headed outside and dashed through the rain for the first bit of cover – the veranda of the staff accommodation. She waited, her eyes on the sky, but it looked like the storm had discharged its electrical fury already. Sighing, she headed to the communal bathroom for some cleaning supplies. The light in the cupboard had died, so she grabbed a bucket and a bottle of detergent and took them to the sink to fill them. She needed a cleaning cloth, too, so she reached into the cupboard and found a damp cloth.

The door to her old room gaped open, already looking deserted. She set the bucket on the desk and dropped the cloth into the hot water. A green streak leaped out of the bucket and smacked into the wall, making her jump. A frog! The little bugger slipped behind the desk.

Audra swore. She wouldn't miss the frogs, that was for sure. Had it been hiding in the bucket or the cloth she'd been holding? Shit, what did it matter? She had to get the bloody thing out of there. Dumping her camera bag on the bare mattress, she dropped to her knees to crawl underneath the desk just in time to see a tiny, green foot disappear between the skirting board and the narrow strip of laminate at the base of the desk.

"Little bastard," she muttered, looking for something she could use to pry it out of its crevice. The plastic pen looked like it'd do, so she grabbed that and thrust it into the gap, levering it up to lift the frog out of its hiding spot.

A white corner emerged and Audra dropped the pen in surprise. Was that the envelope with Jay's money? Had it slipped behind the desk?

Carefully, she inserted the pen again, but nothing came up. Oh, this was useless. Audra clambered to her feet and shoved the desk aside. The frog made a flying leap for the door and landed with a splat on the veranda. The fat envelope lost its fight with gravity and keeled over on its side, spilling out yellow notes.

Audra fell to her knees and gathered them up. It was Jay's money, all right – every dollar. She wouldn't have to repay him from her savings, but she would have to take it to him personally. This much cash was a temptation to anyone. Not like a cheque.

Swallowing, she tucked the envelope into the bottom of her camera bag. She would return it. Today, she promised herself. But it could wait a few hours while she dredged up enough courage to face him. At dinner in the restaurant.

FIFTY NINE

"Table for how many?" the bored waitress asked without looking at her.

"One. Just me," Audra replied.

"ID." She stabbed her finger at the scanner.

Audra scanned her wristband as the waitress nodded.

"Pick any table you want. We switch to a new a la carte menu tonight, so no more buffet. I'll send a server over to take your order when you're ready."

She ordered the first thing she saw on the menu and a beer to help relax her wound-up nerves. What would she say to him? Here, let me refund your money because I didn't sleep with you? I can't keep this because I'm a liar? She couldn't tell him the truth — that she wished she could go back to that night and take what she'd really wanted. Him.

That was the hardest part. Admitting to herself that the

money was the only reason she hadn't slept with him, because she had wanted to. She'd wanted to lose herself in everything he had to offer.

Serge's final words to her rang in her mind: "If life offers you another opportunity, don't hesitate. Grab it by the balls and climb on top."

Not that she intended to assault Jay and sit on him. Well, unless by some miracle he asked her to. She'd hurt him enough already. Hadn't she driven him back to drinking bourbon out of the bottle?

Her entrée arrived and she dug in, barely tasting it as she fixed her gaze on the door. Even if Jay ignored her, she'd throw the envelope on his table.

A well-dressed couple arrived and the waitress guided them to a corner table lit by a candle. Audra glanced at her casual clothes and wished she'd thought to wear something better. If she'd had anything more appropriate. All her good clothes were back home in Perth.

Her waitress returned, switching her empty entrée plate for the one containing her main course. Audra glanced at her wrist to see how much time had passed, but her wristband was mute. She should have put her watch on, but that was tucked into her backpack in her hotel room. Time didn't matter as much any more when you weren't working on the clock. Still, she missed knowing. The restaurant wasn't open all night. What if Jay came late, or didn't come at all?

He didn't eat in the restaurant because he didn't want fans interrupting his meal, she remembered now. Room service only. Shit. She'd have to go up to his villa whether she liked it or not. Suddenly Audra wasn't hungry any more.

She shoved her plate aside and stood up. Throwing her napkin down, she lifted her chin and forced herself to leave the restaurant.

The humid evening air didn't clear her head at all. It curled around her in a caress that reminded her of Jay's hands on her. How she'd wanted to beg him not to stop, to coax burst after burst of pleasure from her willing body. If he appeared in front of her now, she'd drop to her knees and…

Make a fool of herself, Audra thought angrily, striding out into the rain. The drops pelting her head matched her mood, making her wish she could go into the gym and hit something, but Serge was gone and Adam wasn't anywhere near as accommodating. Even if she did have a guest ID today…

No. She'd go for a walk with her camera instead. Maybe photograph the stars here, if the clouds parted for long enough to let her.

Parting is such sweet sorrow…

The line of Shakespeare popped into her head as if someone had spoken it. Why Shakespeare? Was it because of Jay and the lines he'd splattered on the wall of his villa? He hadn't quoted *Romeo and Juliet*, though – his lines had come from a different play. One she hadn't been as familiar with, though she did remember a few lines of it.

"All the world's a stage,

And all the men and women merely players;

They have their exits and their entrances,

And one man in his time plays many parts…"

She muttered the lines to herself as she strode through the downpour. Why had Jay written that quote? He'd said it explained everything, but it didn't mean a damn thing to her except that it compared life to a play. But life wasn't like fiction. Only romance novels had happily-ever-after endings. The chapter of her life here had a happy ending — or it would, once she left for Antarctica.

Cold comfort now, she told herself, smiling at her inadvertent pun. She wished she could ask him the name of the play. Or she could just search for it when she reached the laptop in her hotel room.

The rain seemed to have stopped. Audra glanced up. No, it hadn't stopped. She had marched her reluctant feet all the way to Villa Maxima, and the light glowing through the frosted glass door told her Jay was inside. Before she could think about the consequences, Audra rapped on the door.

"Who is it?" his deep voice purred.

Audra glanced down. Her soaked clothes clung to her as if she'd gone for a swim. This wasn't the way she'd wanted to look when she saw him again. If she reached into her camera bag for the money, her precious camera and the notes would get wet. "It's me." Even as the words left her lips, she cursed herself for her stupidity. "Audra." She almost added that she was from Housekeeping, but she held her tongue. She didn't work here and she wasn't from anywhere right now. She was just plain Audra Zujute, soon to be Audra from Antarctica.

The door flew open and Jay stood there, a delighted grin on his face. "You finally came!" He grabbed her and folded her into a fierce hug, wet clothes and all. "Talk about leaving it to the last minute."

Audra stiffened. This wasn't how she'd imagined things

at all. She struggled out of his embrace. "Don't. You'll get wet."

His grin turned devilish. "I can see you are." His hand slid between her thighs before she could stop him, awaking desires that she tried to ignore. "Not wet enough, though. We can fix that." He rubbed his hands together.

"Jay." His name sounded so pleading, so needy on her lips. If she didn't tear her gaze away from his, she was going to drop to her knees and beg for what she didn't deserve. Not from him. Audra swallowed and unzipped her camera bag. "I have something for you."

"I have something for you, too, but ladies first."

The corners of the envelope were crumpled, but she slid it resolutely out from under her camera.

"How do you like your present? I wasn't sure what model you wanted, but this was the best I could get at short notice in town."

"It's fine, thanks. Better than I would've bought. I haven't really had a chance to use it until today."

"Well, better get a good one of us together, then." He seized the camera and clamped an arm around her shoulder as he raised it in front of them. "Smile." The flash blinded her. She blinked through the retina burn as Jay flipped the camera around. "Not bad."

At least she was smiling, Audra thought. Jay looked like he was posing for a shot with a fan, which he probably was. A fake smile for a photo of a moment that meant nothing to him.

"Can I get you to send me a copy? I'll give you my email address later. Afterwards." His grin didn't falter in the slightest. Fine. She'd wipe it from his face with the envelope.

"If you want." Audra wet her lips. "I have a confession to make." She thrust the money at him. "I lied to you."

He shrugged, shoving his hands in his pockets. "I know."

SIXTY

Rain pattered on the roof as the silence swelled between them.

"What do you mean, you know?" Audra asked finally.

"I've been with a lot of women. Your body tells me way more than your lips do." Jay's gaze travelled down. "I felt you lose control. Utterly lose it. That's when I knew I'd won the bet. It didn't matter what you said. Your body knew what you wanted, even if your head was a mess."

"I was in complete control of my actions!" Audra snapped.

"No, you fucking weren't. You took a blow to the head and a beating, remember? It didn't feel fair, taking advantage of you when you were confused. I figured you'd be back, and here you are!" He spread his arms wide. "I admit I was pissed off for a moment when I saw you'd taken the money, but I figured you needed it for something.

287

It's true, isn't it?"

Audra bit her lip.

"Yeah, I'm a rock star now, but that place in Cottesloe…I shared that shithole with five other guys and their occasional girlfriends. The place was falling apart and the landlord wouldn't repair it, not for the dirt-cheap rent he charged us. Some days the water at the beach was warmer than what came out of the so-called hot water system. I slept on a mattress on the floor that was so stained it had probably come from a brothel. If it had, the brothel had thrown it out." His eyes bored into hers. "I remember weeks when all I could afford was a packet of instant noodles for dinner. First year uni. First and last year, too." He gazed down at the tiles. "I failed everything. All I wanted was to play and drink and smoke and shit. So they kicked me out of uni and I had to move back home, because I couldn't get welfare payments. Unemployment ones, instead of student ones. So many times I nearly sold my guitar. I was still living at home when Chaya got our first recording contract. Fuck, I would've done almost anything for a couple hundred bucks, let alone five grand."

"I won't," Audra bit out, holding out the envelope.

"Now, it doesn't matter to me. Five grand is nothing. I don't need it back, Audra. Keep it. It's a gift, like the camera."

She wanted to stamp her foot and scream at him for not listening. "I can't. I'm not a prostitute, Jay." She threw the money at his feet.

"No, you've told me that. A few times now. Fair enough." He stooped to pick up the envelope and dropped it on the hall table. "Right, so are we done with all the talking? I won a bet and I want to claim my winnings."

Audra felt more confused than ever. "What winnings?"

Jay pointed at her chest. "Fuck, you're torturing me. Those perfect tits. The ones your soaked shirt is sticking to. And those nipples. Quit teasing me and take your shirt off."

Her head hurt. None of this made sense. "I came here to apologise and beg you to forgive me, and you're talking about my breasts. Why aren't you mad at me?"

Jay sighed and reached down to adjust himself. "Because I knew you wanted me and I was just waiting for you to come back. Everyone wants me." He flashed the same grin he had for the photograph. The one that didn't reach his eyes.

Realisation dawned. "You're joking. That's a joke. I don't know how many times I've heard you say it, but I just got it. You say it to bait people for a reaction, but then the joke's on them. Because everyone wants Jay Felix, the rock star. Not the man who only plays the part. Hence, the Shakespeare on the ceiling."

Jay's grin finally vanished and he held out his arm.

Audra followed his gaze to the tattooed words she'd noticed but never read. Now, she did: "All the world's a stage."

He pointed at her camera. "That's a gift for the girl who wouldn't let me die. I left a pub full of girls who thought they owned the rock star. I came back here for a girl who'd seen me at my worst and stayed to listen to the man in a moment of doubt. Audra, not Audrey. In *As You Like It*, Audrey married a fool. But Jacques stayed alone. He's the one who said we're all players. I don't want to be a fool or alone. I want you."

Audra sucked in a breath, not sure what to think any more. "Jay, don't you think —"

"Don't think," he replied. "We had a bet. That I'd give you the best orgasm of your life, you'd beg for more, and I'd give it to you after you got your tits out." He groaned. "Fuck, that wet t-shirt. Quit torturing me. Did I give you the best time of your life?"

Audra closed her eyes, remembering the heat of his fingers inside her as his tongue sent her soaring to undreamed-of heights. No one else had ever come close. She swallowed and nodded.

"Do you want more?"

"Yes," came the barely audible whisper.

"Then I've had enough of this fucking shirt." Cheap cotton ripped as Jay yanked hard at her top. Now the front hung free, dangling from one sleeve as it exposed most of her bra. "Fuck."

With trembling hands, Audra took off what remained of her t-shirt. She should have been shocked or annoyed at the destruction, but she didn't care. All that mattered was Jay. She reached to unhook her bra, but Jay's hands were already there, expertly freeing her faster than she could release herself. Wet lace fell away, replaced by his warm hands as he cupped her breasts.

"Oh, yesss…" The blissful look on his face made her smile. His eyes snapped open and he pulled his shirt over his head and threw it on the floor. He snaked his arms around her, holding her tight to his bare chest. Her nipples tightened in response and she gasped. Jay kissed her open mouth.

The moment his tongue touched hers it was as if

lightning had struck her, coursing down her spine to her core. Oh, but lightning only started in the sky. The blinding white light came from below.

Well, she was named after a storm for a reason.

Audra shimmied out of her shorts, leaving them with her underwear in a puddle on the floor. Now she was standing naked in Jay's arms. Talk about crazy.

Their lips parted for a moment as Jay paused to grab a breath.

Don't think. About tomorrow or next week or anything but this moment. Even the weather could wait.

She reached up to stroke the stubble on his jaw. This time she kissed him, focussing all her passion into the pressure of her lips and the twine of her tongue around his. His hands crept down her back to cup her arse.

He swept her up in his arms, carrying her through to…the bedroom? No, the bathroom. He dumped her unceremoniously into the spa and tossed her the plug as he turned on the taps. "Can you sort the temperature while I get these off?" He struggled with his shorts, which seemed to be stuck on his…

Audra tried to smother her laughter as she turned her attention to the taps. The water was comfortably hot when she heard Jay climb into the tub behind her, but an attack of nerves seemed to have frozen her. She squeaked when Jay's arms encircled her, pulling her into his lap.

"Do you trust me, Audra?" The seductive purr was sexier when his breath tickled the back of her neck. She could feel her insides melting. "Trust me to give you the best night of your life?"

His thumb circled her nipple, then trailed down her belly

and slipped between her thighs, circling again. He brought her expertly to the edge of a storm front, as if he knew one more well-placed circle would unleash the storm's screaming fury. "Do you want it?"

"Yes," she gasped, feeling him press harder. "I want you, Jay. All…night…JAY!" Her words ended in a scream to the skies as she soared up past the clouds to the stars above.

SIXTY ONE

When she returned to Earth, Audra found that the bath had filled with water, or maybe it was the space their bodies took up that had let it fill so fast. Or had she been too lost in Jay's magic hands?

"Turn around," he breathed in her ear and she complied, sliding around in his lap as she realised Jay was hard as all hell beneath her and with one thrust of his hips he'd be inside her. Shit, all that inside her? How would he fit? The man was massive.

He must have seen the fear in her eyes, because he leaned back and said, "Oh, you won't be getting that until you're ready. I promise you that. Ready and begging for it, and not before. I'm not into pain. Yours or mine. Just pleasure and plenty of it. Trust me, Audra."

"The rock star or the man?"

Jay laughed. "Mostly the man. The rock star – " He took

her hand and guided it to his cock. " – is ready and raring to go, but even he's going to wait until you're satisfied."

This time, she didn't manage to smother her laughter in time. She pulled her hand away and covered her mouth. "Shit. Now it all makes sense. Every time you make some comment about being a rock star, you're thinking with your…"

"Say it. You'll be riding it soon enough."

Audra swallowed. "Cock."

"It sounds so hot when you talk dirty. You should do it more." He pressed a hand to her back, between her shoulder blades. "Now, lean back a bit."

Audra did, and found herself floating up. She wrapped her legs around Jay, anchoring herself around his torso.

"Perfect." He leaned forward and licked her nipple, sending a jolt right into her core. "Oh, you like that. So do I – sweet pink pearls." His teeth grazed sensitive flesh as he sucked her so-called pearl into his mouth.

"Oh!" His tongue tickled as he sucked harder. Desire sparked at his touch and spread like forked lightning, electrifying her breast until he set her heart ablaze. His hair tangled around her fingers as she held him in place. "Oh my God, Jay."

"Told you I was a rock god. Now, I bet the second one's sweeter." He caressed her still-tingling breast with one hand as he devoured the other.

Heat engulfed her chest, racing through her veins to the juncture of her thighs. "Jay, I want to feel you inside me. Now."

"Inside where?" His finger traced her lips. "Tell me where."

"Inside my…my…ohhh."

Something warm and hard brushed against her thigh, the lightest touch before it traced a circle around an even more sensitive pearl. Not touching but so close.

"Here, maybe? You know why this is called a pussy? Because if I stroke it just right, I can make you purr. Tell me." A deliberate stroke, hard enough to spark her nerves again.

"In my…pussy. Deep in – augh!"

On command, his long fingers plunged into her, straight at first and then curving around to touch a spot inside her that crackled into life with another fork of internal lightning. His tongue entered the fray and she couldn't think. He'd unleashed another storm and she was helpless before his onslaught. Sobbing, then shrieking his name, Audra's body became a nebulous cloud swirling around the commanding eye that was Jay.

When she peaked this time, she swore she saw stars.

Audra came to in Jay's arms, curled against his chest with tears streaming down her cheeks. She couldn't have been senseless for more than a moment, surely.

Jay tilted her chin up for a gentle kiss. "That's the first time I made a girl come so hard she cried. Fuck, you're awesome, Audra. I want to do that again."

His lips claimed hers as Audra felt his fingers slip inside her once more.

"No," she gasped. "I want…more." This time she only hesitated for a moment. "I want to feel your cock inside my pussy. Nothing…less. Please."

Jay closed his eyes. "Fuck, say that again."

Audra's voice sounded a little less shaky this time. "I

want your cock in my pussy."

Jay surged to his feet, sending water cascading everywhere. "Let's move to the bedroom, then, where I left the condoms." He stepped out of the bath.

Audra reached for a towel to dry herself, but her eyes were fixed on Jay. His cock jutted, pointing right at her. Long and hard and hot as…

"Bed, or I'm going to take you right here on the floor."

Audra found herself in his arms again as he strode across the living area. This time, when he set her on the bed, she spread her legs wide in invitation.

Jay knelt between her thighs, so close and yet so far. With agonising slowness, he rolled a condom down his length.

"Jay, please," Audra begged.

He leaned over to kiss her and she felt his heated flesh ready to enter her. She held her breath, wanting to savour the feel of his first thrust as he filled her.

"Scream for me one more time." His musician's fingers entered her instead, playing a bass line her core responded to with a flood of searing heat. Then his tongue joined in, singing a melody perfectly tuned to send her up a stairway to heaven. The song he played with her body reached a crescendo and she couldn't help screaming his name, not once, but over and over until her heaving lungs ran out of air.

His fingers still strummed her nerves as his cock started its slow plunge into her molten core. He held her thighs firmly as he slid inside, inch by glorious inch until she wasn't sure whether the heat boiling her blood came from him or her, and she didn't care.

Jay's eyes never left hers, watching her until he filled her so completely it was like he'd been made for her. Or she'd been made for him. Made for a rock star.

"Don't let me slip out," he whispered as his hands grasped her arse. Audra tightened around him, moaning at the sheer pleasure of having him inside her. Jay leaned back, pulling her with him until he lay on the bed with her sitting astride him. Audra rocked her hips, humming with joy at the feel of him sliding in and out of her.

"Fuck, yes," he groaned, releasing her to reach for her breasts. "I could come just from watching your tits bounce as you ride me."

She drove down hard at his next thrust, meeting every rise of his hips with a dip of her own until the pounding rhythm became as natural as the beat of her thrumming heart. But another storm was brewing inside her, bigger and more powerful than before, already blowing her away with its intensity though she hadn't reached her peak yet.

Jay was close, too, she was sure of it. Audra reached for his balls, caressing them delicately as she felt the tightening within. He responded by changing his angle slightly, tipping her over the edge until she flew apart around him, clinging desperately to Jay as the only eye in her swirling cyclone of joy.

A warm hand caressed her cheek and Audra forced her eyes open. "Fuck, we were made for each other, Audra," Jay breathed. "Any time you want an encore, this rock star is all yours."

The story continues in
The Rock Star's Email Order Bride

ABOUT THE AUTHOR

Demelza Carlton has always loved the ocean, but on her first snorkelling trip she found she was afraid of fish.

She has since swum with sea lions, sharks and sea cucumbers and stood on spray drenched cliffs over a seething sea as a seven-metre cyclonic swell surged in, shattering a shipwreck below.

Demelza now lives in Perth, Western Australia, the shark attack capital of the world.

The *Ocean's Gift* series was her first foray into fiction, followed by her suspense thriller *Nightmares* trilogy. She swears the *Mel Goes to Hell* series ambushed her on a crowded train and wouldn't leave her alone.

Want to know more? You can follow Demelza on Facebook, Twitter, YouTube or her website, Demelza Carlton's Place at:

www.demelzacarlton.com

Books by Demelza Carlton

Ocean's Gift series
Ocean's Gift (#1)
Ocean's Infiltrator (#2)
Ocean's Depths (#3)
Water and Fire

Turbulence and Triumph series
Ocean's Justice (#1)
Ocean's Trial (#2)
Ocean's Triumph (#3)
Ocean's Ride (#4)
Ocean's Cage (#5)
Ocean's Birth (#6)
How To Catch Crabs

Nightmares Trilogy
Nightmares of Caitlin Lockyer (#1)
Necessary Evil of Nathan Miller (#2)
Afterlife of Alana Miller (#3)

Mel Goes to Hell series
Welcome to Hell (#1)
See You in Hell (#2)
Mel Goes to Hell (#3)
To Hell and Back (#4)
The Holiday From Hell (#5)
All Hell Breaks Loose (#6)